MURDERS AT GABRIEL'S TRAILS

I0680604

The Complete 5 Part Series
with unreleased bonus story

SINS OF BAIN

Mirika Mayo Cornelius

Murders at Gabriel's Trails: The Complete 5 Part Series Plus Bonus SINS OF BAIN

This is a work of fiction. Names, characters, places and incidents are either products of the author's imagination or are used fictitiously. Any resemblance to actual events or locales or persons, living or dead, is entirely coincidental.

ISBN: 0970851758

An Akirim Press publishing

Acknowledgements

All glory, honor, praise and total worship to God Almighty, Jesus Christ and Holy Spirit.

For my loved ones – son, husband, parents, siblings, nieces, nephew and grandparents - I love you all, those both here and that have passed on. You mean so much to me.

To all fans of this written project,
thank you.
God bless you all.

For anyone living in struggles of any type, keep your eyes on Jesus. He brings calm to any storm. Fight the good fight, and He will stand you up in the end where others tried to keep you down.

Table of Contents

MURDERS

AT

GABRIEL'S

TRAILS

An Alexis & Bain Love Story

Murders at Gabriel's Trails: An Alexis & Bain Love Story

"Mom," Alexis yells to her mom who is upstairs working hard on another project that she has to complete due to a self made deadline, "I'm off to school now. Love you!" She waits by the front door because she knows that it usually takes her mom about five seconds to respond when she's engulfed in writing major scenes of her novels. This is the norm, and it's so normal that Alexis counts down the seconds until she sees her mom bolt from the office and make a mad dash downstairs.

"Like clockwork," Alexis mumbles. "Morning, mom. I'm about to go. You didn't have to get up and run downstairs half naked either just to see me off," she grins. "I understand how it is with you and your work."

"Well thank you, Lexi, but I need to see you off in the morning, and I feel bad when I'm so engulfed that it steals my attention. In about two weeks, I should be all finished with things and it will be back to making that full breakfast and even driving you to school three times a week."

"Or maybe it will finally be me driving you. I want my license," Alexis whines, slouching her shoulders over and tilting her head to the side making her hair's heavy layers fall to one side of her body. Her locks are stunning, and since the day she was born, people would marvel over how thick, rich and naturally beautiful it would grow. To Alexis, it has always been the norm, and she hasn't ever seen much special about it.

11

Alexis comes from a bi-racial home where her mom is a dark brown skinned African American woman, and her dad, who works from sun up to sun down as a surgeon, is Caucasian with a tinge of Cubano, or Cuban blood. This particular match poured out a sort of light pecan brown color on Alexis while her hair was naturally curly until she would blow-dry it straight as done this morning.

Alexis's mom, Lorah, beams at the idea. "That's a bet! When we get to driving again, I will make it my duty to help you pass the driver's test, and let you have one of the cars. How's that?" she asks, fixing her daughter's hair as if she's still a small child.

A great big smile stretches across Alexis' face, but then it goes south as she places her hands on her mom's shoulders. "You said that the last time, remember? You should probably hurry and follow through on your word before I turn twenty, ma."

"Don't be too funny. The longer I can keep you a teen, the better for me. I don't want you growing up too fast, Lexi, I really don't. I wish I could stop time and force you to stay fifteen forever."

"But," Alexis raises her finger in the air, "you can't, and thank God!" She then gives her mom a kiss on the chin, and her mom brings the kiss back up to her only daughter's forehead.

"Love you, baby, and have a nice day."

"You too, mom. Love you more."

As Alexis hops off of her wide porch of five stairs and heads off, she gets about two blocks away from her gated community after failing to get on the school bus and points her sneakers in the direction of Gabriel's Trails. Gabriel's Trails is the location of one of the more dangerous communities on this side of town. On the outside of the community, a passer-by sees nothing but flowers, well behaved insects and even a patrol that circles from time to time, about every hour, which gives the impression that beyond those four well manicured trails that lead inside, there is nothing but tranquility. Unfortunately, that's not the case.

Gabriel's Trails isn't the original name of the seemingly well kept neighborhood. In fact, the original name of the community was called The Stills. It was renamed Gabriel's Trails after an onslaught of criminal activity bombarded the place, and what was supposed to be so still about these condos turned into chaos after murders, rapes, muggings and drug activity continuously happened on those same entry trails for those without a car, such as Alexis. The name Gabriel's Trails was supposed to signify a change when many older people, in what was turning into a lost community came together, tired of all the crime, and named it after the angel Gabriel. They scratched through The Stills sign and carved in Gabriel's Trails. They felt it would bring more life and less death into what had turned into the worst streets on this side of town. This change hasn't worked yet.

This doesn't terrify Alexis for the simple fact that she knows some of the people who live here via her secret twenty-seven year old boyfriend, Bain. Alexis attends a private school, so by any other means outside of Bain, she would have never crossed paths with the people of Gabriel's Trails. It just so happened that she and Bain met during one of Alexis' first fits of curiosity about the Trails, and it was Alexis who allowed her curiosity to run wild with no objections from Bain. Bain is her first real kiss and first love. They have been dating for one solid year.

As Alexis walks toward one of the four trails that leads into Gabriel's Trails, she whips out her cell phone and sends Bain a text at seven in the morning. She knows Bain is probably asleep because she failed to speak to him last night which was a total disappointment, meaning he could have had a long night. She constantly called him last night, however, Bain never answered, and he never returned the call. This has been on Alexis' mind all morning because it just isn't like him to ignore her messages, especially when he works at night.

"Hello, Bain? What happened to you last night?" she questions him on her stroll toward the neighborhood.

Bain answers like he is feeling down and out, almost as if he's recovering from being hit by a truck or mauled by a mut, the latter of which isn't a rarity in Gabriel's Trails. "Hey, baby girl. How you doing this morning?"

"Bain, I called you all last night because I want to see you today, like now. Can you meet me halfway down the trail?"

"Which one, baby?"

"Number two, Bain. You know I always come down number two," she answers with a slight smile being that she thinks it's cute to wake him up while he doesn't have all his wits together. "It's the one that leads closest to where you live."

"My bad, baby, my bad. I had a long work night. How close are you away so I can throw on some clothes and meet you down there?"

14

"I'm about twenty feet away from number two now, so if you run and get me, that would be good."

"That's a bet. Love you, girl."

"Love you, too." Alexis' heart races each time they are together. Even speaking on the phone to Bain gives her the goose bumps despite the fact that they both know it's statutory rape. She voluntarily gave up her virginity, nothing was forced, and Bain also took her word that she gave of a seventeen year old age, which by the law is legal age of consent. He found out later, two weeks later, that she was only fourteen yet very mature all the way around for her age. The love affair continues.

Alexis spots Bain walking casually down the trail with his confident swag and cell phone to his ear. Whoever he was talking to, Alexis doesn't care. For the most part, she's just ecstatic to see that he is coming up the trail to meet her like her knight in shining armor. She trusts him so much until she feels like absolutely nothing can hurt her in the world, including in Gabriel's Trails. Besides that, Bain is well known for his handsomely strong stature and no hesitations when it comes to taking care of any trouble that comes his way. He's never killed anyone, however, but after he's finished dealing with anyone who crosses him, the word is that the victim of his anger wishes Bain had taken his life.

Bain is about six feet two in height, medium build but built into a brown skinned body that any woman would love, including young girl. He has a youthfulness about him that appeals to all the women because although he is all about no nonsense when it comes to what belongs to him, he's also tender and respectful and can make any woman blush, let alone a teenager. It is Alexis that has his heart though, and most ladies know this.

He's finally within arms' reach of Alexis and pauses before reaching out to embrace her. "Why did you walk this far up, Lex? You know I don't let you walk this far up the trail…"

"I'm a big girl, babe," she responds, tip toeing to plant him a kiss on the lips while he stands there and takes it all in, rubbing the small of her back like he wants to undress her on the spot. The trail is lined by trees on both sides, and as Bain pulls back from the kiss, he gently turns her backwards so that she can see why coming this far into Gabriel's Trails is dangerous.

"Do you see the main road anymore, Lex?"

"No, Bain," she drags.

"Nothing but a trail that ends, curving back into where you came from. Nobody can see you anymore, Lex. At that point," he explains, pointing to a boulder that's painted red on the side of the trail, "Coming in here beyond that rock this far up means that you're on your own." He turns her back around so that he can look her in the eyes. "I don't ever want you to be on your own, Lex."

"Like I said, I got me."

He shakes his head. "That's what you think. Give me your bag and let's go."

She faithfully grabs his hand and walks.

"Why didn't you go to school anyway? You know I don't play that, not for me or anyone. Can't have no dumb girl on my arm."

16

"Shut up, Bain!" she says, punching him in the stomach. He playfully leans over like she has a mean hit. "I didn't feel too well, so instead of staying home with mom, I decided to fake it and come your way, especially after you didn't call back."

"All my fault, Lex." He wipes his hand across his eyes in another attempt to wake up, added with a yawn.

"I'll race ya!" Alexis takes off.

"Ah, girl, wait," he stammers, and then groans under his breath as she runs down the trail, "Damn running this early in the morning." Then, he takes off behind her as if it's all good.

When he finally catches up to her as she giggles in delight like the school girl that she is, Bain hears his name being called.

"Yo, Bain, man, you finished work?"

"Yeah, man, can't you see I'm with my girl, man. Cut that short, dawg, cut it short. I'll holla atcha. Later." he yells back highly irritated.

"Why is he asking you about work?" Alexis asked, totally clueless about the life he leads at night.

"Sometimes I go right back," he answers while looking her directly in the eyes, "for overtime. I worked hard last night, so I didn't even hear you call my cell at the factory. It's loud in there, you know that, babe."

"Yeah, I do. Sorry for getting a tad bit upset that I didn't hear from you. I brought you something though, like I do every month, but this time it's a bit extra."

"Ahh, baby." He lifts her from the road and places her on the back of a car's trunk. "You do me really good, you know that? Here." He pulls an eighteen karat gold bracelet with charms out of his pocket. "It's yours."

"Bain!" She jumps off of the car, snatches the bracelet from his hand and gleams. "Put it on, put it on!"

"Inside, Lex, inside."

Indoors they go.

Bain dumps her bag on the bed while she snatches her change of clothes to get out of that private school uniform. Along with the clothes that came falling out of the book bag is money, and lots of it. Alexis gets a sizable allowance each week, and each month, she believes that she is too well off, so much so that she feels for Bain living in the not so nice Gabriel's Trails.

Her goal is to help him move out so that they can marry when she is of age. At least that's the story Bain gives her which made her a ride or die for him type of girl. Alexis has been contributing to the cause with her money for about six months in now, giving just enough so that her mom and dad won't wonder that anything is too far off. Today, the drop is two hundred dollars.

"Bain," she says a little puzzled coming out of the bathroom from freshening up, wearing tight booty shorts with a tank top and her new bracelet. "Either you wear female lotion or this belongs to another woman you have in your condo but me."

He looks up and Alexis is holding a strawberry scented body scrub and lotion which is so not manly. "Lex, baby, that's my sister's. She drops by from time to time. No lie. You're the only lady in my life, and the only one I'm planning the rest of my life with."

"And I'm putting in on that future, too. How much do we have saved now, Bain?"

"Not enough to make a mark, but it's coming." He flops on the bed that's layered in unmade black sheets with gray and black striped pillow cases. "About five grand."

"That's a good start for us, don't you think? By then, I'll be able to date you openly in front of mom and dad instead of having to skip school," she says, jumping atop him in full straddle position. "Like my outfit today?" She swings her arms from side to side.

"Sure do. I'm gonna like something else more in a minute," he says slapping her on the butt and yanking at a piece of flesh.

Alexis giggles and then she gets undressed again. Thirty seconds later, they were having sex on top of a loose total of two hundred dollar bills.

To conceal the fact that those two are ever together from the world outside of Gabriel's Trails, Bain only walks Alexis to the red boulder on trail number two and watches as she walks until she turns the corner in the direction of her house. The time is about three fifteen in the afternoon, and the bus should be turning the corner at any minute, just in time for her to appear that she's been in school the whole day.

Approaching her house, Alexis notices that her mom isn't anywhere near the front door. This means that going inside will be easy as pie. Alexis watches as the bus rolls by and gives her a beep. She waves at the bus driver who gives her the old you better stop skipping school look, and Alexis cracks a smile. In her mind, school would always take a backseat when she is missing her future husband.

"Ma, I'm home!" She drops her bag at the front door and locks it as she enters. "Ma!" She calls but gets no answer, so since she hasn't passed the kitchen yet, she turns to go check the garage to see if her mom's car is missing. Surprisingly, Lorah's gone, so Alexis whips out her cell phone and dials. Lorah picks up.

"Hey ma, what's up? Where are you?" she asks snatching an apple from the bowl that sits highly decorated in the center of the kitchen table.

"Oh hi, honey! Listen, one of my good friends is in the hospital from a really bad car accident, so I'm up here where your dad works. Do you remember Cathy?"

"No ma'am, I sure don't. Is she going to be okay, or is it up in the air?"

"Right now, sweetheart, it's up in the air. Anything could happen, so I'm praying hard to the Father that she comes out of this. They induced a coma…"

"Mom, are you okay?" Alexis hears her mom drop silent on the phone for a split second, but then continues.

"Yes, baby. I was listening to the doctor who is now speaking to the family. Listen, Lexi, I put some cold cut sandwiches in the fridge, and there is also some spaghetti and meatballs there as well. I might be here for a while, and you know your dad is going to be at work until about eleven so eat carefully and put the chains and immediate alarm on. I'll call before I come for you to disarm, okay?"

"Sure, ma. I'll be praying for her, too, and you, ma."

"Thanks, hon. Love you."

"Love you more."

When Alexis hangs up, she walks into the entertainment room, turns on the radio, and starts to dance all alone. There's a huge mirror in front of her that's planted almost wall to wall, and she admires herself in the midst of her thoughts of Bain. He's all she can think about, and then in the middle of prancing in front of the mirror, she gets an idea. Bain.

She plays with the bracelet Bain just gave her and calls him. "Bain?" He picks up on the first ring.

"Hold on, Lex." He starts to speak to someone else. "Yeah, Cease! I'll catch up with you, man. Much love to your moms, playa. Take it easy now." Coming back to the cell, Bain's tone is much calmer when he speaks again. "What's up, babe? You got home alright?"

"I did, but I have an idea."

"An idea, huh? What's that, Lex?" he asks, blowing out smoke from his cigar.

"Are you still smoking? You know I'm allergic to that, Bain, come on now."

"It's not a cigarette. Cigar. I just puff on it after we do our thing, you know?"

"Stop lying! You're stupid," she exclaims, taking the cigar smoking after sex as sort of a compliment.

"Nah, but what's up? I'll put it out."

"Thanks, babe."

"Ain't no problem. Talk to me. What's this idea you got?"

"I want you to come over. My mom and dad aren't at home, and there's been some emergency at the hospital with a friend of theirs. It's sad, I know, but...I'm wondering if you can come over and spend more time with me until about eleven. I miss you again!" she laughs. "Besides that, don't you want to see the inside of my room for a change?"

"Man, I don't know, Lex. This thing we're doing here is all private. It doesn't leave beyond the trees of these trails, girl. You want your man to catch a charge or something? You setting me up like on that show?"

"Bain, no! If I was setting you up, don't you think you would have already been locked up by now. We've been doing this for a year now. That's cold, Bain."

"I'm sorry, Lex, but you know I have to check up on us with that shit."

"Bain, you know me."

"Yeah..." he pauses, "And you know me."

"Good, so you coming?"

"Yeah, give me about thirty. I'll be there. Look out for me, okay, and hit me if things aren't clear."

"Okay," she says, expressing her out of bounds joy by clapping her hands and jumping up and down a mile a minute.

"Lex, I'm serious. Look out for me. I always do the same for you."

"Bain, okay! Just hurry. Do me a favor though, come through the garage. I'll have it open so you can come straight in. If you see a car, keep walking."

"Cool, baby. Bye."

Bain gets to Alexis' house twenty minutes after they concoct the plan on the phone. It was a bit early for Bain to leave Gabriel's Trails, so as he leaves, people who are keen to his goings and comings are on the prowl for something strange to happen, but nothing did.

Alexis already has the garage up, and Bain hustles inside, wearing a white hoodie and the same jeans he had on earlier. Of course, the hoodie is pulled over his head in order to conceal his facial appearance just in case someone sees him.

"Come on in," Alexis greets him at the garage door entrance.

"Girl, take your hair down out of that pony tail. You know I like your hair loose. Gimme kiss," he says, stealing one from her lips while sliding the rubber band down her hair. Alexis' hair dropped around her shoulders. This makes Bain smile, and that makes Alexis feel like she's on top of the world.

She wraps her arms around his neck. "I love you."

"Well," He moves her back. "I'll love you far more than this if I can check this pad out. You are really living over here, aren't you, Lex?" he says, checking out the house while holding her hand, dragging her behind as if it's him who owns the place and he knows where he's walking.

Suddenly, Alexis snatches her hand back, away from Bain's grasp. "What the hell is that in your pants, Bain? Don't bring that crap in my house around me! This is me, Bain! What are you gonna do or need with that here – in my house?" Alexis is clearly upset and ready to call the whole visit off.

"Wait, baby, see look. I have it because of the Trails. When I leave here, it'll be dark. This has nothing to do with you or yours. Here, you take it," he says, handing it to her handle first. "Don't touch the trigger, Lex. Hold that shit tight, and put it where you want. I'll close my eyes. Get it for me before I have to go, okay?"

"No, take this thing out of my hand, Bain. I trust you."

He opens his dark brown eyes, approaches her while the gun is still in her hand, and kisses her with the pistol up against his stomach. "I trust you, too." Then he calmly takes the weapon and places it on the kitchen counter, barrel facing the opposite direction. "Are we good now?"

"It's just that I've never done this before," she says still eyeing the gun. Then, he places his finger up against the bottom of her chin, moving her attention away from the gun and back on his face.

"We...we've never done this before, Lex. Hell, my ass will rot for some shit like this." He takes both her hands, after noticing a slow jam come on the radio, and leads her in the direction of the music. Alexis follows without hesitation until they enter the scarlet red walled entertainment area. He then pulls her gently in front of him so that her back rests on his chest, and they start to dance facing the mirror.

"You're beautiful," Bain describes her as he massages her stomach and kisses her on the neck while moving her long, thick brown strands to one side with his other hand. Bain, then, stares back at her in the mirror while Alexis' eyes are completely closed. She's enjoying the moment, and she really wants it to last forever, unaware that Bain is looking her over as if she is a jewel to be protected from any harm.

When Alexis opens her eyes from the slow dance fancy Bain is giving her, she notices that he's admiring her from the rings on her toes, through the cut off jean shorts and ripped short white top, on up to her spotless face. "Why are you looking at me like that, like you've never seen me before?"

"You just don't know how fine you are, do you?"

"It doesn't matter what I think. You're my man, and I want you to always see me as beautiful." Then she pulls away, turns off the radio and takes off running. "Think you can find me?"

"What? Not this chase stuff again, Lex. Come on now, I'm not going up those stairs...trap my ass in this mansion." Quickly with a change of mind about the stairs, Bain follows behind, but hesitates as his pistol sits on the counter. Unfamiliar territory is something that Bain rarely does without a full check while fully loaded. In this case, however, he shrugs it off and gives chase while understanding that this is fun for his very young love who doesn't know much about the real world.

For one year, he's not only been her boyfriend, but her father in a sense, being that grown man in her life replacing her constantly working and absent father whom she sees, if lucky, on the way to the toilet in the early hours of the morning when he gets up. Her only real world experience is Bain, and he's careful about shielding her from the rest of it and himself. Bain's smart. He knew how to get her and still knows how to keep her all to himself and happy.

Bain gets much out of it as well. He gets to pretend to leave his real life which really isn't factory work. His life is wrapped up in the streets from sun down to sun up, but it's Alexis that brings goodness and innocence back into his life, something that is very odd to him. There are times when he realizes that he could take full out advantage of this rich situation Alexis has brought to him, the way she's intrigued by him, how he can develop any emotion that he wants her to have, but he figures that he'll play along with the fantasy, mostly for her sake, until it runs out. Bain is well versed in the differences between fantasy and reality, unlike Alexis. All things end when reality comes full circle. Until then...

"So this is your room, Lex?" He catches up to her and then leans on her bedroom door, rubbing his go-tee.

She falls back onto her pink and yellow comforter set, crosses her legs, and places her hands behind her head that's resting on her frilly pillows. "Yep, this is my own little world."

"This is some unreal shit for T.V. land right here, Lex," he laughs. "It's nice though, real nice. I already feel like a hardened criminal just standing in this spot."

"You coming in or what?" she asks. "Nothing in here bites or has teeth, so come on. Enjoy while we still have time."

"No, Lex, I'm good right here at this door, babe."

"You scared?"

He stares directly back at her, not believing that she's taunting him over fear. It was new to him, and he actually takes the taunt as quite funny.

"Me? Scared? No, Lex," he responds, kneeling down to graze his hand on the soft plush carpet that was also dyed a light pink and then stands back up. "I'm not scared to come in. Just ready for you to come out is all."

"Why?"

"The last place I want to accidentally get my DNA on is your room."

"Mine is in yours," she quickly responds.

"Sure it is." He looks back behind himself and down the stairs. "Sure it is, but that's my place. I'm in control of that."

"Oh, Bain…" she complains, jumping off the bed. "You're so paranoid! Stop it and come on! I want your scent in my bed so I can sleep better tonight. I love the way you smell," she says, grabbing his hand and pulling him forward.

Her forceful pulling doesn't work, and Bain gets a bit annoyed, yet doesn't show it. Instead he pulls her back toward him with the strength of one arm, and it startles Alexis so much that she goes speechless and even puzzled.

"Let's go back downstairs, Lex. This isn't good for you. For that fact, me either."

"Are you mad or something?" Alexis notices the serious look on his face, one that she's never seen in the full year they've been together.

"No, I just don't like feeling trapped is all. Right now, that's how I feel. Can you respect that, baby?" He loosens his grip on her hand. "I'm not angry at you. Never that. Just don't want this to end too soon."

"Bain, we are getting married! We're never going to end. You're my man, and I'm your girl – for life." She places her left hand on the side of his face, rubbing the short unshaven newly growing hairs, but he removes her hand right after it starts the caress.

He glances back into her room and then back at her. "Yeah, Alexis, we're getting married someday, just not today or any day if I get caught up these stairs. Let's go."

"Whatever with that not any day junk you're talking, Bain," she turns, waves her hand in his face and proceeds to walk down the stairs as he follows a strategic four paces behind.

"Look, Lex, I have things I have to do for myself and for you if you want that marriage thing, and I'll be happy to do that with you, so just be patient."

"What things other than wait for me to turn eighteen?" She blocks his way at the bottom of the stairs.

He grins from the side of his mouth and watches her clueless gestures that entertain him at times when she gets angry or bothered. "Just some shit I have to deal with. It's time for me to go though and get ready for work."

"Yeah? This early?"

"Yeah, Lex, this early." He tosses on his hood and gives her a kiss. "I love you."

As he walks out the same way he came after retrieving his pistol, Alexis responds, "I love you, too."

By eleven o'clock, Alexis isn't hearing from her mom or dad, so she assumes that things are still critical. Completely bored out of her mind, Alexis derives an idea from the bowels of her curiosity to find out if Bain is really going to work tonight. Her instincts are on full blast now, and she's tired of always alerting him to her whereabouts and comings and goings. Therefore, she grabs her sneakers, some long jeans from the drier and tosses on a loose fitting sweater for the chill at night that she will meet as she finally decides to enter Gabriel's Trails completely on her own.

The trek won't take long, and if Alexis knows her parents well, they won't be back until they extend warm welcomes and a place to sleep from the youngest person to the oldest. They may even eat an early breakfast with the family, so she still has nothing to fret about them coming home until the early hours of the morning.

On the way down the street, Alexis is only slightly nervous. Nighttime isn't a great time for any young girl to travel, however, she has her kicks on her feet and a pocket knife of her dad's in her front pocket with her hand tightly around it. There are plenty bad things that she's heard about Gabriel's Trails that go on at night, but for all she knows, those stories are wives tales because nothing is hardly ever on the news. Fact is, Alexis is fairly certain that she'll be fine entering and exiting the Trails with or without Bain who is the sole reason why she's coming.

Alexis stops at the carved Gabriel's Trails sign before entering, listening for any voices or movement that sounds suspect. She can barely see down past ten feet into the trail because the night light is only flickering, meaning it's about to die out. That isn't good, but it still isn't enough warning to keep Alexis off the trail. She enters. There's no turning back – by her own personal daring choice.

She reaches the red boulder that Bain warned her about on her visit from earlier today, and she looks back. The street will disappear at this point just as Bain said it would, and she backs up. Her fingers grip her pocket knife tightly, and then she decides to take it out of her pocket, brandishing it for whoever may think to attack her as she runs down the trail. Her mom once told her that a weapon seen is much better for safety than a weapon unseen when it comes to a woman. It makes an attacker hesitant. Of course, her mom never was in a situation like this one. That advice came from watching a reality show.

No matter where the weapon theory originated, Alexis is going for it. Still, she hears no noise in the trees besides the leaves blowing, so she runs as fast as her sneakers and strong calves take her until she reaches the end of the trail and the beginning of night life inside Gabriel's Trails.

There's a car show going on, or what Alexis believes is a car show, as she comes to a complete halt, quickly shoving the knife back into her pocket before anyone notices her. Too late. They already see her concealing her small knife in her pants' pocket. There are men and women, boys and girls her age and younger everywhere, and they don't flinch at the sight of her. Some even laugh and point, but still, they continue doing what they do best – whatever that is.

Alexis puts on a strong face as she decides to keep moving. It would be crazy to turn back around now because she could potentially be followed. At the most, she's stuck in the Trails until she can get to Bain who can then lead her back out. She could potentially find her way to the main road from the from the other side of Gabriel's Trails, but that would mean walking through the entire neighborhood, and it's fairly big. She's never even been to the opposite side on foot, ever. Bain's place is closest to the trails which is the back way inside.

"Look who's here! Oh shit!" she hears a male voice yell.

"She must be looking for Bain," a lady laughs as Alexis walks directly in front of her. Alexis looks up at

Bain's condo that sits on a slight hill. "Gone on up there!" she continues to laugh.

"Stop right there, sis." A guy jumps in front of Alexis, holding a beer in one hand with a young boy not more than five years old in his other hand. "What's in your pocket? I saw that shit. Pull that shit out before I do."

Alexis looks around while others wait on the big reveal. She has no choice but to remain silent and do as he says. As she reaches in her pocket, the guy lets go of the little boy's hand, and the child walks behind her to someone already there waiting on him, a woman who is licking a lollipop.

"Uhmm hum," he nods, directing Alexis to put the pocket knife in the palm of his hand. "I know you. Go on up there and see Bain now."

"Thank you," Alexis responds, not knowing what else to say while walking around him, nearly in tears from terror. The crowd disperses while the guy who took her knife grins.

"You're welcome," he laughs. "That's a first for that polite shit." He continues to drink and then takes the little boy back by the hand.

Alexis finally realizes all that Bain has said. She really shouldn't cross over without him, and this is absolutely no place that she's familiar with. In the day, Gabriel's Trails is totally different. It would be a ghost town if you didn't know it, but it looks like the place wakes up at night and only at night.

A couple of women lined the only two stairs of Bain's condo which takes Alexis by surprise, and they wouldn't move out of Alexis' way as she tried to go inside.

"Excuse me, please," Alexis requests, and all the ladies do is roll their eyes and laugh. They don't budge one inch, and Alexis looks back nervously because she feels like the butt end of a bad joke. Her eyes then land on the guy who has her dad's knife, and he looks irritated at the sight.

"Get y'all asses up! Move! Stupid ass mother…move! You see her trying to get up the steps. I know her ass said excuse me." He turns back around to finish talking to whomever it is he's talking, and the ladies only make a path small enough for one foot to go by at a time, meaning it's a tight squeeze.

"How you doing?" a lady standing near the edge of the steps asks.

"Fine." Alexis clears her throat. "I'm fine. Just looking for Bain."

The lady then points her finger to the front door, holding a cigarette in the same fingers. "All I asked you was how you doing. I could give a damn who you looking for." She walks off.

Bain's door is open to her shock with all the people running rampant outside, and to more of her surprise, Bain's place is still as tranquil as it is when she visits. Everything is in place, but there's no Bain.

"Maybe he really is at work," she says, sitting down uneasily on his leather chair. Then, she pops back and quickly walks over to the front door, locking it. "I'm stuck until in the morning. Mom is gonna kill me," she says to herself, not believing Bain is really inside until she hears noises coming from the down the hall.

"Bain?" she calls, but she gets no answer. She decides to walk down the hall and call his name again, "Bain?" His room door is shut, but that only means to open it. When she does, there's Bain, naked and underneath the body of a woman, a beautiful woman, just not her.

Alexis stands there in tears, silently crying and taking it all in. She thinks about that strawberry scented lotion that she saw in his bathroom earlier when they made love, but that's not the worst of it all. Bain is making love to another woman on what looks to be the same two hundred dollar bills she brought to him for their future savings. He's on the same sheets, the same money, the same...

"Lex?"

Alexis stands there with a blank expression floating in tears, her hair down like Bain likes to see it, as she watches the lady continue to ride him as he calls toward the door.

"Lex, baby," He turns back to face the woman on him who is now smiling at Alexis and slaps her face so hard that she falls off the bed to the other side of the floor.

"You ain't 'bout nothing, Bain! Don't hit on me for a bitch that came in here to watch!" she screams, getting her naked body back onto her feet.

Bain rises up from the bed fast in all his nakedness, unwilling to walk toward Alexis in this form, no matter how many times they've made love. This isn't how he approaches Alexis ever. He's always as respectful as he can be in their illegal situation, however, tonight, it's nearly impossible to turn off the lack of respect that Alexis is seeing before her very eyes.

34

Grabbing his pants, Bain rushes to put them on as the woman shoves past Alexis with only a tank top and some underwear on, causing her to fall up against the bedroom door's hinges. Then she backs up to create one more tear in Alexis' heart.

"You ain't know your man is a pimp, child," she says, looking directly into the side of Alexis' face. "Because that's what he is," the lady says, turning her glaring eyes at Bain, "Nothing but a low life pimp. How you in love with that, huh?"

"Get the fuck out my house!" Bain yells, and Alexis covers her ears, terrified as Bain grabs his pistol off the dresser and shoves it in the back of his pants. He paces toward Alexis slowly, but she won't let him come any closer.

"Stop! Stop it!" she screams. At this point her tears and screams blend together like a chaotic mass of thunder. Alexis sounds like a woman who has lost a child. The pain from her voice is so bad that Bain immediately grabs her and holds her tightly as she fights to get him away.

"Lex, baby, please. She ain't nothing to me. Forget that shit, please. I'm right here with you, okay? What are you doing here, Lex?" He holds her tighter. "Stop fighting, Lex, calm down, baby, calm down. Stop screaming, please. You can beat me up. I'll let you, just calm down. I'm sorry, Lex, I'm sorry," Bain continues, out of breath and not knowing what to do.

Alexis snatches the pistol from his pants, and Bain immediately throws his hands up because he knows what's about to happen. The gun is pointing directly at his chest, yet he still fails to treat Alexis like an enemy.

"Lex, baby. Put the gun down. I love you. Did you not just see how I knocked the shit out of her? You have a gun on me, Alexis, and I didn't do one thing to you yet... and I won't try. I love you, Alexis."

"Well, I hate you, Bain! I hate you with all my heart!" she screams, the gun still aiming at Bain's chest. Then she runs. She just takes off running, pistol in hand, out the front door, prepared to shoot anyone who tries to stop her. No one does try to stop her, especially when they see Bain standing at the front door about to go after her.

"Get the fuck off my porch." Bain orders the ladies who are now in shock that he's actually about to chase behind a girl.

"Bain, I have to talk to you about some money..." one of the ladies begins.

"I said clear my porch. Sit on the grass and wait."

Bain then takes off down the street after Alexis unarmed because Alexis is dangerously carrying a weapon, his weapon, that can go off at any given time at the wrong touch. Bain has more guns inside his place but he refuses to chase after her with one. His plan is just to get the pistol back and bring Alexis back up to her fantasy with him. Besides that, if she makes the wrong move in her anger and sadness by drawing the pistol on someone as a threat, she could end up dead because there will be no hesitation from any other person in Gabriel's Trails to blow her brains out as a result.

As Alexis reaches trail number two, Bain calls her with no luck. Alexis is clearly delirious as she is running thoughtlessly, not looking up but down, with the pistol pointing down as well as she clutches the handle tightly. Alexis' race through the trail isn't like before when she first entered tonight, but it's a loose jog because she's out of breath from starting off too fast from Bain's place while trying to breathe from all the weeping.

Finally, Bain catches up to Alexis deep inside the trail.

"Lex, I'm serious. Give me the gun so I can get you back home safely. That's all I'm asking tonight. You don't ever have to see me again or come back here."

She turns around furious. "They were laughing at me! All of them! On my way to see you, all those people...they knew me. They know me!" she screams. "Am I your big joke, Bain?"

"Lex, don't do that again," he says referring to her lifting the gun. "Put the piece down, and if you don't want me to, I won't even walk you home. I'll watch from behind."

Alexis raises her gun. "A pimp, Bain? You sleep with your whores, is that it? That's your work? You were trying to get me in...is that the real reason you took my money, Bain?"

"No, Alexis, shit! I have all your money. Every last dime. I never spent it. Listen, Lex," he walks toward her, but she warns him.

"Don't come near me. You took everything from me!" she screams. "Every single thing!"

"Lex, you haven't lost anything, baby. Calm down." Bain silences and checks around him, making sure no one is there. "This is some dangerous shit you're doing, Lex. I'm coming to get the gun. You're too loud out here in these trails..."

"I love you, Bain," she cries. "I loved you more than you'll ever know."

"I love you, too, Alexis. Ain't no loved, Lex. You still love me like I love you." He pauses and stares into saddened eyes on her for the first time since he's known her. Then, he kindly reaches forward. "Come on, give me the..."

She shoots him in the chest. No words come out of their mouths. Alexis stares into Bain's eyes as he smiles back at her, still standing though stumbling to remain upright. When he finally gets it together, she's confused that he hasn't fallen yet, so she shoots the pistol again. The bullet penetrates Bain's chest, and he falls backwards onto the hard concrete.

Alexis drops the gun, but nervously retrieves it again. It's over now. She runs. She runs so fast, leaving her love back there dead on the ground for no one but the night to watch over him. She remembers what Bain taught her as she passes the red boulder – *"Coming in here beyond that rock this far up means that you're on your own. I don't ever want you to be on your own, Lex."*

Clearing the boulder, she turns to look back. She no longer sees anything beyond the red as Bain said. Just then, she hears a patrol coming down the road, as it does every hour. Alexis pulls her hair to the side, straightens up her face, hides the gun, and walks patiently toward where the trail begins.

The security guard nods his head as he passes by, shines his light into the trail beyond the trees and keeps going. He sees nothing, and Alexis continues to walk until she turns the corner heading for her house. She then dumps the pistol into a pile of sticky bushes. It's hidden at the very bottom.

It's Monday morning, and it's time for school again. Alexis' mom is upstairs tending to her novel while her dad has already gone back to work.

"Mom, I'm on my way to school!" she yells.

"Wait, honey, here I come." Lorah bursts through the door with a full manuscript in her hands and a big smile. "Tah dah! I'm finished my novel, Lexi!"

"That's good, ma. I'm sure it's going to sell better than all the rest," Alexis responds with the best smile that she can muster. She's cried throughout the whole weekend unbeknownst to her parents who are, for the most part, too busy to notice anything. There's a continuing report on the news about a pimp who was found dead in Gabriel's Trails of gunshot wounds to the chest, however, the investigation is at a standstill with no leads. All weekend, Alexis just knew that the cops were going to come knocking, but no one ever came. Her parents just came home that night of the murder, and that's who's been coming in and out of the house since.

"Are you okay, Lex?" her mom asks trying to see beyond the sunglasses covering Alexis' eyes.

"I'm fine, mom. The morning sun…I may need to see an eye doctor."

"You're right. I'm on it! Love you, Lex. Have a good day. She kisses her daughter on the forehead, and Lex returns the love with a kiss on the chin.

"I love you more, mom." She leaves to catch the bus. Alexis can't bare walking to school anymore because she fears someone may catch a glimpse of her from the edge of the trail. They know who she is. They must know. For some reason, they won't tell.

As she boards the bus, her friend nicknamed Lace pats the seat next to her. "Girl, where you been? I called you over the weekend."

Alexis sits down. "I wasn't feeling too good, Lace. Flu or something. What's up?"

"You know they normally don't report all the crap that goes on down the road, but peep this. There was an actual pimp that lived there, a real pimp that got shot up by some crazy on Friday night. From what my cousin said…"

"Your cousin?"

"Yeah, my cousin…anyway, from what he said it was a friend of his named Bain. That shit is too close to home, don't you think. A pimp is a friend of someone in *my* family and he ends up shot? No boo…too close. Anyway, those people are crazy in the Trails."

Alexis looks out the window. "Yeah, they are kinda crazy."

The bus driver closes the bus doors, turns the corner and drives past Gabriel's Trails. Alexis wipes a tear from her eye. Her fantasy is over.

MURDERS AT GABRIEL'S TRAILS

II

A Son's Sacrifice

Murders at Gabriel's Trails II: A Son's Sacrifice

"I'm a nut…in a hut…I stole your mama's pocketbook, so what," sing the children outside on the street as they play a more criminal form of patty cake that pertains to stealing. It's a summer day in Gabriel's Trails, and things are all good for the new people who are just moving in named the Moores. The Moores have three sons, the oldest named Javis, the middle named Derek, and the youngest named Joseph after the Moores got saved, thus naming the child after a prophet. The boys are seventeen, sixteen and fourteen in age, and they even look like twins though separated by one to three years from oldest to youngest.

Gabriel's Trails is the most decent place they could move that provides a livable in house atmosphere. Unfortunately, the outside atmosphere is a bit more damaging, however, the plan is to keep the children in house, and on the days they need to spread their wings and get fresh air, they are driven out to do what they need to do in another area. The truth is that the Moores are very protective of their boys, and will do what it takes to provide them a safe household.

"Summer's almost over, man," says Derrick to Javis. "Two more days left, and it's time to start this new school."

"I'm so tired of this," Javis responds to his younger brother as he peeps back at the cracked window to remind Derrick that mom and dad could hear. "All that happens nowadays is us running low in the bank and having to move every three to six months. It's embarrassing. By the time I graduate, I will have attended every school in each district at this rate. What's even the point in dating or even

43

finding a place in school when moving is around the corner, D."

"I know, but look at the bright side…"

"There isn't a bright side to look at," he says forcefully in a whisper. "Man, look at us! Look," he exclaims, hitting the chair he's sitting in. "We can't even leave off the dang porch!" Then he points to the children across the road on the sidewalk playing patty cake. "Even *they* get to walk up and down the sidewalk, Derrick."

"You're almost out of here, Javis. It's me that has two more years."

"I'm thinking about packing it in sooner than that. I'm tired of school…"

"Javis you can't drop out!"

"Man, shhhh. Be quiet. Dad is right there on the couch asleep when she should be out there working. Mom, doesn't make enough money to hold this together. Either I drop out and get a job to help her or I leave. It'll be one less mouth to feed. I'll be alright."

"Pops is trying, man. He got laid off and he was out all day long looking for work yesterday, until night fall without anything to eat."

Javis looks back at his dad and then back at Derrick. "Yeah, I know. I'm sorry for saying that. Father, forgive me," he states looking up at the sky, referencing the location of God. "I'm just upset, D. I might not be quitting school, but I will start to work. Mom and dad are just going to have to realize that I can't sit home anymore while they struggle. I'm able, plus I'm willing. I can do it."

"Tell 'em then, man. I'm with you."

44

"Yeah, I will." He glances at his dad again. "I will."

"Hey, here comes mom."

The boys get up from the porch and walk down to the car to help her get her things. No matter how bad the times, Mrs. Moores always relies on her sons for smiles because she's proud of all of them individually and will break her back to keep them happy and safe. Unfortunately, it seems the money woes are making that hard to do.

"Mom, let me get that for you," Derrick offers as he reaches inside the car to grab her purse and umbrella. It rained this morning before she left but the day turned out sunny and far too hot.

Mrs. Moores is a gentle looking lady with naturally curly hair that bounces with each movement and nice, dark brown skin that would make any man take two glances and a third. She's what *sinning* men call holy and hot at the same time, but don't think she's a softy. Mrs. Moores is a third degree black belt with full on boxing training so she can throw down if need be. Gabriel's Trails doesn't scare her. She's born and bred from worst streets, but she always says she won't die in them.

"Mom," Javis begins, helping his mom out of the car by her hand, "I'm going to get a job to help out with the bills after school or on the weekends. Does that sound good to you?"

"I don't know, does it? Let me see." Mrs. Moores places her hand up to her ear and squints her eyes as if she's trying to hear a soft whisper, and then removes her hand from her ear to place it on her hip. "Nope, no sir, it doesn't sound good to me." She kisses Javis on his cheek, thanks him for opening the door, and scurries around him to go start dinner.

"No? What do you mean no, ma? We have no money right now! You guys need me to step up and…"

Mrs. Moores grabs him up by his chin and cheeks quickly before he gets another word out. Javis' lips are poking out like a duck's bill as he stares back at his mom who has a look on her face like she could mash all his teeth out of his mouth.

"I don't think it's a good idea, Javis." She watches Javis' eyes fall to the ground and his shoulders slump over before she continues, "I think it's one of the best ideas you've had since you turned seventeen." She lets his face go as his face lights up like the sun. "You're starting to think like a man. That's one of the first signs of it – responsibility." She nods and winks. "Sure, you're ready, but before you do it, let's let your dad know your thoughts tonight. Then, we'll pray that your path at work is blessed. Does that sound good?"

Javis recalls what his mom did at the car and puts his hand up to his ear, squints like he's trying to hear something and then says, "Yep, sounds great to me!"

Derrick's head is pressed against the window's screen with both his thumbs up. Mrs. Moores looks at him grinning from ear to ear.

"Looks like you already shared your idea with your brothers, huh?"

"Just Derrick. Joseph is in the bed reading his Bible or either asleep.

"Well, let's get ready to share the news at dinner."

They both enter their new home with smiles on their faces and a new hope for the future.

"So what's this good news you have to announce, Javis? Your mom sure is pleased about it, but she won't tell me one word. She tells me that you have to spill the beans this time, just don't spill it over here in these beans I simmered up for your mom before she got home. I put my foot in that," Mr. Moores laughs, stuffing his face and bragging about his cooking.

"Well, go on, Javis," Mrs. Moores encourages him as she takes her seat at the table with fresh squeezed lemonade and a pitcher of water on the side.

"Well, I see the hard time the family's having as a whole, and I know, dad, that many places tend to believe they have to pay you top dollar to give you a job, making it hard to find work for yourself."

"You got that right," he interjects.

"Exactly. Thing is, I want to work. I'll try to get a job, but in the meantime, I can cut yards for about fifty dollars and up per yard on the weekend or after school during the week. Shoot, I add that up with just four yards, that's two hundred dollars!"

"So you want to work now, son, huh?"

Javis sticks his chest out. "Yes sir. I'm ready."

Mr. Moores picks up his napkin and wipes his mouth. "Karen, I think it's a good idea. I prefer the yard cutting over a job because he can control his own pay and when he needs to take time off. Those jobs care nothing for you, and he's still in school. We didn't use the lawn mower anyway in the last couple of places we've moved because there was no yard." He looks up and points in the direction of the neighborhoods surrounding Gabriel's Trails. "All those rich people over there may cut you some slack and let you cut their yards if you do a good job, Javis. Just let me know and I'll even help you from time to time if you need me, but until then, I need to find a job with benefits. Shouldn't be too long now."

"Preach," Mrs. Moore chimes in with a giggle.

"Amen! Let me know when…"

"Tomorrow," Javis interjects. "Dad, I'll go door to door tomorrow and schedule with the neighborhood. I might even take the lawn mower with me, but for now, I want to be professional and introduce myself."

"Hey! Why didn't anybody come wake me up to eat? You guys are foul!" Joseph says finally coming out of his room to greet everyone for dinner. They all burst into laughter at the sight of Joseph standing there in his boxers and one sock.

"We just decided to let you get your beauty rest!" Mr. Moores teases.

"Man…Derrick scoot over." He walks over to the table and plops down angrily. "You guys are wrong for this. That's alright though, as hungry as I am. There's always get back. Always get back. Bet you took the best pieces of meat, too."

They smile and eat. Even though the Moores have hardly any money or benefits, they, for the most part have a good attitude about it.

Sunday comes and right after church, Javis' parents drop them off in the neighborhood right outside of the back of Gabriel's Trails called Dominion Lakes. Javis wants to look at the medium sized to bigger yards where he figures the owners have the money to spare to a young man trying to earn an honest living.

Early this morning, he shaved up really clean, creating the look of innocence and youth. He may be young, but Javis has already had his fill of being a chocolate brown young man. When he was younger, he remembers women of all races calling him handsome and cute, even giving him a dollar. Now, he has to keep his cute as best he can because any gruff found around the collar, it seems like people take him as an immediate threat. Javis even cut his mustache down to the bare minimum.

"You look funny, J," criticizes Derrick. Your mustache is what makes you look distinguished, as dad puts it. Now, all you look like is a scrub."

"Well, you can sit on the sidelines while I make my scrub money. Do you see all these yards? Forget that…I'm making my money. As a matter of fact, let's stop right here. This will be our first house because it's right on the corner, looking big, rich and ready to give me some money for my service." He stops and places his hand in front of Derrick. "You stand about five feet behind me and look like a kid. Sink that chest in some and put a smile on your face."

"Man, what if it's a girl in that house that comes to the door."

"I'm not cutting her, Derrick, I'm cutting the yard! Stay focused and smile," Javis responds irritated but ready to put the plan into action. He walks up, knocks on the door and takes four steps back as to prove he wants to do no harm.

"You should have rang the doorbell," Derrick says under his breath but loud enough so that Javis wants to karate kick him upside his head.

When no one comes to answer, Javis returns to the door and follows the hint that Derrick gave him which is to ring the doorbell. He returns to his nonviolent, give me a chance stance about five paces away from the door when he hears a voice from the upper floor window.

"Yes?"

"Excuse me, ma'am…" He looks up, placing his hand above his eyes to shield the sun.

"I'm not a ma'am. I'm a Miss. M.I.S.S….that kind of Miss."

"I'm sorry, Miss…" Javis waits for her to finish the name, however, she doesn't. There's about a three second silence, so Javis continues to talk. "I would like to offer my services to you, Miss, my yard services. My name is Javis Moores, and if you allow me, I would love to schedule a time when I can come and upkeep your yard weekly, biweekly or even monthly."

"Well, can't you make up your mind, Javis Moores?"

"Excuse me?"

"Your mind…"

The front door opens, and another woman comes peeping out. "Yes, may I help you? Why are you screaming at my daughter from the upstairs window, young man?"

"Your daughter?" Javis glances at the woman at the door and then quickly back at who he now knows is a girl. Then, he immediately expresses his apologies to her mother. "Ma'am, I'm so sorry. My apologies, I thought that she was the owner…"

"Of the house, mom. It's not his fault. I misled him, just joking around. He wants to cut the yard for a fee, weekly, bi-weekly or even monthly. It all depends on what you want and need."

"Quiet!" she shouts up to the window. Then she turns back to the young men. "Your name?"

"Javis Moores…and this is my younger brother Derrick," he responds, pointing behind himself.

"What are your ages?"

"I'm seventeen, and Derrick is sixteen."

"Church going boys?" she asks, noticing their clean dress clothes.

"Yes ma'am. Twice a week and sometimes three times depending on…"

"You're hired. Where's your lawn mower?"

"We're only scheduling today, ma'am."

"You need my name to do my yard, and it's Mrs. Balentine. Do you have a sheet of paper?"

"I do, Mrs. Balentine." He waves his brother to whip out the pad and pen.

"Teamwork, I see, and coming prepared. Listen, I do need some yard work done as you can see. We never have the time, and our yard man moved away…"

"So yes. Saturdays good?" interrupts the girl in the window.

"Didn't I say be quiet?" Mrs. Balentine shouts up to her daughter who is still hidden by the screen. "Saturdays, Javis, is fine. Your charge?"

"Fifty dollars."

"Front and back?"

"May I see your back?"

"Smart young man! Go on around back and peep at the rest of the yard to see what you're working against. Come back around and then let me know."

"Yes, Mrs. Balentine." He looks back at his brother who can't believe it's this easy to make a buck. "Did you get that? Saturdays – every Saturday. B.A.L.E…"

"Man, I heard her. I got it." Derrick looks up at the window, and the girl is gone. "Where'd she go?"

Javis looks up. "Who cares? She had me looking like a herb."

"You do look like a herb, with or without her help."

"Man, shut up. I hope this lady's yard looks like a dump so I can up the price."

As they go around back, the young lady who was speaking to them from the window meets them at the ajar fence to introduce herself once more.

"Alexis."

Both Javis and Derrick freeze. She's the best looking girl that they've seen since they moved to Gabriel's Trails, and it's far too obvious that they are tongue twisted at her generous smile, long hair and gorgeous face.

"Since you and I said you look like a herb," Derrick says out the side of his mouth, "Hi, I'm Derrick. This is my herb brother, Javis, up close and personal." Derrick extends his hand only so that he can feel hers, and Javis knocks his hand out of the way, clearly already irritated with Alexis and her antics.

"We're not back here to talk." He glares at Alexis. "We're here to check out some grass," He walks by them both. "Thank you, however, for hiring us, miss, and your mother."

Alexis laughs and can't believe he is getting that upset with a joke. "Are you really that much a herb like your brother says? I was joking. Really, sorry. Alexis." She extends her hand toward Javis, and he finally accepts.

"It's cool. Nice to really meet you." From there, Javis pretends he's not that interested in her or her looks, but more interested in the grass. Derrick isn't putting on a façade. Instead, he just shoots right for the target.

"I'm sixteen, how about you?"

"Sixteen."

"Yeah, this looks like a fifty dollar job for the front and ten dollars extra for the back. Sixty bucks. Let's go."

Javis passes by his brother and Alexis to go and let Mrs. Balentine know that it will be sixty dollars each week.

"Mrs. Balentine," he calls, turning the corner with Derrick close behind, "It'll be sixty dollars for the front and the back each Saturday. If that's fine, I'll be here on Saturday morning or evening, when the sun is going down or before it comes up."

"That's fine, Javis. We'll be looking for you. The only thing is, don't enter my home under any circumstances or this verbal contract is null and void. Got it?"

"I understand, Mrs. Balentine, and thank you for the opportunity. You don't know how much."

"I think I might, Javis. I was young and needed money, too, at one point. I still need it now, however, it's not as hard to come by. I like to give back to young men trying to earn an honest living."

"Thank you again. Come on, Derrick."

Derrick nods to Mrs. Balentine, and catches up to Javis who has already reached the street, walking toward the fast food restaurant about five blocks down the road which is the long way around to get into Gabriel's Trails main entrance. Mr. Moores is sitting at the restaurant waiting on them to make their way down the road from finding work.

There are two more homes that open the door for Javis and Derrick on the way down to meet their dad, and they declined the offer. So far, on this street, Javis has future solid earnings of over two hundred dollars a month. When they reach the intersection, Derrick starts.

"She's fine, man. I hope she goes to our school. Sixteen, too. I'm changing my schedule to all her classes," He jumps up and down like a boxer in church clothes. "Long hair, creamy brown skin, great personality...she'll make a nice wife, kids and bedroom loving."

"Derrick, shut up. Did you see her house? It takes money to date a girl like her, and since all we do is cut her yard, we can forget it." He hits the traffic light button three times because it's not changing fast enough for him.

"Javis, calm down. The only place we have to go is home. Enjoy this freedom."

"I can't argue with that, Derrick," Javis responds, giving Derrick pound. "And she is a dime, man."

"Oh! Oh! So you did see that?!" Derrick shouts, pointing back at the house and covering his mouth.

"With both my eyes, man." he laughs. "All both of them." They both cross the road, meet with their dad, tell him the good news of some extra money coming in, and go home.

School starts and Javis and Derrick are disappointed that the one person they met on Sunday is nowhere to be found in school. They already let Joseph in on how gorgeous she is, and begin to plot on who'll get the goods. Every last one of them are virgins that perpetrate otherwise to each other.

"I'm not ashamed, guys. Love me how I am. I'm a vir-gin. Holla at me!"

Derrick slugs Joseph in the arm at the cafeteria table. "Man, shut up, dude. Javis, man, you sit by him.

That ain't cool that he's all loud with that." All Javis does is laugh as Derrick changes seats, continuing his rant. "So what! Nobody needs to know all that. Play the role, Joseph, play the role."

"The only role I play is my own. Bump you." He nudges Javis. "Big bro, what do you think? You're a money maker now, is it play the role or be the role model?"

"It's be the role model, Joseph. Be the role model," he responds, taking a deep breath and then swigs his chocolate milk. "Any time you can be or are forced to be."

"Aw, man, that's that herb talk again." Derrick takes a bite of his burger, and they all finish lunch.

Saturday rolls around after a full week of school, meeting new people and more, and Javis, who is finally in his senior year, is ready to make that money, not only for himself but to help out his family. It took all he had in him to not drop out and cut grass all day long, but he knew that his dad's heart would be broken as well as his own jaw when his dad punched him in it. Therefore, he buckled down to the desks until school let out each day and left.

Javis backs away from Mrs. Balentine's front door after giving it two knocks and one ring on the doorbell. After waiting for two minutes, someone answers, but not from the door. It's Alexis, and she's speaking from the window again, but this time, with the curtains pulled around her face.

"Hi, Javis. I didn't see you in school all week so I assume you aren't private."

"You assume right? Is Mrs. Balentine home?" Javis answers, swatting a group of gnats that he's incidentally walked into.

"No," she pauses. "No, she's never home on Saturday. I have your money though. It's safe with me until you finish both the front and the back for fifty dollars was it?"

"Sixty...sixty dollars, it's Alexis right?" he asks pretending to have a lapse of memory when it comes to remembering her name.

"In the flesh."

"In the window," he says under his breath so that Alexis doesn't hear him. "Is the gate open. I prefer to start in the back and make my way to the front, if that's cool?"

"Sure, whatever you want. And yes, it's open."

"Thanks," Javis responds as he reaches for the bottom of his shirt to pull it off, wrapping it on the handle of the lawn mower.

"You're welcome," says Alexis eyeballing Javis' well toned chest, but Javis doesn't hear her because he's already turned on the lawn mower, headed to the back. As soon as Javis turns the corner, she heads downstairs and out the back French doors.

At first, he starts to cut without noticing Alexis looking at him as she stands beneath the only tree in the backyard that is hovering over their deck, providing the best of shade. She watches Javis and begins to tear up with each minute that passes by until he looks up and notices her watching. Javis turns off the lawn mower, and she slowly wipes a tear away from her eye promptly as to conceal the fact that in her admiration of him, she is still saddened by memories of a lost love. Believing that Alexis could have said something to him while the mower was running, Javis asks, "Did you say something?"

"Do you want a glass of water?"

"My brother should be here later. He may bring one, so..."

"I'll bring it anyway." She immediately returns into the house to do just as she said while Javis shrugs his shoulders, wipes the sweat from his face with his shirt that's tied tight on the mower's handle, and continues to mow the yard. About ten minutes later and with a quarter of the yard already finished, Alexis is back with the water. She sits it on the deck's table, watches him and waits, but he never stops mowing. He doesn't even look up. Finally, Alexis pours him a glass, takes her hair down and shoes off, and delivers it to him while attempting to calm her nerves.

"Here ya go," she sneaks up behind him at the edge of the yard before he turns the mower. Javis doesn't flinch because he already knows it's her. He's been watching her, too, but he's not about to let her steal the money his family truly needs right now by her obvious flirting and his not so overt scoping. Therefore, he pretends to not pay her any attention when the truth is, she's hard to miss.

"Thanks," he says, releasing the lawn mower's handle to take the glass of water from her hand.

"You remind me of someone I used to know."

"Really," Javis laughs while taking a sip. "Is that why you're serving me and treating me so nice?"

"Why would I treat you any other way? To be honest," she takes a deep breath, "I'm bored as hell around here."

"Say what? You can have anything you want and go where you please."

She rolls her eyes. "That's what you think." There's a bench two feet from where they're chatting and Alexis goes to take a seat. "I haven't left this house for about a year."

"Why not?"

Watching her words, Alexis responds, "Just trying to make it. Sometimes I feel so stuck, like I need to go. I want my parents to move, but it's a waste of time for me to keep begging. We don't get along anymore, and now, I just feel like no one understands me, ya know?" She kicks the grass with her feet, knowing full well the true reason behind the mental anguish in her life. Even though Javis feels uneasy in his client's yard chatting about moving and boredom, he shares a seat next to her on the bench to finish his water.

"If it makes you feel any better, this job does more for me than making money," he admits in a round about way, referring to her presence, but he options to make it about freedom. "It gets me out of the house, too. It gets me some freedom to think, to clear my head," he continues. Then he leans over, slowly reaching to move her long, beautiful hair from her face as she stares at the ground. He continues, "And meet new people like you."

Alexis doesn't need Javis to spell it out, and Javis knows he doesn't have to cast too many lines to reel her in. They are both attracted to each other at this point, and words need not say anything that will mess up what just started.

"Hey man, I've been ringing that doorbell about two hundred times! Let me go tell dad to drive off." It's Derrick coming around the house, and as Javis told Alexis earlier, he has some ice cold bottled water in his hands. As Derrick turns around and walks back around to the front, Alexis stands up, walks directly in front of Javis, purposely positioning her body in this fashion, and removes the sixty dollars from her pocket, placing the neatly folded money into his hand.

"Are you finished?" Alexis asks, glancing at the glass of water in his other hand.

"Yeah, I'm done. Thanks again," Javis responds to her body and then her face.

"You're welcome." Alexis turns and walks away. Javis watches, of course, all the way until she closes the French doors. When he looks down at the money, her phone number stares back at him requesting he call soon.

Of course, Derrick is pissed, but what can he do but listen to Javis all week long call Alexis after dinner. Each and every breath makes him cringe, but he's happy for the sort of couple that he sees blossoming because he found his own girl at school, maybe not prettier, in his mind, than Alexis, but she's pretty enough for his taste.

"Hey, man, can I help you make that money so I can, you know, take care of my girl's lunch or something in school. I feel tacky, J. I don't ever have any money, and what kind of man can't help his woman out with lunch?"

"If you help me cut instead of what you did last Saturday, sit around and wait on Lexis to come back down, maybe I will give you twenty bucks a month to spend on your little girlfriend."

"That's it?"

"Okay, ten."

"What!"

"Keep asking and it'll be nothing. That money is for me to pocket and help mom and dad out. Simple. When dad gets a job, then I'll front you more for helping me out."

"Yo man, how is she?" he asks flipping on the television and diving on the other side of the couch.

"She's cool. Deep, really. Sometimes she even sounds sad, but I don't bother her about it. I try to keep her smiling, man. That's the way to a woman's heart…"

"And panties."

Javis shrugs his shoulders. "She doesn't come off as that type of girl, D. She's cool people. Cool, rich people. Her dad's a surgeon, and get this…Mrs. Balentine is an author."

"Don't get her pregnant. Her ass will clean you out in court. You'll be cutting yards from sun up to sun down."

"Derrick! I hear you! Shut it up!"

"Yes, ma'am! I'm sorry, ma," he calls.

Javis gets up and goes outside. "That's exactly why I have to get out of here. Ears in the walls," he mumbles.

Saturday comes back not too fast for Javis because he and Alexis have grown quite close over the past week. Something that they both found out about each other is that they need a change. Javis obviously wants to make a good living after school, and he finds out that Alexis is tired of the same ole same, wants different experiences with different people. She's opted into more advanced classes to graduate at the same time as Javis coincidentally. This elates Javis in every way.

Mrs. Balentine isn't at home again, and this leaves Javis alone with Alexis again until Derrick gets back, being dropped off by dad. Instead of getting straight to cutting the grass, Alexis calls Javis up to the deck.

"I'm so glad you're here," she squeals, elated that she finally has enough nerve to start a relationship again and to a guy that reminds her so much of her first love. Alexis has her hair pulled up in a high pony tail, allowing Javis to see the full scope of what he believes is a beautiful face.

"Good to see you, too, Lexis," he says as she pull him up the deck by his wrist as if he needs help. "Does your mom know…"

As soon as Javis looks up from watching his step during mid sentence, Alexis plants a passionate kiss on his bottom lip. Javis reciprocates…but he doubles up while placing her hands inside his. Javis is about to get lost in all this forwardness, and he doesn't know how to stop it until his eyes look up and land on the house. He moves away, but she moves closer, seeming to gaze and want to graze through the skin on his bare chest.

"Do you want to come in?"

"Yeah, I wanna come in, but that's not a good idea."

"What is? Not coming in?"

He laughs, and then she laughs after him. The only thing about her laugh is that he doesn't know just how serious she is about the invite.

"You may need to talk to your mom about that, Lexis. I'm not about to get shot by your moms or your dad for being in their house with their daughter without their permission. Your moms gave me..."

"Who said anything about getting shot, J?" she asks calmly, but a bit perturbed. Javis can tell by the look on her face that he hit a nerve. "You think we have a pistol in this big ole house?" She walks closer to him, close enough to kiss his neck with no effort. "What if I told you that I did have one? Would it matter?"

After her response, Javis backs up a little, enough to feel the distance between them. "You alright, Lexis? I didn't mean it like that, I was just saying, I might get beat down and lose my gig. I'm not paid like you, and I need the money."

Alexis about faces. "She already knows you've been calling me if that makes you feel better. I told her you're really smart, helped me with my homework issue and all during our conversations."

"Say what, Lexis?"

"She thinks you're a nice young man, is her description, especially since you respect her rules."

"One rule. Don't go in her house."

"That'll change." She walks over to the corner of the deck and listens to voices she hears from the front of the house. "Derrick's here. It's time for you to get to work... while I watch," she grins.

"Well, guess what?" It's Alexis' mom turning the corner with Derrick. Alexis simply leans over the deck's post shooting a quick glance at Javis while he starts backing slowly off of the deck altogether. "I just met your father out front, Javis. He tells me great things about you and the family, and he's a very intelligent man." She glances at her watch and then back at Alexis. "Baby, go run and grab my credit cards out of my drawer. I forgot that I have a shopping date with some friends. Do you want to come with us, baby? It'll be a lot of fun."

"How are you, Mrs. Balentine?"

"I'm well, Javis. Thanks for asking," she responds while Derrick tosses him a water. "It's commendable that you want to work to help the family out with the bills."

Javis immediately nods, glances up at Alexis a bit embarrassed by what Mrs. Balentine reveals, and then walks to start up the mower while his brother shakes his head in disbelief at what he just heard Alexis' mom say about the family being broke. Alexis, in tune to what just went down, interjects.

"No, I don't want to go this time mom, but I was actually thinking that me and Javis could catch a movie this week, maybe Friday night, since you seem to get along great with his dad. You think? I haven't hung out in a minute, ma."

Javis stops cold in his tracks at the mower and stalls at starting up. He's waiting on Mrs. Balentine's answer, hoping and praying that Alexis' mom isn't as strict as his mom nor as paranoid.

"I don't see why not," she states, glancing over at Javis who purposely starts the mower just in case she starts to ask him any questions about her daughter's concoction. "You have your license now, and I'm sure Javis does. Sure," she shrugs. "Have fun with your back up driver because that's the only way I'm allowing you to go is if you drive, Alexis."

Derrick drops his water on the grass and walks away. Javis smiles and pushes the loud lawn mower. The motor never sounded so good.

Friday night comes after a long week of anticipation. Alexis gets ready with every detail about herself in order, from her hair to nails, both the fingers and toes. Alexis' mom steps out with her, looking like newer money, pearls, rings and all, for an anniversary date with Dr. Balentine who will meet her at this posh spot for dinner and whatever else Mrs. Balentine has planned.

Alexis wasn't stupid when she chose Friday for her movie date with Javis. She knew full well that's her parent's anniversary date, and earlier that day she put her gifts before them and encouraged them to have a long night out because she didn't want to hear the nasty stuff going on in the house. Her parents laughed at the remarks, but felt it was a great idea. Besides that, they've trusted Alexis with the house for a long time, so Friday night is not the exception. Alexis is on her own with their permission.

For the very first time, Alexis enters Gabriel's Trails, not from the back, but from the main entrance. Her stomach knots up, but forces herself to pull through it for her own sake. It's been so long since she killed her ex, one whole year, and it still eats at her every night and day, thinking the cops will come and arrest her. What consumes her is when and where anyone will finally snitch or get pay back.

This is her first time going out with anyone since that time. It's only been school and back, never showing her face back at the Trails. The good thing is that her car windows are heavily tinted, and the car is unrecognizable to anyone in Gabriel's Trails as far as Alexis knows. Even better is that Javis and his family are the first people on the corner which is always that last condo to fill and the first to go empty. People living in the middle seem to get stuck there for a while.

As she pulls in to the driveway, the sun is making its way down in the sky. Instead of getting out to knock on the door, Alexis sits and waits, hoping Javis is waiting near a wall or window and hears the car humming. He does. Out the door he comes, mother behind him.

"Well hi there," his mom says on her stroll to the car. Alexis is already rolling the window down to the red hot like fire interior, silver on the outside paint job her mom got done on the older model mustang. "Can you control a car like this, young lady? It's nice."

"Yes ma'am." Alexis hesitates to open the car door to greet her, but thank goodness for her, Mrs. Moores pardons her and reaches inside the window.

"No, honey, don't get out." They shake hands as Mrs. Moore examines all there is to see about her and the car. Unbeknownst to Alexis, Mrs. Moores trusts no one, but is willing to unleash her son for a date because the relocations have been difficult on him. "Javis tells me good things about you."

Alexis turns to Javis smiling as he gets into the car while Javis is impressed and a bit amazed that she's even giving the yard cutter the time of day. As Javis looks up to spot his dad standing in the window, Alexis continues speaking to his mom.

"I'm glad, Mrs. Moores, and nice to meet you."

"Well, get going. Get back safely." She cuts a sharp eye at Javis, and he knows what that means, thus, giving her a salute. Javis looks back at his dad who seems to be admiring the type of man he is becoming, and that's when Javis tells Alexis to hold on a minute.

"I need to run in the house really fast. Hold on a sec." He exits, leaving his mom to chat with Alexis for a short while longer. His dad has a puzzled look on his face as Javis jumps onto the porch and through the front door, pulling him away from the window.

"Boy, you better get out there with that girl! She's picking you up for right now, but when I'm able to put money down on your ride like I've been planning to…"

"Dad, I don't want to talk about that," he laughs. "What I do want to say is that things have been rough for you, but you never shunned me or the rest of us. Thank you for letting me help the family, and thank you for being a good father to me."

Mr. Moores gives Javis a hug with a manly pat on the back. "Better days are coming," he says, pulling back and staring Javis straight in the eyes. "We're going to make it happen, me, you and the Father in heaven, no matter what rough times we go through. We will make it. You will make it. Love you, now go have a good time."

"Love you, too. We got this." Javis heads out, kisses his mom, and they drive off. Mrs. Moores stands outside, listening to the noise rise in the neighborhood the later it gets. She inconspicuously allows her eyes to follow a strange woman that has already pointed toward the house twice. Then, she walks inside.

"I thought we were going to the movies?"

"We are," she affirms, however, her face is all a lie. Alexis pulls into her driveway, opens the garage door with the automatic remote, drives inside, turns the car off, and tells Javis to wait inside. "I have to make sure the alarm is set. That means that my parents won't be coming back for at least two hours."

"Wait, Lexis…" Javis calls, but it goes unanswered.

"Shh! Just wait!" She scrambles up to the door, opens it, and when she hears the beep, she runs to turn it off. When she gets back to the garage, Javis has already gotten out of the car, appearing more nervous than ready.

"Lexis, this isn't cool. I'm typically straight up, and I don't do that sneak stuff. Either I do something or I don't, and people know about it, one way or the other." Javis is generally an obedient young man, never pushing the envelope usually. In this case, he is extremely uncomfortable, yet highly tempted because of his adoration of Alexis.

"Javis, it's cool. Things are cool. I prefer to watch a movie here tonight. I just had a change of mind. It's nothing sneaky. I invited you into my home. I'm allowed to do that right?"

"Are you sure you mom and dad are gone for the night?"

"We'll only be here for two hours tops." She wraps her palm around one of his fingers and clicks the garage door shut. "It's alright," she confirms, swinging his hand back and forth. "If you knew how alone I am most of the time, you wouldn't even sweat it. I know my parents like read books."

Javis doesn't think anymore about it. He's at the house now, and he's really feeling Alexis because she's already inched closer to him as the garage lights turn out. The only light that shines is from inside the house, allowing them the capability of seeing a silhouette of each other's bodies. The more Alexis sees, the more she thinks about Bain. Javis is the same height, just a little lighter in weight than her first love she gunned down. Each night she has nightmares about the bullets, his smile as he took his fall and how she became invisible. Since then, she's cried every night to try and make it right, but nothing erases pain and secrecy. Now she needs an outlet, and her outlet is Javis.

"Well, let's go inside," he interrupts her as she begins to lift up his shirt.

"Let's."

Upon entry, Javis is floored by the size of the home. At best, the homes he'd lived in prior to moving to Gabriel's Trails were half the size of the first floor. The kitchen is decked with the latest appliances while the stainless steel shines like it's never been used. The only item out of place in the kitchen is Alexis' keys that she tossed onto the counter as she heads to the entertainment room.

"Come around the corner. I've just downloaded a movie. It's a horror, so I hope you're not as chicken to watch that as you are of being in my house," she taunts.

He looks around at the red walls and the wide load mirrors against the wall as he turns the corner and takes a seat in one of the three loveseats that sit in the middle of the floor. The loveseat he chooses faces the television that's hanging on the adjacent wall. As Alexis returns to take her seat next to Javis, she can tell he's still nervous to be inside the house.

"Relax, Javis. I don't want to get killed either so…" She glances back at door which is directly where Javis continues to look. "We both need a break, right? Get some space here with me and I with you."

Javis doesn't have to turn his head much until his eyes end up connecting with Alexis. The movie starts, not taking Javis' attention of off her, and without much more hesitation, he takes a gentle kiss from her lips, and she accepts. They enjoy the beginning of their first night together as the movie plays. Alexis is refreshed. It's been a long time.

She never got the opportunity to love Bain the way she planned. Each and every kiss from Javis, takes Alexis back to when he was alive, their future plans of getting married, and she begins to cry. Javis doesn't notice any tears streaming down her face, and despite them all, she continues to imagine Bain instead of Javis on the loveseat with her as she rubs the back of his neck. He suddenly pulls back.

"Are you alright?" He moves her arms from behind his head, confused as ever at the tears he's seeing fall from her eyes. "Yo, Lexis, I'm sorry…" His hands up in the air like this is a set up.

She wipes her eyes. "No, I'm sorry, Ba…Javis." She turns to face the movie, continuing to clear the tears off her eyes. Alexis tries to shake her emotions, but Javis sees that she can't, therefore, he reaches over and gently pulls her back in toward him, letting her know that things are going to be okay with his actions, not words. Locking her hands inside of his, Javis turns her away from himself, allowing her to become cradled in his arms as they become comforted by each other to finish the movie.

"I'm really sorry about what happened tonight." Alexis explains nearing Gabriel's Trails.

"Stop the car, Lexis. I don't think you get the type of person I am. Just stop the car. We're cool," he says, looking around down the road from Gabriel's Trails entrance. Alexis doesn't just pull over on the side of the road. Instead, she enters into the parking lot of a twenty-four hour grocery store and allows the car to hum.

"Listen, Lexis, the only reason why I went in your house was because you wanted me to, not because I had anything planned with you. There's nothing to apologize for. You're beautiful…" he pauses, touching her cheek. "Look at me, Lexis." She turns his way, for the first time bashfully. "And I just want to continue this thing we got, nothing attached. We don't do what you don't want to do, and we don't do what I don't want to do either. The thing I want to do though is talk with you every night, hold you when you need it and whatever else comes much later than now. I'm not that other dude, Lexis. I'm Javis."

"Other dude?"

"It's obvious. It was written on your face back there. Whatever he did, I'm not him." He then laughs while sitting back. "I'm probably the brokest, most straight up guy you've ever known. Honest and simple, and that's all I know how to be."

"I wish things were that easy my way. Thanks, Javis." She leans over and gives him a friendly kiss on the cheek.

"Maybe one day you can tell me about it."

"Maybe." She puts the car in reverse to back out of the parking space. "One day."

The main entrance to Gabriel's Trails is right across the street, so since there's no traffic, Alexis inches up to the edge of the intersection slowly without fully stopping.

"What you doing?" Javis looks at her suspiciously and starts to laugh. "Don't even think about doing what I think…"

She then darts across the road on a red light, straight into Gabriel's Trails, speeding into his driveway and coming to an immediate stop. Alexis is all smiles at her show off move, and Javis' mouth is completely open. "Next time," she turns the car off and tosses him the keys, "You'll drive because a girl like me is too dangerous behind the wheel."

72

The keys land in Javis' lap as he continues to cling to the seat. "You got me looking like a real punk, Lexis. A real punk."

"A herb like your brother says."

"I'm herbed out right now." He picks up the keys. "You're right I'm driving next time." He unlocks his door. "Are you getting out?"

Alexis looks startled by the question and doesn't answer right away. Instead, she remembers the last time she stepped foot inside Gabriel's Trails. It's much quieter on this end of the neighborhood. Still, she can hear the ruckus from the back end near the trails.

"Are you getting out, Lexis?" Javis sings slowly, noticing her stall, and his voice causes her to jump. "What are you thinking about? I know it's Gabriel's Trails but…"

"Yeah, I'm getting out," she rushes to answer. She didn't need him to give his philosophy on the neighborhood because her memories serve her good enough. "I was just wondering if I locked the back door to the house when we left."

"You did. I watched. Now get out, we're not finished with our date yet," he smiles, as Alexis joins him outside in front of the car. She looks up the road where she only sees slight movement from the hustle that goes on up the street, but she's anxious to get back in the car to drive away. Instead, Javis picks her up off of her feet and sits her onto the hood of her car. This brings a smile to her face because the last time she felt comfortable off of her feet with another male was when she was with Bain.

Finally, Alexis beings to settle more into her more playful, youthful side and Javis notices the change, though he says nothing about it because he doesn't want to end up in another counseling session for reasons unbeknownst to him. He spends enough time being the mature one, so he wants to be young, think young, and maybe even fall young and in love. As he leans in to give her a kiss on the cheek as they talk about whatever, Javis catches a fast glimpse of a car immediately behind Alexis, and as the window of the car comes down, a barrel comes out, creating a round of shots toward the house.

In the middle of Alexis' laughter during his kiss on the cheek, Javis slams her down onto the concrete, falling on top of her. The gun starts blasting, and Alexis begins to scream hysterically, covering her ears as Javis' head is pressed against the concrete and his arms lay on top of Alexis' head.

"Alexis, calm down, calm down!" Javis yells, as he looks looks back, underneath the car and to both sides of the wheels, being sure no one is running up near them as they shield themselves.

"They're trying to kill me!" Alexis screams, "Please!" She makes an attempt to get up and run, however, Javis' weight on top of her won't allow her to even get one foot on solid ground.

"They're gone, Lexis! Nobody's gonna kill us. It's over," he says breathing deeply, "Just stay low, stay here." He feels her still pressing upward as if she wants to run, so he orders her in a more forceful way, pulling her forehead back by the palm of his hand. "Calm down, Lexis, and don't fuckin' move, I said. Stay put."

Alexis' hair falls all over the concrete as she buries her head down into it. Then, Javis crawls with his elbows as they get ripped by the hard driveway's surface. He doesn't see anyone or anything anymore except a bullet that's landed, shining on the edge of the grass.

Just then, he hears screams from inside the house. It's his mother. There's no fear anymore as Javis jumps up and runs to the porch, fumbling with his keys to open the door. "Mama! Ma!" Alexis is still on the ground, but she looks up to find Javis entering his house. She follows as fast as she can as the screams begin to echo in her ears like death.

Mrs. Moores is on the couch, leaning over her husband who is in an upright position. The television is on, and all the lights are out. The only sound is Mrs. Moores' screams as she shakes Mr. Moores vigorously, yet he won't respond. Alexis falls against the wall and she shakes her head back and forth while the wall behaves like her personal sliding board until she hits the floor.

Javis stands in shock as he sees his father with a hole in his head as his mom starts to blow air into his mouth. Javis' knees hit the floor hard, and he pants quietly, "Dad," but gets no answer. "Dad," he begins again, but his voice is cut short by a loss of air, clogged by a fountain of tears that begin to tumble from his eyes. Finally, he snaps out of it and rushes to his dad who dies before his very eyes. Pulling him off the chair and onto the floor, Javis then shoves the center table out of the way so hard that it turns over onto its side. "Daddy, wake up, daddy, come on." He wipes his eyes as his mom runs to the kitchen phone to call emergency. "Things are gonna work out, dad. Get up…get up!" Javis' palms and arms cradle his father's head and neck as his father's eyes roll back into his head. "Somebody help!"

"Dad! Mom, dad…" Joseph wakes up from his sleep, watching from the hallway as his mom rushes to connect with him in a large embrace.

"Joseph, don't look, baby, don't look. Go back in the room. Daddy's gonna be fine, just…"

Joseph doesn't listen. Instead, he resists his mom's embrace that's meant to contain him in one spot, and he lunges down near his dad's side. Joseph looks up and notices a girl he's never seen staring at the scene before them. Then his tears begin to hit his father's face as he stares back at his older brother Javis and then back at the hole inside his father's head. Reality sets in. Dad is dead. He's been shot to death in a drive-by shooting.

Javis looks back into the eyes of Alexis, and Alexis looks back into his eyes that are soaking in tears. She instantaneously removes herself from the home and walks slowly back to the car, but she doesn't leave. Instead, she enters her car through the passenger's side, and reaches into the glove compartment to retrieve a pistol.

As she places her hands around it, she recalls dumping this same pistol into the sticky bushes on the way to her home after shooting Bain to death. That night, she couldn't sleep out of fear, anger and heartache. The fear overruled her heartache, causing her to return to the very bottom of the sticky bushes the next night, scratch up her arm and pull the pistol out. She tucked it into her book bag and ran home. Her parents never knew she left the house. She feared the cops would find the gun, then link it to Bain, thus, linking it back to her. She couldn't survive being popped for a homicide. Her life would be an open book, and at that point, she needed it closed – then, now and forever.

Alexis placed the gun in her glove compartment this night - the night she knew she would return to Gabriel's Trails. Javis walks onto the porch slowly and watches Alexis standing on the other side of the car. Tears stream down her face, and her hand begins to tremble as the gun remains locked into her grip. Javis doesn't take his eyes off of her. Instead, he walks over to her, unable utter any words after leaving the scene inside the home with his mom screaming on top of his dead father. He's in a daze, and the rage is slowly seeping through his worn down soul.

When he steps around the passenger's side of Alexis' car, he not only sees her but also the pistol hanging from her hand as she hands it to him. Javis doesn't question it, almost as if he knew before stepping out of the house that he would be coming for his next move. He's ready to kill for his family.

The ambulance pulls into the yard as they stand there, looking into each others' soaked eyes. Javis hides the pistol in his pants pocket and returns into the house to watch them lift his father away. Mr. Moores is pronounced dead before he enters the emergency room at the hospital. His first date with Alexis ends in his father's murder.

MURDERS AT GABRIEL'S TRAILS III

Paths of Revenge

Murders at Gabriel's Trails III: Paths of Revenge

"Leave him alone, Trent." Karen, his wife, pulls him by the arm near his elbow, but he snatches away in a fit of frustration at the sight of his son blatantly ignoring him while walking down the street. "Trent?" she questions his action in amazement. Trent has never shrugged her off nor pulled away from her at any time since they've been together, but tonight was different.

"I don't know what's gotten into that boy lately," he responds, turning toward her revealing the rage in his eyes. "I'm telling you, Karen, when he comes back into this house…"

"I agree. He's going to have some explaining to do, but right now, the one thing you don't want to do is get into a fight with him in the middle of the street," she states calmly, trying to diffuse the situation without any harm coming to her son and her husband. "Trent, listen to me."

He rams his fist into the brick on the outside of the rundown condo, looks back at his sixteen year old son who still has his fists balled up continuing to walk down the sidewalk, and then forces himself back into the house at his wife's wishes. "I don't know, Karen, I don't know." His anger is releasing through the heavy breaths that he takes as he paces in front of the sofa, staring out the window as the image of his son disappears. "It's not safe for that boy out there. The problem is, he thinks he knows everything, but he knows too much about nothing. I never want him to learn what I know!" he shouts, hitting himself in the chest. "I don't want that life I knew to come slide in on him."

"Trent…" his wife tries to interrupt, but he tosses his hand up in the air alerting her to the back room. The bathroom shower has stopped.

"Listen," he quiets down. "I'm sorry for raising my voice. Lord, knows I am. Please forgive me for shouting and carrying on the way I did, baby." He reaches for her hand and she accepts as they both take a seat on the sofa together. "I just want everything to be fine with them, poor or not poor. I don't want this world to eat my sons alive. Derrick doesn't know how much I love him. The boy just doesn't know that my tight hold is for a reason."

"He'll understand later, Trent. He will," she says looking out the window, making an attempt to not show how worried she is about Derrick when the fact is, she's praying nonstop mentally and emotionally for her son's well-being. Times have been rough monetarily for the whole family, and the one thing she wants to hold on to through it all is their sanity. "Right now, he's at that age. Besides that, he's probably just feeling the pinch of his brother going on..." She's cut off again.

"A date? Jealous because Javis is going on a date?" He leans over and gives her an are you serious look.

"Yes, Trent," she rolls her eyes with a sigh. "He just may feel like he needs that same freedom. You know he told me about a female friend he has now, and according to him, she lives up the road somewhere." She sits back on the chair, lifts her legs up, and starts to rub her toes.

"Really? He has a girl now, too?"

"Yep. Sure does. So you see," she continues, picking up the newspaper, "His disobedience only means that he may want you to not only trust him and give him a chance, but he also wants to see that girl!" she laughs.

Trent can't help but grin. "Yeah, I remember those days." He looks at her. "You're right. I'll talk to him when he gets back. I didn't even know."

"You cut him off before he told you, baby."

"I did, didn't I?"

She nods.

"My bad, Karen." He stares out the window again. "I just love my boys. Never wanted them to live in a place like this, and as soon as I can…"

Karen places her finger over his lips and turns his head back to face her. "Let's just not ruin the night for Javis. You know how bothered he gets when there's an argument between us. Things will be okay. We'll be alright, Trent. God is good and able."

He wipes his head, takes a deep breath and says, "Amen."

"Hey, ma," Javis calls from the hall, just stepping out of the bathroom noticing that Derrick isn't in their bedroom. "Where's Derrick? I want to ask him if I could borrow his shirt. The one I have like it is dirty."

She holds her husband's hand as she replies, "Your father let him go up the road for a change, to a friend's house."

"Get outta here, pop!" Javis exclaims, excited for this new found freedom that has suddenly come out of nowhere. In the back of his mind, Javis believes that his taking responsibility to help out with the finances in the house literally bought him the extra freedom he craves. That freedom must have softened his parent's hearts, allowing Derrick to go out as well.

Trent stands up and addresses Javis, pushing what happened with Derrick into the back of his mind. "Yeah, I hear he has a girlfriend that lives up the road, so I thought why not?" He cuts his eyes at Karen as to alert her to stay quiet.

"Yeah, he does have a girl now, dad. I told him I would give him some money later so he won't look like what he always calls me – a herb."

"I suppose you two are older now," he pauses. "I trust you, trust you both."

"Alright, well, I have to go get dressed before she gets here to pick me up. Dang, I wish I had a car," he complains walking down the hall, but it's fine by him anyway because it beats staying home.

Tryina's home is in the distance and in complete view for Derrick as he makes his way there, still making extreme efforts to mask his anger from the disagreement he just had with his father.

"Telling me I can't go anywhere or do anything, and I'm just two years out of high school." He punches at a limb hanging from a low tree, but thankfully, he doesn't cut his hand. "I promised Tryina that I would come see her today," he says to himself quietly, angrily looking around at his new neighborhood that he's never even seen before in full on foot. "And that's what I'm gonna do." All of a sudden, remorse enters his heart for being disobedient to his father, and he feels like turning around until he comes to the next street. Tryina's home is directly in front of him, closer than what he thought, as he reads the numbers on the door - 554. He turns back around facing the direction of his house with a bad conscience, but then pushes forward, convincing himself that he'll make it up to his father later on tonight.

"Floss, come here!" Tryina screams over the loud music playing in the background as she raises the short strands of hair from flying loosely at the back of her neck and repositions them in the rubber band. "Floss!" she continues, rolling her eyes because the brush falls into the wet sink. "Crap." She yanks it out quickly, flings it in the air, and starts to brush the neat pony tail she's made.

"Girl, what you want now?" he asks, leaning on the bathroom door entrance with a cap pulled so far down over his forehead that his eyes are invisible. "And what are you getting ready for? You ain't going nowhere but in that kitchen to clean it up. My lady coming over tonight…"

"Clean up a kitchen?" she cuts in, spinning around to face her twenty-five year old brother. "Noooo, Floss! Remember that guy I told you about, the new one at school. Well, he told me that he's coming over, and he should be here about now." She turns back around to face the mirror to give her face one last look, and then she adds more clear deodorant under her armpits.

"It ain't that deep, Tryina," he complains. "So what you call me back here for?"

"I want you to open the door for me. I don't want to look like I'm waiting on him at the door, Floss." She reaches back to clutch his wrists, hanging off if it as she pleads, "Please! And will you do the kitchen?"

He lifts his cap with his free hand and looks at his younger sister like she's half crazy, but then he softens up when he sees the excitement in her eyes. "How long this dude stayin'? You really like him, don't you?"

"If I didn't like him, I wouldn't have invited him here…especially when he'd have to meet you."

"Me? And what's wrong with me?" He shoves her softly out of the way while he peeps himself in the mirror, removing his cap and rubbing the top of his bald fade. "I look damn distinguished today."

"Come on, Floss. Are you gonna get the kitchen and the door for me, huh?"

"Sugar."

"What?"

"Sugar," he says, pointing to his small, cheek tattoo of a dripping cube.

"I'm not giving you a kiss on your nasty cheek, Floss. Cut it out," she responds, folding her hands, however, knowing she has no way out of kissing his cheek if she really wants Floss to perform any of her requests.

"No kitchen, no…"

"Okay, okay! Here dang," she barely places her lips on his cheek, smacks her lips for the kiss sound, backs away and wipes. "Happy now?"

"Nope." He puts his cap back on. "But it'll work. You know I'll do anything for my lil sis, right?"

"Yeah, right. Bye then, Floss!" She shoves him out of the bathroom. "Go ahead and do that," she orders as she slams the bathroom door in his face, surprised he's giving in to her demands for a change.

"Youngsters." He yawns again and starts to walk toward the sink to tackle the dishes when he hears two knocks at the door. "This lil nigga here already," he complains. Just to make sure it's Tryina's boyfriend, he leans over to the window and pulls the curtains back. "Yeah, that's got to be him, his cleaned up ass."

Floss pulls his cap down even further, and then opens the door to meet Tryina's boyfriend for the first time. After opening it, he just stands there as he examines the young man, who at this point, is obviously nervous.

"Hi, is Tryina at home? I'm Derrick."

Floss doesn't flinch as Derrick reaches out to greet him with a handshake. He tilts his head back in order to see the guest better from underneath his cap, and then he lowers his head, looks around behind him and finally speaks, "Whassup, Derrick?" He reciprocates the handshake, forcing Derrick to

86

return the hand he'd already placed back by his side. "Come on in, man. Tryina's in the back. I'll get her in a few minutes after a word with you about my sister, man."

Derrick confidently steps inside, passing by Floss, as not to allow fear or anxiety to seep beyond his pores. As he walks in, Floss doesn't move completely out of the way, staring directly into the side of his face. Derrick feels Floss' eyes penetrating his profile, but he keeps cool as he searches for a welcoming spot in the middle of the floor to stand.

"Come on over here, man, and sit down a minute," Floss says, walking away from the door, leaving it cracked. As he approaches the cream leather couch sitting directly in front of the sliding door, he points Derrick in the direction of a wooden upright chair positioned next to it. "Name's Floss." He removes his cap, but ends up putting it back on quickly.

Derrick assumes the name Floss isn't his real first name along with assuming that Floss can't be her dad either so he replies, "Good to meet you, Floss."

"Yeah, man, but listen, what you like about Tryina?" He sits up from his slouch and starts to toss some dice on the floor in front of him while cocking his head slightly up and to the left to wait on Derrick's response to his question.

Derrick doesn't quite know how to respond to the question as he begins to feel like the school boy that he is sitting in the wooden chair. Before he gets the chance to answer, Tryina walks out, unaware that Derrick is in the middle of being grilled by her brother.

"Floss!" She stops at the hallway in some sort of state of shock, glances at the dirty kitchen and then back at her smirking brother.

"Tryina," he responds with a wide smile. "This is Derrick."

"I know who it is. Why didn't you tell me he was already here?"

He leans back and laughs, "I just did." Then he excuses himself with a nod to both of them and heads to the kitchen. "I got some cleaning up to do."

"Yeah, you do that, Floss. Gosh, so embarrassing," she complains as she motions to Derrick to sit beside her on the couch. Derrick is glad to do so, but he still feels uneasy about her brother so nearby.

"So that's Floss. He was about to grill me on you, too," he whispers in her ear.

She smiles back, allowing for Derrick to touch her hand. "Don't worry about him. He'll be gone in a minute. Thanks for coming by. In the back of my mind, I thought you would have changed your mind."

"Why?"

"I don't know," she blushes. "I just did, that's all. I wish we could go out somewhere like your brother is tonight."

"Yeah, I know, but it's all good. Him and Alexis are just going to the movies, and she's driving, while my parents…"

Derrick's chatter comes to a halt when Floss comes back around the counter, exiting the kitchen to face him and Tryina. Tryina gawks at him, giving him the what do you want stare.

"So you have a brother huh?

"Yeah, two actually, one older and the other one younger," he replies, removing his hand from Tryina's after receiving a very cautious and cold look from him. Tryina falls silent when she notices that same look on her brother's face as well.

Instead of continuing the conversation, Floss puts his hand into his pocket and continues to look at Derrick for about five more seconds. Then he takes a shorter glance at Tryina before abruptly walking back down the hallway, leaving the kitchen water running. After about fifteen seconds go by, Tryina rushes from the couch to turn the water off.

"Excuse me, Derrick," she says nervously. "My brother left the water running. Sorry about him. For some reason, he's trippin' today. You like my hair?" she asks, twirling her extended pony tail she bought just one hour ago after school let out from the girl down the street, fully packaged and stolen. This is her first attempt at trying to shake what feels like her brother about to ambush her date.

"It's cool," Derrick states, slowly regretting coming to Tryina's house without anyone from his home being able to pin point exactly where he is. He wants to cut the visit short after the uncomfortable stares coming from Tryina's brother, however, doesn't know how. "And your hair always looks nice."

He listens as Tryina is inside the kitchen turning off the water, but he fails to see her face. She picks up the rag, still not facing his direction and begins to wipe down the counters. Her expression carries the appearance of apprehension and worry, however, she tries not to have Derrick notice it at all. She continues in the kitchen, picking up the broom, still not facing her date, and begins to sweep, all while Derrick sits alone and unattended during his first visit to her home.

"I'm coming. Just give me a second. Floss left the kitchen a wreck," she laughs, attempting to bring the awkward tension down. Just as she finishes her sentence, her brother's footsteps re-enter the situation that he left except he doesn't come to the kitchen. Instead, he takes a seat in the wooden chair he told Derrick to sit in when he first came inside.

Floss scoots the chair up closer to the couch, nearly touching the armrest that Derrick is leaning on, causing Derrick to remove his arm to place it in a slightly defensive mode.

"Chill out, man, I wanna ask you something."

There's no response from Derrick because Tryina quickly returns to the couch, still trying to create an atmosphere of calm from what she senses is becoming a more volatile situation. She's never told Derrick much about her older brother and his ways nor did she ever want to do so. In fact, the less she talks about him to anyone, the better she feels. She can almost manage to live a normal life, a normal dating life, as a teen. She hasn't been able to do so until now, and that's because Derrick doesn't know her family's history, really her brother's history. Luckily, no one has told him, and to be frank, people are probably afraid to tell him because it's safer for them to keep quiet.

"I wanna ask your opinion about this." He reaches in his pocket, while daring Tryina to talk with his eyes, and pulls out a knife. It's a rather small blade with jagged edges, obviously meant to rip through meat and muscle. The handle of the knife is thick, and it retracts in and out like a switch blade. Carved into the wood of the handle are the initials M.B.

Derrick is confused as he looks at Tryina, back at Floss and then at the blade beneath him that sits on the coffee table. "What about it?"

"Does it mean anything to you?"

"No, I mean, other than I don't want it in front of me like this…"

"You ever seen a knife like this one before?"

"There are plenty switch blades around, but I can't say I know about that one."

"Floss, why…"

"Shut the fuck up, Tryina," Floss orders her without looking her way, eyes still planted on Derrick. Tryina's eyes begin to water up, but she doesn't get up to leave. She realizes that this is probably going to end up in a bad place, leaving her love life as a ghost town once again.

"Look, man, I don't know anything about that knife. It's probably a good thing if I go ahead and leave," Derrick explains as he stands up from the couch, looking back at Tryina as she sits there in silence.

"No you won't, man. Sit down." Floss gets up from his seat, looks down at the blade that's still open and shining a reflection of light onto the ceiling. "Didn't you come here to see my sister?" Floss is still watching how Derrick reacts to the knife closely.

"I did but…"

"Well sit down. Ain't no problems here. I just had to see where your head is at, Derrick," he says as he reaches in his pocket to pull out some money, "before I treat you two to some time alone while I take care of some things. Here's thirty dollars. Order some wings and a pizza or something. It's good, D," he continues, holding out his fist to give him pound, and suddenly, flashes a smile.

Tryina isn't amused, and in the back of her mind she hopes Derrick takes off, but instead he sits back down, taking the money from her brother's hand with a grateful response, yet not sold on the gesture.

"Thanks," Derrick responds with uncertainty.

Floss picks up the blade from the table, shoves it in his pocket, pulls his cap even tighter down on his head and then asks, "You live down there in that house on the corner, don't you? The new people," he says looking again at Tryina. Tryina realizes that his smile is fake, but can do nothing about it. "At least that's what Tryina told me earlier, is that right?"

"Yeah, on the corner. We just moved in right before school started."

"See, you, your brother and your brother's girl could have all come in here for a double date. All expenses paid, ain't that right, Yina?"

91

She doesn't respond due to her fury, but Floss walks over to her and gives her a kiss on the cheek. "I'm sorry, baby girl. I'm sorry for cussing at you and all that, and checking your man out. I like your man, Derrick, but I had to make sure he wasn't a crazy mu' fucker like me before I leave him alone with your ass. Cheer up. Here."

Floss places more money in her lap, and then leaves. Just like that he's gone. Tryina's whole date is torn to pieces by the look on her face, so Derrick chooses to remain there to comfort her despite the sick feeling in the pit of his stomach.

Dusk is settling into the day, and the people of Gabriel's Trails are starting to make their way to the outside of their homes. Floss walks slowly up the sidewalk, on his way to the same post he fills night after night, and this is the same location where his homies hang out as well. Though the night is falling, it's still too early for the Friday night parties to sound off.

As he walks, he takes the knife from his pocket that he perplexed Derrick with at the house and continuously opens and closes it between his hands. Since the sun is going down, Floss lifts his cap up a little for relief. His eyes are bad in the day due to the sun, but instead of buying sunglasses with his money, he prefers to wear a cap to shield his eyes. That's only one reason. The other reason he wears a cap most times outside of the home is to be unidentifiable. He knows that eyes are what make most people recognizable because it's the first place anyone looks at when dying or living. Floss hates being recognized by those who shouldn't know him which is why he lives by Gabriel's Trails street code – all business stays within the neighborhood where all who live here are afraid to snitch.

Crossing the street, he watches like clockwork as his friend, who sticks closer than blood, walks up to meet him under the flickering night light near the trails. Just about every night, their work starts right here and ends where they rest.

"Tonight's not the night for this, Chief," Floss begins as he stops fiddling with the blade in his hand, and instead, closes it, handing it to his partner in crime.

"Man, I gotta make that money. What's happening?" Chief asks, swapping the blade and money at the same time. "This for me?"

"No, man, take a look at that shit."

"What about it?"

Floss looks around and then answers, "This is the same blade I took from Bain's young thing the night he was shot. Remember that?"

"Oh shit, yeah, man. You still have this shit, too."

"Her ass left it with me on her way out when Bain was going after her, so I kept the shit ever since. I was going to give it to Bain that night, but he never came back." After he leans on an old tree that looks to be struck by lightning, he continues, "She's in the Trails tonight. It's time to go get her." He looks in the direction of the Gabriel's Trails main entrance which is the location of Derrick's home.

"How you know she came back in here tonight?"

"This young blood that's dating my sister. His brother is supposedly out on a date with a girl named Alexis. I overheard them talking, but he don't know shit about what went down with her. Lil' nigga just as innocent as my baby boy, but I still don't trust it."

Just then, a car rolls up to the curb, and it's full of females who are dressed like they're going to a house party later on that night. One of the ladies gets out of the car, walks up to both Chief and Floss, but only acknowledges Floss with a kiss to the lips. He kisses her back.

"Tell your friend to wait," Floss commands.

93

"Who?"

"Her." He looks into the backseat where he sees one of Bain's former whores who he definitely knows has seen and remembers the face of Bain's killer. "I need both of you to do something for me real quick."

"What's up, baby? You know I got you as long as it doesn't get me in jail. You know I don't sling this dope."

"No, baby, I need you to take your friend to identify somebody for me. Go get her. Hurry up, too." he says, smacking her butt as she turns around to coerce her friend to get out of the car for a favor.

A woman gets out of the backseat known as Faye, at least that's her street name. She has no last name because she hasn't had a family since entering Gabriel's Trails, and since then, she's never left nor let anyone in on any family ties or full real name. Her way of life is out of pure choice, however, she's made herself known as being loyal until the death.

Faye is dressed in red heels that scream scarlet red, a tight animal print dress that she has to continuously pull down just to walk, and a fake pony tail that reaches beyond her butt. She's dressed to party and more, but this is the first time that Floss has ever requested her services, therefore, she figures that there's more to it than a regular favor.

"I don't do threesomes, Floss," she explains, planting one heel on the curb while she balances herself with the other foot on the street and hand on her hip. She cuts a side eye over at Floss' main girl who told her to get out of the car, and smiles. "And I really don't do them with my friends. It causes too much confusion."

"Don't nobody want you, girl." He waves his girlfriend back over to his side. "I need you to do something for me, and my baby's gonna drive you there real fast."

"I am?" Floss' girl says, approaching his side. He ignores her question because she knows better than to question him, thus, it's a joke.

"There's some people that live down on that corner house at the main entrance."

"I know," Faye responds. "It's a nice family. They look real homely," she grins.

"Well, Bain's young thing, Alexis, might be down there, so I need you to identify her for me. You probably got like fifteen minutes tops."

Faye's sarcastic smile fades slowly into the background of her highly made up skin that's plastered with ruby red lipstick, thick black eyeliner, hazel contact lenses feathered with long fake eyelashes and drawn eyebrows. She removes her heel from the curb, looks in the direction of the entrance, and then back at Floss who is waiting on her response. Five seconds go by, and then he speaks due to her silence.

"Isn't that the girl who had Bain slap the shit outta you? Isn't that her name?" Floss is talented at manipulation, and manipulating Faye's emotions is what he has to do in order to keep his control of a situation that's long overdue to be handled.

Faye remembers that day, one full year ago, when she was making love to Bain, the man she desired all for herself. Anything he wanted, she would do because she was crazy about the prestige of being his woman. It was her way out of working hard, and in her mind, he enjoyed it when she would stop by during the week and give him some of what any man needs. She did it all for free. Bain was the only man she sexed for free and raw. Anyone else had to pay and was covered up double.

When Bain knocked her to the floor the night Alexis walked in, she knew that although she had his body, Alexis had his heart and had it for good. Little did she know that after her uncontrolled rant against Bain and Alexis, it would be the last time she would see him alive. Faye remembers crying her eyes out while the festering anger built in her body after authorities found his body lying in the trails. This is her chance to deliver due punishment. If Alexis is really in the Trails again, she's going to pay.

She quickly responds after a fit of rage and bitterness creeps into her heart. Faye looks at Floss's girlfriend and son's mother and agrees to the job, all the while reviving her jovial facial expression with a slight smile. "Let's go. Time's ticking." As she walks away, she stares Floss in his eyes. Floss returns the look with a nod.

Faye sits in the car as Floss' girlfriend allows the motor to hum at the corner of the Gabriel's Trails entrance. Faye watches each car that turns in, but that isn't good enough. She feels like she's missing something, so she gets out of the car.

"Faye, what are you doing? Get back into the car before someone sees you."

She ignores her at first, but then sees what she needs to see. There she is. She spots a silver mustang with a tint so dark that it's impossible to see through.

"Give me my cell phone and take off," she tells Floss' girlfriend as she keeps her eyes on the back of the car as it pulls into Gabriel's Trails. "I'll walk back, and I'll call you to let you know if that's Alexis."

As the car drives away, Faye rushes to get off the side of the road because she doesn't want to get popped for prostitution based on how she's dressed. Her hustle doesn't ever leave Gabriel's Trails unless it's on strict assignment, and that's been much slower since Bain got killed.

There's a large tree immediately behind the short brick wall that makes up the entrance to the Trails. Before she can tell if anyone sees her, she takes a seat behind it, hiding herself from view. As her heels dig into the dirt beneath the grass, she twists her body to see beyond the tree and into the yard where the silver Mustang pulled up.

"Bingo," Faye states as she watches the person driving the car roll down the window. It's Alexis, and the presence of her inside Gabriel's Trails makes her blood boil. She watches the activity in the yard for a while behind the tree until her cell phone lights up and vibrates, so she answers.

"What you got?" It's Floss calling from his girl's phone.

"Floss, it's her."

"Bet your life on that, baby girl?"

She goes silent because she realizes that Floss isn't just throwing around words. If she confirms to him one more time that it's Alexis, she's really just bet her life. If she's wrong, she dies. Therefore, she looks again and confirms.

"Yeah, Floss, I bet my life." She then gets up and walks, unhidden, continuing to talk to Floss. "That's that bitch," Faye states as the car is pulling out of the driveway. She's so angry that as she walks up the street, she points in the direction of the house, cursing as she describes the car that just drove by. "Her ass was right there at the house, picking up one of the guys that live there, Floss. You're right I bet my life on it," she says angrily, taking her heels off to finish her trek into the middle of Gabriel's Trails. She hangs up the phone and looks back at the home to find the woman of the house on the porch. By then, Faye could care less. She's finally getting her vengeance.

Time passes as Floss and Chief sit one block up from the house he knows will deliver the goods. Before driving to this location, Floss stopped back by his house to check on his sister, but most importantly, be certain that he makes Derrick feel more welcome than he did before. Being that he knew he had more than one hour to spare, he pulled out Tryina's favorite video game and played with them for about thirty minutes, ate a slice of pizza, laughed and then left again after allowing Derrick to use the phone to call his parents from a spare cell phone. Floss' whole plan was to keep things running smoothly and comfortably for both his sister and himself while he does his dirt.

"It should be any minute now, Chief. We finally get to repay. No witnesses as long as this stays inside the Trails. She can bring her ass in here, but she won't drive her ass back out."

"She must have been crazy to come back in here like that. As long as she was with Bain, her rich ass should have known better."

"It's like they say, Chief. Some people are fascinated with the things they don't understand. She probably thinks she got off because nobody snitched."

"Welcome back to Gabriel's Trails," Chief responds as he wipes down his pistol, getting ready for what is to take place.

"Shhhh…." Floss alerts Chief to a silver car driving fast into the Gabriel's Trail's entrance. He starts up the black, untagged car, and orders Chief to start shooting when the traffic light at the entrance turns green. "It'll be at my go, Chief. Hold until I say when."

Slowly, Floss pulls up with his lights off just enough to watch a young man place Alexis on top of the hood of her car. As Floss watches them talk, he moves the car forward fast when he notices the light turn green at the intersection.

"Now, Chief," he says, grabbing the blade that originally belonged to Alexis. At the same time, he rolls the passenger's side window down and allows Chief to open fire in their direction. Then, Floss comes to a screeching stop behind a bush located at the front of the yard as Chief pulls his gun inside. Then, Floss steps out of the car and runs toward the house to be sure the intended target has fallen. If not, he plans to finish the job up close and personally, but he knows the traffic light won't stay green too much longer. Out of time, he pulls down his cap, and runs back the car. As he feels for the blade that he shoved in his pocket before he jumped out of the car, it's gone.

"Shit!" He glances at the light which is still green but has no choice but to enter the vehicle and go.

"What the hell was that, Floss?" Chief asks angrily.

"Did you get her?" he responds, breathing heavily while checking the rear view.

"Yeah, man, I think so. They went down so, I can't know for sure. What the hell was that shit about?" Chief asks in reference to Floss stopping during the drive-by. "It's called a drive-by, damn!"

Floss doesn't answer. All he does is drive. He messed up.

Across the street in a parking lot opposite Gabriel's Trails, Faye sits awaiting the outcome of Floss' murder attempt. No one knew she would be watching, but she just couldn't help it. Drive-bys are no guarantee, and since she put her life on the line to get Alexis capped, the least she is going to do is see if the job is done.

"Bain, baby," she says, talking to a dead man, "We got her. We got her. I always told you that you should have made me your girl. I wouldn't have shot your ass."

Faye continues to watch the yard as the young man Alexis is with gets up from the ground and runs to the front door, and then she smiles. The smile is cut short, however, when the next thing she watches is Alexis running inside the front door behind him.

"He fuckin' missed." She can't believe what she is seeing. She calls Floss' girlfriend's phone. There's no answer, so she simply drops the phone inside the cup holder and waits. "I got a beef to pick with this bitch anyway." Instead of trying to contact Floss again, she turns her phone on silent so she can purposely ignore any call back as she tosses the phone in the backseat. Then, she waits on the action.

The ambulance gets there before the cops, and it's right before the EMS arrives that Faye watches Alexis come back out of the front door and walk toward the passenger's side of her car, followed by the guy she's with for the night. Then she gets back in her car and leaves, just as the ambulance pulls in the yard.

Faye follows her as she pulls out of the entrance, sticking closely behind so she won't lose her. As she rides two car lengths behind, Faye fumes, "Why didn't you just die?" The memories that Floss brought back to Faye were starting to become unbearable. Alexis is the reason for her decreasing pay scale and having to make ends meet. When Bain was living, no one disrespected her because she brought him the most work and money. The only time he hit her was because of Alexis. Somewhere deep in Faye's mind, she begins to place Alexis at the center of her ruin, and she feels the urge to confront her in the worst way.

Turning onto the next road, she notices a garage door coming open where Alexis is getting ready to pull in, so she accelerates to meet her before she goes inside. At this point, Faye doesn't even care if someone is inside the home waiting for Alexis return. She's furious, and she's about to let it all out.

Alexis notices the bright car lights pull in behind her causing her to halt the garage door halfway. Then, she exits the car hesitantly, thinking it's a cop, or detective, wanting to question her about the shooting since she left the scene. Instead, when the woman steps out of the car, Alexis is made well aware that it isn't a cop, but a woman that she's seen only one other time before in her life. It's the woman who Bain knocked to the floor, the woman who smirked at her while having sex with her ex. Before Alexis has a chance to get one more foot in front of her, she feels a tight tug on her arm, and she yanks away, striking the car with her elbow.

"Oh now you want to act like I don't have a right to touch you, Alexis, after you touched something of mine? Look at you," she taunts, waving her arms out to the side as Alexis looks on terrified. "This big ass house and a fucking three car garage. You just couldn't stay away from the Trails could you?"

Alexis shoves her out of the way and rushes into her half open garage on foot, but Faye follows her inside, reaching for Alexis' hair until she grabs it and pulls her backwards, slamming her against the wall.

"Your little lucky ass is supposed to be dead tonight, see. Guess what we know?" Faye states, gritting her teeth tighter and tighter, her words coming out like it's all she can do to not break Alexis' neck as she controls Alexis' every move by yanking her hair. Faye then leans in toward her left ear. "We know you killed Bain."

Tears fall from Alexis' eyes, and through it all, she doesn't say a word. Faye is breathing down her neck while her solid grip forces her nails into Alexis' neck each time Alexis pushes back against her. Wanting Faye to just leave, Alexis puts her hands against the garage wall in surrender, causing Faye to let go after she inflicts more pain by shoving her head against the same wall she's leaning against.

Faye continues to look around inside a garage that's half the size of her residence, and a fit of jealously begins to fester in her heart. "How would you like to be taken away from this big, huge mansion you live in now and be thrown into a small ass box, huh, Alexis, baby?"

Alexis turns around slowly to face her attacker, visibly shaken after already being shot at and watching the bullet that she knows was meant for her, kill her boyfriend's father. Then, she glances over at the car that's still running in her driveway as she thinks about Javis slamming her to the ground while a car drives by in an attempt to kill her. Alexis stares back at Faye and starts to carefully look around for something to grab because in her mind, this is the woman who just tried to kill her. She's getting ready to do it again.

Faye approaches Alexis again. "Just what if I change your life for good by not killing you, but turning your ass in for shooting Bain out there in them trails, huh little girl?" she taunts, pointing in the direction of the wooded trails. "You should've never tried to live like a grown woman if you couldn't hang, Alexis, baby."

Alexis begins to panic because all the thoughts of getting caught by the cops return full force. Her heavy breathing begins to reveal the surge of adrenaline her body is giving off in order to do anything in her power to maintain her freedom. In Alexis' mind, death would be better than prison with her face plastered all over the news.

Faye notices the fear she evokes in Alexis and smiles, deciding to destroy the teen even more by her words. "Bain was my man. Bet you didn't know that, and we spent all that damn money your ass brought him, too," she lies, feeding off of Alexis' crushed emotions. "I got some proof tying you to him, too, ole Lexi," she continues, coming nose to nose with her. "Yeah, I'm glad you're not dead, pretty baby. It's time for me to snitch. Your pathetic, rich ass. Don't get scared now." Then, she backs away slowly with that same smile she gave Alexis while she was sexing Bain, turns around, and starts walking to her car, not intimidated at all by Alexis.

Before Faye ducks down to exit the garage, Alexis grabs a long, thick wrench from the shelf and swings, knocking Faye to her knees. The hit is so hard that Faye isn't able to respond in voice or action as she lands hard on her knees. Alexis finishes knocking her to the ground by cracking her skull with another blow to the temple. Faye drops completely to the ground, and

Alexis shakily drops the wrench, reaches down and covers Faye's mouth and nose until she feels no more pulse.

A car passes by, and Alexis looks up quickly but is completely blocked from view by the dead lady's car that's still running in the driveway and her own car. In a mad rush, Alexis moves the woman's car to a diagonal position in the driveway so that the passenger's side of the vehicle is facing the house, creating a perfect V at her garage. She hops out of the car through the passenger side door, and pulls the dead body inside.

Blood creeps onto Alexis' shirt, but she doesn't care. She wants to erase strong bodily evidence linking her to any murders and erase the murders from her memory. She decides to drive her to the back of Gabriel's Trails, the same spot where she left Bain shot dead. She hopes no one will recognize that another car was ever in the yard because the encounter was only about five minutes. Alexis sees the dead woman as a whore, so as she drives the car, she decides to rip the shirt of the bleeding dead woman to make it look like a rape gone wrong. With headlights turned out, Alexis grabs a cloth she spots on the car's floor panel and begins to wipe the steering wheel vigorously. After that, she leans over to lift the lever of the passenger's side seat, forcing the seat backwards as far as it can go by the weight of the woman's body so no one will see her sitting there dead.

Alexis makes sure all is clear outside, and she listens for that guard that drives by each hour, but hears nothing nor does she see the car lights. She zones in on trail number two and recounts her first murder that she's gotten away with, giving her confidence that she can do it again. After checking the rear view mirror and seeing nothing, she jumps out to wipe off the sides of both doors and latches and runs, mostly hidden by high bushes.

Alexis' senses are on high alert, and as she turns the corner, her garage is still partially opened and car still turned on. She slows down and shoves the cloth she used to wipe down the car in her pocket, and then she becomes aware of something else. She still has the woman's car keys in her hand. Although her heart plummets to her feet, she continues to slow her pace as to look as normal as she possibly can to any onlookers just joining the evening lookout. More than likely, no one is looking out the window in the front because in this neighborhood, all hanging out takes place in backyards on decks making things of criminal nature much less obvious. Besides that, Alexis is the only teen on this street. The rest are in elementary school, well in bed by now.

When she enters her car, she continues to raise the garage door and then she drives inside, quickly closing it behind her. Remembering the wrench she used for the kill, Alexis turns her car off, exits with cloth and victim's keys still in hand, and retrieves the wrench from the garage floor, placing it back on the shelf. From there, she rushes inside the house, wets and suds a rag to clean the wrench and the spots of blood that linger on the garage floor.

When she's done, everything, including her own clothes and the victim's keys that have her name, Faye, hanging from the loop, enter into a black garbage bag that Alexis folds neatly to fit underneath the middle of her mattress. She plans to dump it in school next week before the janitors come by to take the trash from the restrooms

Now she waits, hoping the cops don't come to her door for anything at all. Before leaving Javis' driveway, she requested he not mention her name to the cops because she's too afraid to be involved. He accepted, so now she can only hope he has her covered.

"How was your date night, Tryina?" Floss asks, arriving at the house looking like his normal self while scanning the front room to see if Derrick is still present.

She runs up to her brother and gives him a big kiss on his cheek, unlike the one from earlier that day that she loathed dearly. "Thank you, Floss!" she squeals. "I had the best night ever."

MURDERS AT GABRIEL'S TRAILS IV

Littered Deception

Murders at Gabriel's Trails IV: Littered Deception

Derrick is elated after leaving the date with Tryina after it started off so rocky with her brother Floss corrupting the first half by pulling out a switch blade plus other verbal jabs. As he walks and observes all the never before seen action dead center of Gabriel's Trails, he realizes what his dad was speaking of about the dangers that could potentially go wrong. There are so many people out, not doing anything in particular, but hanging out. Some are obviously up to no good while others, such as small children, are out as well with their parents, some arguing and some playing cards, but no matter the potential, things seem put together, despite the rumors about Gabriel's Trails. Everyone knows one another, and Derrick begins to feel like he belongs as he's finally able to walk the neighborhood alone, at nightfall, and with a sense of freedom.

Nearing his home, Derrick notices some people causing a slight bit of commotion that appears to be directly across the street from the mailbox of his home. As he approaches from only three quarters of a block away, he watches his parents' car pull out of the driveway, making their way out of Gabriel's Trails.

Triggered with a rush of adrenaline to catch them, Derrick runs his fastest home, waving his hands and shouting loudly, however, it does no good. The car turns out of the neighborhood, leaving him twenty feet away from his front door. Before moving toward the front door, a strong sensation of something is wrong moves over him as he examines the crowd of people across the street scatter as soon as they see him. When he looks at the house, the night light isn't on as it normally is every night, and the screen door is still wide open as if someone is lifting groceries in and out, from a car to the kitchen.

Derrick reaches for his house keys from his pants pocket and begins to rush the front door. He immediately enters his house, shuts the door behind him and begins to call for anyone in the house, but there's no answer. That's when he notices the living room's center table turned over, cushions off of the chair, and the television is still running, playing one of those old black and white cowboy movies that his parents love so much.

Even though Derrick didn't hear anyone in the house after he called, he continues to try to find someone. He paces down the hallway like a madman, grabbing the room doors and calling everyone's names as if he hasn't already, but still no responses. Finally, he collapses onto a kitchen table chair near the phone that's off the hook.

"What?" he asks himself completely afraid of what could have gone on inside his home, and then he sees red on the floor by the couch. He gets up from the table and hangs up the phone while becoming mesmerized by the red spots he sees decorating the scraped up and aged hardwood floor dad always shines up so brightly on his hands and knees as if the floor is brand new. As he approaches the red spots, fears begin to bubble up in his stomach, almost creating a full episode of vomit because the red spots don't look like anything other than fresh blood.

Time seems to stand completely still as Derrick imagines all that could have happened while he was gone at Tryina's house. His mind is in a fog as his eyes tear up from the what ifs that plague his thoughts of a robbery, an attack, or even a fight gone wrong between members of his family which has never, ever happened before, thus, hard to believe could. Finally, Derrick breaks from the trance his thoughts put him in, and he runs to the telephone that he just placed on the dial. As soon as he picks it up, he slams it back down. They don't have call waiting. If he calls from hospital to hospital, he could potentially miss their call to home from wherever they are.

"Crap!" he yells, punching his fist onto the table until he eventually yields to a more direct idea to call Alexis to see if she and Javis are still out on their date. If Javis is still with her, that's even better because they can drive to pick him up to find out what's going on or even call from Alexis' cell to locate them at some clinic which would leave the home phone open.

"Hello?" Alexis picks up her cell phone assuming it's her boyfriend, Javis, calling, however, when she hears the voice on the other end, she's regretting even picking up. After what has happened earlier at Javis' house and what happened ten minutes ago at her own, she can't hang up. Being on the phone is the perfect alibi to cover her second murder.

Alexis purposely moves into the bathroom quickly to turn the water on full blast. The running water will alert any callers to the fact that she is at a home, her home, busy taking a shower. Also if the cops come knocking because word gets out that she was on the scene of the drive by, she has a reason to not answer the door. She'll sit in the shower, or pretend to do so, until she hears her parents open the garage door.

"Alexis, it's me, Derrick. You and Javis still out on a date?"

Alexis hears the panic in his voice, but she's trying to figure out exactly how much he knows about the situation that just took place at his house. "No, I'm already home." Alexis' nerves are shot from only minutes ago killing a woman inside her garage, and just the sound of Derrick's voice brings things to another level of severity. Her hands start to shake violently because things are getting to her psychologically, and she's finding it hard to hold it together. Instead of holding the cell in her hand, she reaffirms that she's home alone by listening, and then places the cell on speaker. Then she sits with her back up against the bathroom door, eyes completely sealed shut.

"Do you know why our house is in a wreck, and there's blood on the floor, table knocked over, people pointing into the yard..."

Alexis begins to fumble over what to do or say as she listens to him grow worse in his concern for his family until she interrupts. "Derrick, wait a minute. Slow down," She slides up the bathroom door, picks up the cell phone and relocates it to the bathroom counter top as she tries to get the nerves up to tell Derrick what happened.

Alexis begins wiping away the tears that are flowing from her eyes as she remembers his dad lying there with a bullet in his head. Derrick has also unknowingly triggered another memory inside of Alexis, one of the first worst memories of her life, that makes her stomach turn inside out, but she plays it off. "They aren't at home, Derrick," she continues, bracing herself with her hand leaning on the wall, head over the sink, in case she vomits. "There was a drive-by shooting, and it was in front of your yard. Someone was shot." The tears begin to hit the sink quickly as she pushes the complete truth back from her mind in order to reveal what's necessary. "The bullet," she chokes back tears, "shot your father."

Alexis listens to the phone drop on the other end, and then her ears pierce as she hears Derrick's voice holler out as if his soul is departing from his body, ripping away from every organ and tissue, bone and all his blood. The sound is so heavy that Alexis begins to rock back and forth, holding her stomach, knowing that all of this family's problems are stemming from her, and she can't seem to slow it down. She never should have re-entered Gabriel's Trails.

Finally, she hears Derrick pick the phone back up, weeping uncontrollably and finding it difficult to hold back any of the emotions that are racing through his body. "Do you know if he's dead, Alexis?"

"I don't know…" she starts, but then he shouts hysterically.

"Tell the truth, Alexis, damn! You sound like you're hiding something, now just say it!"

Alexis cries out, "I don't know, Derrick, I don't know! I left before the ambulance left, and Javis promised me that he wouldn't include me in the investigation. I swear I don't know if he made it or not, Derrick. I promise on my life. It happened so fast…"

There's a knock at the door, and Derrick wipes his eyes as he walks to the window where he confronts the bullet hole staring back at him. The police officer stands to the right on the porch awaiting an answer at the door. Instead of opening the door right away, Derrick imagines the bullet, following its path from the hole in the window directly to the seat where his dad was probably shot. "I gotta go."

"I told Javis not to mention me, Derrick, so please don't."

There's a strange silence between the two before Derrick hangs up, a bit bothered that she wants nothing to do with assisting cops on who shot his dad.

Outside Derrick's door is a female officer who has come to scan the scene and ask onlookers if they witnessed anything during the drive-by shooting. She truly looks uninterested and doesn't seem to care about solving the case one way or the other because she knows the policy of the neighborhood which leads to dead ends each and every time. Derrick watches as she barely scans the scene with her flashlight, walks down the driveway, shining her light on a couple of stray bullets, and then crosses the street to talk with neighbors as more cops pull up to the scene. Derrick simply goes out on the porch and waits.

Four hours later, the rest of his family pulls up into the driveway without his father, and he gets the confirmation he doesn't want when he looks into their eyes. His dad is now dead. His mother enters the home first, followed by a crying Joseph. Before a blank faced Javis even reaches the first step, Karen nearly faints to the floor when she comes face to face with the murder scene she just left. Derrick catches her along with Joseph as they carry her back to her bedroom where she will now sleep alone. On the way down the hall, Derrick peers back outside the front door and watches Javis pick something up out of the yard, but he can't make out what it is. He's never seen his brother so distant, not even attentive to their own mom. Javis seems gone.

After Derrick tucks his mom in and Joseph goes into the bathroom, before getting his mom a warm cup of tea along with her Bible, he catches Javis in the bedroom, his fingers full of a pistol as he stands over the dresser. He then tucks it back into the deepest part of the drawer and starts to cry. Derrick asks no questions because no matter

114

where the gun came from, protection is a must now more than ever.

Back at Alexis' house, she's on her hands and knees weeping all across her bathroom floor as she consumes herself with the gloom and guilt surrounding her existence. For the first time in her life, she wishes she would have died instead of an innocent man.

She finally hears the garage door open and knows it's her parents coming back from their anniversary celebration. Alexis gets up off of the bathroom floor, undresses, and remains in the shower until the water washes away her tears. Each time she closes her eyes, she sees Faye's dead body, clothes torn, lying in the car dead where she left her to be found at the trails of Gabriel's Trails.

The cremation ceremony is held on Tuesday at the church where Mr. Moores attended along with the family every week without missing a beat for the most part. Mrs. Moores requests that the funeral be very private with only relatives of the family and close friends from church and the life of the late Mr. Moores. The pastor, of course, obliges, and makes for invite only at the church's double doors. Because the family is in such distress after the death of Trent, the church gives them relief in the form of a refrigerator full of food, bills paid for two months and two thousand dollars. The family is grateful and attempts to carry on with what seems as less full lives. On Thursday, the boys are back at school, and their mother back to work.

Javis is quiet the whole day of school after they decided it would do no good for them to sit out the whole week. The brothers do their usual at lunch time, however, Javis is completely shut down for the most part. After the shooting, no one in the house even heard him talk much nor did he chat on the phone with Alexis at all. Derrick and Joseph both leave him alone the entire day in school when they see him in passing, even at the points he looks like he could just sit and weep. They know him well enough to give him his space until he decides to talk. He's just become the man of the house and that has to weigh hard on him now.

Outside of Javis' silence and back at home, Mrs. Moores is overworking. Since she requested more hours at the job, God is providing, but that leaves no time for those great, hot, home cooked meals the teenage boys are used to their mother putting together. Instead, they have to warm up leftovers in the oven because they don't have a microwave. That particular appliance had to be sold a while ago just to keep the lights on in a previous residence.

"Wake up, Derrick."

"What's up, J?" he asks, looking at the time on their alarm clock that reads two thirty in the morning. His pillow has a load of slob on it, so he flips it over on the dry side while raising his head, shocked that Javis is finally initiating conversation.

"Man, look." Javis pulls out the gun, and Derrick jumps clear to the other side of the bed, thumping the wall extremely hard, possibly enough to wake up their mother.

"Man, what the hell you doing pointing that thing at me?"

"Shut up, Derrick, dang man!" Javis throws the covers over the weapon and walks to the doorway. Joseph is in his room still asleep, and instead of being in the bedroom, he hears the purr of his mom's soft snore from the living room while the television's light blinks the movements of different scenes as it plays on mute. He shuts the door and then returns to the side of Derrick's bed.

"Listen, Derrick, keep the noise down, and if I was about to shoot you, I would have never woke you up, now would I have?" he asks matter of factly.

"Sleep people don't think about the rules of rational when it comes to guns, Javis. One rule counts – move," he responds. "Now move it off my bed. I already saw you with it once, just didn't say anything."

Javis uncovers the gun and places it back inside the drawer. "Alexis gave it to me."

"She owns a gun, man?" Derrick asks wiping his eyes off, still in a sleepy stupor.

"She can't own it. She's too young to own it, but she gave it to me. It could belong to her parents, a friend, I don't know, but when dad got..." he pauses and changes the direction of what he is saying. "When the drive-by happened, she took it from the car and gave it to me." Then he looks directly at Derrick like a man who needs some guidance. "I took it without hesitation, D, and no matter how hard I try not to think about it, I still imagine myself using it. I'm fighting everyday not to kill somebody to right this wrong." A tear falls from his eyes as he struggles to contain himself. "I also hear mom and dad in my head telling us that vengeance is the Lord's, but I'm stuck, man. I'm going crazy, D. I feel lost without doing something. I'm about to explode." Javis' hands wrap around his head as if it's in a gruesome amount of agony. The veins are popping out of his arms and hands, stressed from a lack of sleep, sadness and being worn down overall.

At a loss of what to say, Derrick answers, "Man, it's gonna be alright..."

"No it's not. Alright is over. I used to be able to think for the future. Now, the future stops each time at the same place, finding who killed dad. It doesn't go any further than that, D. Daddy was just trying to make it. He wasn't doing anything but trying to make it with what he could make it with."

Derrick doesn't know what to say or do, but let him cry. At this point, Derrick feels that while everyone was letting things out in their own ways, Javis held it all in, and this must be why his mind is tilting off balance and his words are making the sense of a man headed for the penitentiary or the grave. The best thing for Derrick to do, he figures, is to let him talk, with no disagreement or agreement. He realizes how serious a person Javis is, and he can't afford to lose his older brother to a crime nor can the family.

"Here," Javis says, wiping the tears from his eyes as they start up again while he reaches back at a shoe box from underneath his bed. He pulls out all the money he has. "I talked mom into going on government assistance for food earlier tonight. I told her that I would take care of you and Joseph's clothes. We're not going to touch the money the church gave us until we have to. On Saturdays, mom drops us off up the road to cut grass and we walk back home. Joseph is going to be taken to the church where they are teaching mechanics and painting classes to learn a trade. You can go, too, if you like but…"

"No, I'm walking with you. Two is better than one." Derrick remembers his dad's voice loud and clear.

"Cool."

Javis gets back into the bed and lies there awake like every night since the death of his dad despite the fact his eyes are closed. He can't run from the dreams or the feeling of vengeance that he's constantly praying to let go of for the sake of his mom, brothers and his soul. God would have it that way. His dad would have it that way. That's the way he was raised. He wasn't born a killer, and doesn't want to die one.

Saturday morning is one of early rising, but instead of being dropped off at Alexis' house to cut the yard as early as Javis planned, he and Derrick opt to walk to her house later on in the evening because they want to try their luck in the other neighborhoods nearby, see if anyone else would like to schedule their yards to be cut. Mrs. Moores isn't too happy about the plan, however, she has no choice. She can't keep a firm grip on them too much longer now that she needs their help, so she has to trust the way she and Trent have raised them, leaving all things in the hands of the Lord.

Javis and Derrick start off on foot, without the lawn mower that morning, but by noon, the sun struck their skin like a match causing them to return home to grab a bite to eat and cool out.

"Man, the yards in that last neighborhood look like the kind you see in magazines and on movies. I've never seen grass that green and people that scared to walk on it in my whole life." Derrick flicks on the television to pop a movie in as he chews on a bologna sandwich.

"Your life hasn't been that long and neither has mine." Javis shuts the refrigerator after pouring a big glass of cold water and taking a big swig. Choosing to sit at the table is the only option for Javis right now, facing away from where his dad was killed. "People are serious about their grass though, and since that's what we do for now, we'll treat their grass like gold, too, as long as they want to pay us to do so."

"When are we gonna go ahead and hit up Alexis' grass?"

"About three or four o'clock. Besides that, I want to get something cooked for ma so she can eat and relax later. This is the perfect time to do it. That way, we can eat a full meal before going up there, too." He turns to face Derrick. "How long you think it takes to get up there on foot though?"

"We can cut through the trails."

"You been there before?"

"No, but I told Tryina that we're going to cut some grass today, and she told me that instead of going the long way around into that neighborhood, we could use trail number four. It puts us out closer to here on the way back, and they even have brand new lights up. On top of that, I told her I would stop by on the way back."

"Man, I don't have time for that girl, D."

Derrick shoots him a slightly irritated look. "But you got time for yours right? I even make time for yours when I get second dibs on the phone." He pauses. "Y'all still together? You haven't been…"

"Yeah, D."

"Why she didn't want to…"

"I don't know, D, now stop asking me questions about Alexis."

"Come on, Javis, man." Derrick says, frustrated with how Javis has started to act. Before dad died, Javis would tell Derrick just about everything, but now, those days are dwindling down. "We can do this, bro."

"You didn't see him!" Javis shouts, taking his glass of water firmly inside the palm of his hand and throwing it full force at the wall. The glass shatters and ends up all over the floor along with Derrick who dives down as soon as he sees Javis lean back for the pitch. "Don't tell me what *we* can do! We can't do a damn thing. It's all on me, and not one mother fucker better not touch my family again!"

The rage in Javis' eyes creates a tension in the home so thick that Derrick feels like he's being attacked by his own brother. In defense of himself, Derrick returns with fiery words after getting up off of the floor.

"What? You think you hurt worse, J, huh…because I didn't see dad with a bullet in his head?"

"Shut up, Derrick," Javis warns, but Derrick continues anyway, walking slowly toward him.

"No, you shut up! That was my dad, too, and how you think it felt for me to argue with him before I left the house?" Derrick yells with tears in his eyes. "How do you think it feels to know that if I would have just stayed home, maybe the bullet would have got me instead because I normally sit right there!" he shouts, pointing at the couch where his father was shot. "I freed that shit up that night. I should be dead, J. Not dad, but me!"

Javis doesn't return fire, but instead, goes to grab his brother and embrace him tightly during his breakdown. They both begin to sob as Javis confronts the place where his dad was shot for the very first time as he hugs Derrick. His brother's right. That's Derrick's seat because he's the one who watches television the most out of everyone, and that seat puts him in direct line of it with the best view. His dad's seat was usually the used recliner in the corner. Dad would have never gotten shot. It would have been Derrick.

"I'm sorry, D. I love you, man. Dad loves you, too, regardless of any argument."

"Love you, too," he responds as he step on a piece of glass. He lets go of Javis in an attempt to man up by the interruption of the glass breaking even more under his shoe. "I guess we better clean this up and start on dinner." He wipes his eyes and gets ready to go get the broom before Javis stops him.

"No, man, I'll get it. I did it, and I'll clean it up." He looks his younger brother in the eyes and repeats his apology. "I'm sorry, Derrick. I miss him, and I know we all feel pretty bad right now, no one worse than the other."

Derrick shrugs, "Dad would want us to keep going. I'm trying."

Javis thinks back to what his dad told him the night of the shooting. "Yeah, we'll make it." They clean up and start dinner.

They make it to Alexis' house at about five thirty which leaves them cooler weather to cut the grass and enough time to return home before it gets too late. It won't be broad daylight, but what's left of the sun will be just enough to see their way through the trails. Just to be sure, Javis packed a mini flashlight before they left because he's never walked that way before, and he doesn't want to be surprised by anything. Derrick made sure he packed about five bottles of water that he made from freezing faucet water in plastic bottles that he'd washed out. They have to conserve where they can because the church money isn't going to last forever, so it makes no sense to pay for water in a bottle while having to pay the water bill at the same time.

Alexis is waiting, looking out of her window as she watches Javis and Derrick walk onto her street, coming from the trails. Just the sight of them walking from the back of Gabriel's Trails makes her nervous, however, she's confident that she won't get caught after removing the visible evidence of Faye's murder from her home. The best thing for Alexis is that a dead woman found down the street didn't make the news at all, so not even her parents discussed it. The shooting of Mr. Moores never made it to the evening news either, and she still hasn't told her mom that the incident happened while she was in the yard. She's afraid her mom will overreact to what Alexis already has under control.

Before going downstairs to open the gate into the backyard, Alexis stops in front of the mirror to get herself together. She takes her hair down from its curly pin up and allows it to fall how it may in a big messy do. It's a brand new look for Javis to see on her, and since their conversation has been little to none during the week, she wants to start fresh.

To complete the fresh start, Alexis layers on a a clean smelling body spray that isn't too sweet or fruity in scent, careful not to put it on her neck or chest so that it doesn't seem that she's trying too hard. Instead, she sprays it on her lower back, navel, inner thighs and hair tips. Her shorts aren't too high, but high enough to keep his attention. As far as the shirt, she allows it to hang of off her shoulder while she ties a knot on the bottom end so that a portion of her midsection drives the imagination. She realizes that she has to make things up to him for more than what he even knows.

There is five hundred dollars stashed in her drawer, and from it, she takes three hundred. More than anything, she wants to help with his family's finances now that Mr. Moores is gone, but she also knows that Javis isn't taking anyone's monetary hand out. That's why her plan is to give it to Derrick if she can. She flattens out the three hundred dollars made from only hundred dollar bills and neatly folds them down into her pocket. From there, she takes a deep breath, checks herself one more time, and then runs to open the gate.

"Hi guys," she greets them, not too cheerfully however because she's still well aware of her memories from last Friday when their dad was killed. Those same memories have replayed in her own mind ever since.

As they walk through the gate, Javis walks inside first, looking at Alexis but not saying a word her way. Instead, he gives her a nod which lets her know that things between them are still on the rocks, and she has to smooth them out.

Derrick responds to her greeting aloud, "What's up, Alexis? How you been?"

"I've been good," she starts with her eyes following Javis until she finally looks back at Derrick. "How have you been considering…"

"We miss him." Then he looks up at her majestic sized home and continues, "But we still have to work. That's what he would want, for us to do the best we can do with what we have until we can get more to do even better."

Alexis' heart sinks as she reaches inside her pocket while Javis is still walking toward the back of the yard and pulls out the three hundred dollars. "I have some money that I want to give to your family. It's three hundred dollars, and if you ever…"

Derrick shakes his head and laughs, quickly glancing up at his brother who just started the mower. "You better put that money up unless you want more problems. You can't buy your way into this family, Alexis. Explain your damn absence since that night. Better yet, go take that three hundred dollars to Javis and see if he won't cuss you out." He unscrews the top off one of the bottles of water. "I'm not a rocket scientist…yet…but he's not feeling you right now."

"Derrick, I'm afraid," she explains the best way she can which is by leaving out most of the story about what, besides the bullets, has her so shaken.

"From what I heard, he saved your life. Don't you think he was afraid doing that? Don't you think you owe us," he pauses as he looks down at the money that's still in her hand, "more than money?" He starts to walk off. "But it'll still be sixty dollars for the yard, though."

Alexis closes the gate and locks it as she thinks about what Derrick just said, and it's all true. That's why before Javis gets into the flow of cutting the yard, she walks toward him to tap him on his shoulder from behind. Javis turns off the lawn mower and faces her.

"Can I talk to you inside the house for a minute?"

"Hey, Derrick." He points to the lawn mower. "Come hook this part up for me real fast. I'll be right back." Javis tosses his shirt over his shoulder, places his book bag underneath the bench, and then follows Alexis into the house. Alexis closes the door behind them and doesn't waste time apologizing for her absence when he probably needed her most.

"Javis, I want to apologize for not being there for you or your family last week. I got terrified and didn't know what to do or think."

Javis stands there as if he's already heard the sob story and could care less, so Alexis, after she starts to feel uncomfortable in her own house as a result of Javis' coldness toward her, continues to further her explanation after reaching for his hand. He allows her to hold it.

"My mom and dad don't even know that the shooting happened while I was there. I don't want them to get so afraid that they won't let me see you again."

He looks at her clothing and rather convincing innocence with the way she stands and speaks, and then he reaches for her other hand gently before he finally says anything.

"For a week now, I've been thinking hard about my father." As he continues to talk, a tear creeps out from behind the strength of his face as he tries to hold it back. "We just moved here, Alexis. No one knows us. No one. This is a completely different school and neighborhood, different people everywhere we look, and the one thing that isn't normal is a new family getting welcomed into any neighborhood with a bullet. A pie maybe, in the worst of the neighborhoods, but not a bullet in a drive by aimed directly at them for no reason. Sure it can happen, but what are the odds it's for nothing?"

Alexis is about to answer despite her knees getting weaker, but he clutches her hands tighter to let her know that he's not finished speaking.

"So I was thinking the whole week you didn't call, who knows me? But really… what I want to know is who knows you? Who would be mad enough at anyone who lives at my home to come blasting in my driveway and in my direction when I have no enemies? The question is, do you have enemies, Alexis?" He rubs her fingers in between his, and waits for her reply.

Alexis' breathing pauses, but because she's grown even more accustomed to lying, she finishes her breath as if his words don't startle her at all. She even manages to muster up the confidence to move closer to him in efforts to show him that she can be trusted.

"Baby, I know many people around here, but the one thing that would make no sense is why someone would want to kill me? I'm a sixteen year old, private school girl, and I live right outside Gabriel's Trails. All I know is that I can hope that it has nothing to do with any of us at all. It could have even been mistaken identity, but the reason couldn't have been me."

Javis leans in and gives her a kiss on the lips, and Alexis returns the kiss passionately as tears roll down her face which only add to her sincerity. However, Javis takes the opposite approach to her tears because he's already

127

cried lakes and streams behind his dad's death. He questions how sincere her tears are and compares those same tears to guilt. Tears look the same, whether they mean something or not.

Even though he wants to believe her, he continues pushing the issue beyond her tears. "I didn't ask you that, Alexis. I just want to know if you have any enemies."

"Well, I told you what I told you, Javis." She pulls away from him. "Give me the third or fourth degree if you want, but if you think I had anything to do with that shooting…"

"You said it, Alexis. When you fell, you said that they were gonna kill you," Javis states calmly, holding his stance as she backs away.

"What?"

"That's what you said, Alexis." Javis is dead serious, and she knows it.

"Well, wasn't it the truth? They were trying to kill us, Javis," she says appearing confused, as if she doesn't know what he's talking about.

"It just sounded like you knew someone was gunning for you when I think back on it," he continues, pausing to examine her gestures for any odd reactions, but he gets nothing out of the ordinary. "It could be my imagination though," he says, grabbing his shirt off of his shoulder, preparing to walk back outside to finish the yard. Then, he looks back at Alexis who is just standing there dumbfounded. He reaches back for her hand, allowing his heart to soften. "If I'm wrong, Lexis, I'm sorry." She takes his hand, and they both head outside onto the deck.

As they walk outside, it looks like Derrick has been waiting impatiently because he takes his hand off of the motor as soon as he sees them exit the house. He then begins walking towards the deck with Javis and Alexis after grabbing a bottle of water from his bag.

"It's hot as hell out here, and I ain't even been there to find out," he says only to take four big gulps of water as he climbs the deck's steps. "Don't plan on going either," he confirms as he grabs a seat.

Javis comes to sit in the chair across from him with Alexis in hand as she centers herself in front of him, sitting on his lap. Javis, with her hand still inside his, wraps his arm around her stomach and leans back. As soon as he relaxes, something falls out of his pocket that startles everyone, taking their attention to the deck's floor. It's a knife. Javis simply picks it up and places it on the table. The setting sunlight reflects light onto the engraved letters M.B. that are settled into the knife's handle, and the water Derrick's drinking comes tumbling out of his mouth. Alexis doesn't even see him choking because her eyes are glued on what is only inches away from her as her heart pumps a mile a second. It's the knife – her dad's knife – the one she took from home the night she shot Bain.

Immediately, Alexis' thoughts begin to race as Javis pushes her to the side while he goes to pat Derrick's back to clear his airway. For one whole year, she's forgotten about the knife, thinking that it was long gone, but not today. Today, she remembers who she gave it to before she entered Bain's condo, and she ran right past him on the way out because she had something better to protect her – Bain's gun.

Alexis backs up to the rail of the deck as she watches Derrick's full recovery from his choking fit, and she's consumed with questions about how Javis got the knife in the first place. Feeling pressed to grab the knife and run inside the house, she goes against her fears and decides to play it cool. No matter how cool she tries to behave though, her hands begin to shake, so she grips the railing with her hands as tight as she can before she takes off back into the house with an excuse, "I'll go get some paper towels." At that, she's gone.

"Derrick, man, you alright?" he asks, still patting his back as his brother catches his breath. "Answer me, D."

Derrick waves his arms and shakes his head up and down to let Javis know that he can breathe again, but his breathing isn't the issue. In the middle of clearing his throat and tossing the water bottle, Derrick gets up and grabs the knife off of the table. He then opens the blade while he stares down at the same M.B. he saw at Tryina's house when her brother brandished the knife in front of him. Then, he remembers that Javis picked up something out of the yard when mom nearly passed out on the floor the night his dad was killed. After completing his examination of the knife, Derrick then looks at his brother who is still concerned about him choking.

"I'm cool," Derrick finally speaks, stalling on unloading information that could be wrong and accusatory against his girl's brother. "But when did you start carrying a knife?" Then he looks up. "You already have a gun, man."

"I picked it up from the yard."

"The yard?" he asks. Even though he already figured that was the situation, hearing where Javis found it, coming from his own mouth, only confirms his thoughts.

"Yeah. When we got back from the hospital, I saw it there, so I've had it ever since. I brought it with us just in case we ran into trouble on the trail. We'll be going back late, so…"

"Well, whatever man. Look, I need to call Tryina real fast. I did my part," he says pointing to the grass that he's already cut. "Now it's time for me to have a minute with my girl like you had a minute with yours." He hands the knife back to Javis, taking one more glance at the M.B. inscription to be sure his eyes aren't playing tricks on him.

"Whatever, man." Javis walks down the deck, on the way to finish cutting while Derrick knocks at the French doors. Alexis comes back to the door with the paper towels in hand that she's been holding a while, but when she sees Derrick at the door, she immediately looks over at the empty deck floor where the knife fell, back on top of the table, and then back at Derrick. The knife's gone.

"Can I use your bathroom and phone a minute, Alexis? Don't worry about the paper towels. It's all good, but I really have to use the phone. Is it okay?"

"Yeah, it's fine." Alexis looks back at Javis who has already started cutting the yard, so she decides to fall back and stay inside after pulling her cell phone out of her pocket, handing it to Derrick. "Here."

"Thanks, and I'll be right out. I just need some privacy to make this phone call," he explains, appearing shaken but trying not to let it show. His eyes are telling it all because they continue to shift left and right as if he's putting together pieces of a puzzle right in front of him.

Alexis remains quiet while she points him in the direction of the guest bathroom. As Derrick walks into the bathroom and shuts the door, her heart pounds as she finds it hard to breathe air into her lungs. Rushing to the sink, she throws some water on her face while her heart continues to protest against the one day of calmness she desires because seeing her dad's knife fall from Javis' pocket is about to send her insane. As she hears Derrick start talking, her uneasy curiosity guides her over to the door to listen after being sure Javis is still cutting the yard.

"Hello?"

"Tryina, it's me, Derrick."

"Hey, babe, what's up?" she asks, sitting up on her bed as she attempts to detangle a knot in her necklace. Because she's tied up at the moment, Tryina puts the phone on speaker.

"I need to ask you about something important. Hello? Tryina?"

"Yeah, Derrick, I'm here. Just can't get this knot out..."

"But I need you to hear this, Tryina," he states anxiously.

"Okay, okay." She puts her necklace down and throws herself backwards onto her pillow. "What's got you so riled up, Derrick? You sound weird."

Derrick leans on the sink of the spotlessly, fancy guest bathroom. The sink is lined in the color of gold along with the faucet handles, and there's even the smell of fresh roses with a floral design that looks hand painted onto the walls. Taking in the whole spectacle causes Derrick to take his butt off the sink and just talk to Tryina leaning up against the door.

"Tryina, where did your brother get that knife he showed me?" he asks sighing heavily.

"How am I supposed to know? And why are you back on that damn knife?"

"Look, Tryina, I'm serious. Do you know?"

"No, Derrick, didn't I just tell you that I don't know where Floss got that knife from?" In the blink of an eye, Tryina looks up as she speaks, and Floss is at her room door. She reaches to take the phone off speaker, but Floss dives over and grabs her arm tightly, flinging both her arm and her over onto the mattress.

"Well, it was in my yard, Tryina, after I saw Floss with it at your house."

Tryina doesn't answer because her brother Floss is looking directly in her face about to smack the living blood out of her if she ends the conversation. Her face is full of terror as Floss leans back on his elbow to hold himself up on the bed, beckoning her to continue the conversation with his eyes.

With a dry throat, Tryina answers, "Your yard?" She uses the smallest amount of words that she can use, but this doesn't clue Derrick in at all. Her mouth normally runs a mile a minute, but not today.

"Yeah, so how did it get there?"

Tryina stares Floss in the face, and he puts his finger up to his lips. Tears begin to fall from Tryina's face as she balls up her fists, reaching back to punch Floss, but he grabs her face after grabbing her hand, shoving her head back toward the phone. She knows better than to make any sound of distress, so she responds the best way she knows how.

"I don't know, D," she says, and then Floss squeezes her cheeks, forcing her to say more. "Has he been to your house?"

"Not invited by me." Being careful with his words as not to purposely accuse Tryina's brother of anything, he continues. "What do you think he was doing in my yard or in front of my family's house? Tryina!" he asks as he grows more and more heated at her slow responses.

"You think he shot up your house, Derrick? Is that what you think?" Tryina's voice quivers as she asks the question to which she already knows the answer. The look on Floss' face says it all. He's behind the shooting, and she purposely asked the question about the shooting just to spite her brother for forcing her to talk.

"My brother found it that same night, Tryina. I saw him pick it up, but I didn't find out what it was until today. Now I know he was with us a couple times during the night," Derrick states, forcing his anger to refrain itself off of this highly possible assumption, "but he wasn't with us when the shooting happened. I just missed it, Tryina. Floss wasn't home."

"I gotta go, Derrick. I'll call you back later."

"Tryina, I know that's your brother, but I had to ask you in case you knew something I could go on. Not accusing him or anything, and I know you love your brother, but, Tryina, that was my dad that died. I loved him, too, and now he's gone."

It's too late. Floss hangs up the phone while Tryina looks at him in disgust. She slides off the bed, away from her brother who happens to be her guardian as well, and she's weeping madly. "I should kill you myself, Floss!" she screams, choking on each word that comes from her mouth. "I hate you!"

He wipes his face in a downward motion, and then reminds her. "Sometimes I wish I didn't have to do things, Tryina. This time, I really messed up, and I have to do what I have to do so I can continue to take care of you." He puts his hand out for her to grab it in order to help her up, but she doesn't flinch. "I dropped it. It fell out of my pocket when I was in his yard, that's it, sis. That's it."

"Why did you do that, Floss? He's my boyfriend, and that was his dad!" She screams, punching the floor.

"Alexis is that chick's name that shot Bain. She came back in these Trails, Yina. I had to get her, so we tried to pop her. I got wind we missed. That was Bain's girl, but Bain was my blood. Didn't that nigga take a shot for you because of me? I owe him. We were made brothers that day." He gets up from the bed. "I should've never let her go in his place that night without clearing that shit better than what I did. I thought her polite ass wasn't a threat, sis."

"Get out of my room." Tryina's eyes are blood shot, and if she could kill her brother she would. She's always been forced to live his life since the death of her parents. He would control her ever waking move and every breath of her sleep. The only one who has more control over those movements and breaths is God, and it's at this time that Tryina wishes God would finally take her dear brother out of his misery and the misery he causes other people, including her.

Floss puts his cap on all the way down to his eyes and asks Tryina, "Where is he?"

She doesn't answer, but she knows what's about to happen if she doesn't. Still, she keeps quiet, assuming that this time she'll be stronger and less of a push over than the other times when she's had to hold it down for him more times that she can count.

"Tryina, what you want this time?" he grins, "Some more money for that damn weave you like to drag down your damn back? Here." He digs down in his pocket and throws money at her, all twenties rolled up in one rubber band. Then, he walks over in front of her and kneels down, tilting his head to the side as he watches her posture up in front of him, like she's about to hit him. "I could give a damn, sis. I really could," he responds to the ruthless stare she gives him. "You just better tell me where he is right now, and I'm not fuckin' counting the shit down."

The only thing Tryina knows to do is call his bluff as she holds on to cracks on the floor with her fingers. Then, Floss gets tired of her stall, lifts her body from the floor like she only has the weight of a rag doll and slams her against the wall like she's a man. She still doesn't open her mouth...that is until she watches Floss pull his gun from the back of his pants.

"Answer the question," he demands.

"Trail four. I told him to come down trail four!" she says, giving up. Floss takes his hand from the gun after shoving it back down his pants.

"That's all you had to say. I wasn't gonna shoot your ass. Sorry." He stands tall, looks at her and then leaves. As he walks down the hall, he proclaims, "Don't need to date no niggas from the Trails anyway."

Because she knows time is running out, she watches through the window as Floss heads out. Then, she snatches her phone to only find she picked up for Derrick from a number that he marked as private. She then hits the floor in tears because she knows that there isn't any way to warn him about the trail and her brother.

Derrick calms himself down before exiting the bathroom. Going up against Floss isn't something Derrick wants to do on a hunch nor does he want his straight up no nonsense older brother to go after him with no proof. It's Floss' knife, but the problem is that it was a drive by. The knife in the yard makes no sense because people don't generally walk in drive-bys.

He exits Alexis' bathroom to find her sitting on the counter top near the kitchen sink. She's fast. If privacy is what he wanted, she is sure that he thinks he had it.

"Thanks," he says, handing her the cell phone and walking back outside with Javis. As soon as she sees Derrick's foot hit the grass, she looks at the recent calls, but is only flicking through recent recognizable numbers.

"He deleted the number," she says to herself as she glances back out of the window. Now all she is left with is the names she heard Derrick say during his private conversation with his girlfriend Tryina. Her brother had the knife that Javis found in the yard, and his name is Floss. This is possibly the same guy Alexis handed her father's knife to before she went into Bain's house. Alexis holds her stomach. "I'm sorry, Javis," she mourns with tears falling freshly down her face, but the brothers can't hear her because they're outside in the yard. She only wishes she could tell them the truth, and everything would go away. It won't though. Nothing will ever be the same. That's why she takes a couple minutes to gather herself together, wash her face and then return outside because she's convinced that she can make everything turn out good, in her favor and in her freedom. She has to get the knife before someone connects the dots to M.B. being her father, leaving her exposed.

By the time, Javis and Derrick finish with the front yard after completing the back, it's well on its way to dark. There's only a portion of the day left, and it's slowly slipping away as they gather their things, fill up on more water and leave the yard. Alexis stops Javis on the way down the driveway while Derrick continues to walk toward the trails.

"Yeah, baby, what's up?" Javis asks tired, not wanting to be bothered about anything, however, not trying to be too rude despite his not looking anywhere near her when he speaks.

"Be careful," she tells him as she takes his hand, trying to generate movement from his eyes into hers. Alexis is well aware of the danger he may be in, and the thought even crosses her mind to give them a lift in her car back home, but that could potentially put the family in more danger, plus get her killed. She continues, glancing at Derrick, still not knowing what to say or do to keep them off the trails, but she tries anyway. "It's dark and going through those trails might not be too nice," she explains, referring to all the other crimes that have happened there besides her own. Before Alexis can ask Javis about the gun she gave him for protection or the knife he found, he starts to talk.

"I'm good. We're good." His eyes finally meet hers with that same amount of distrust he arrived at the house with, no matter how he pretends to be okay. "I have to go now though, Lexis."

"Will you call me when you get inside?"

"Yeah, I got you." He walks on without a kiss or hug which is different for Alexis, but she's not pushing it because she's aware that more than one thing has got his mind going in and out. It's best she leaves him be.

"See that, Javis?" He walks angrily toward the wooded trails.

"Whatever, man. Did you really expect her to give us a ride back in here? I get what you're saying, but like I told you in the yard, if she doesn't volunteer, we don't ask."

"How you even mess with a girl that scary? It's just a ride! What's the likelihood she get shot at again? We ain't no gangsters, J," he exclaims. "Hell, she's the one that gave you a gun!"

Javis holds back on his response. Derrick doesn't realize that it's taking Javis all his might to keep control of himself when it relates to the situation of his dad's death, Alexis, and just living at the Trails now among the people who killed him. The more things don't make sense, the more he thinks about that night, how dad is now dead, being stuck in the Trails, and how to help get his family out.

As they walk, Javis replays the drive-by over in his head as he squeezes the lawn mower handle. He can still hear the gun shots as he dropped to the ground on top of Alexis. The fact that he could have missed seeing the shooter up close and personal makes his blood boil as he remembers his conversation with his hardworking and innocent dad before he died, letting him know that everything would be alright. The more he remembers, the less he can control his temper, so the pain ends up coming out in tears. He wipes before Derrick sees, and he also chooses not to answer him as he continues to sort out items in his mind. He feels like he's going crazy with each day.

"Which way do we go again, Derrick? Trail four, right?" he asks, with his head turned the opposite direction in efforts to continue concealing his face and emotions. He's trying the best he can to replace his father by not behaving like a child because he knows the family depends on it.

"Four, J, it's trail four. You forgot the trail already?" He stares down the trail they are approaching, and continues, "It's well lit from what I can see, but it does look much different in the dark."

Javis stops and checks out the other trail entrances, one of which has some left over police tape near it. "Didn't forget, just double checking. I don't care how close it puts us out, but really, how safe is it at night?" He continues to look around at the huge homes lining the trails, blocked off by brick and fences that are covered in bushes both high and low, thorny and those not so much. The scenery helps convince Javis that it can't be that bad, at least not at the beginning of the trails. Nearing the end may be another story, so he continues with the confidence that there are two of them and not one taking on the trail at night.

Derrick responds stopping to tie his shoes tighter. "You got that knife, right?"

Javis gives him a quick glance and answers, "Yeah, man, I got it in my pocket." Derrick nods, and then Javis pulls out the flashlight, but it's very dim, so he tosses it back into the bag, regretting not changing the batteries back at home.

"You want me to get that bag, man?" Derrick asks referring to Javis' book bag hanging loosely from his shoulders.

"No, but take this." He retires the lawn mower into Derrick's hands. "Just in case something goes down, my hands are free."

"That's a bet." Derrick takes the mower's handle with full knowledge of his older brother's fight skills that need to be free for use. He's always had a natural ability physically whereas Derrick has a natural ability verbally. "Well let's go."

As they head into trail four, both of them are fairly secure about the trek, and Tryina didn't tell a lie. The walking area is well lit and very clean, however, looking from left to right tells a darker story. Because the path is so lit, it makes the visual of the woods surrounding them even darker, and their pupils can't adjust. They fix this by walking in the dead center of the trail as a safety measure.

Javis' eyes are fixed on the road ahead of him, and Derrick is looking from side to side amazed that no one else is coming down the trail. During the day, they passed by plenty people, but now the trail is barren. Further down the trail, the tops of Gabriel's Trails' condos come into view, and they both relax a little bit after being in the middle of nothing but a lit trail and sides of darkness for so long.

"Derrick," a voice calls from behind them out of nowhere.

Derrick lets go of the lawn mower as fast as lightening, turns around but doesn't see anyone. Javis immediately places his hand near his pocket where the knife is located, but he doesn't pull it out. His dad taught him to never draw any weapon, whether it be a stick, brick, bat or book unless a fight is what you want. Javis didn't want a fight, not unless he had to fight. In this particular instance, the unseen person is obviously someone who knows Derrick because he calls him by name which makes both Javis and Derrick uncertain as to the nature of the call.

As Derrick and Javis stand nearly shoulder to shoulder silently with their eyes wide open, the well lit trail has become their worst enemy by casting shadows where they don't need them. The voice comes again, but no matter where they look, they don't see who it's coming from.

"Derrick, I think it's a little late for you to come down this trail. Good thing you're not alone."

Suddenly, Derrick recognizes the voice. It's a voice he's heard before on the same night his dad was shot to death. The voice is that of Tryina's brother, Floss. Derrick looks quickly at Javis who is unaware of anything that's going on between the knife and Floss, but something inside of Derrick's spirit is telling him that this particular meeting with Tryina's brother isn't going to be friendly on either end.

Despite the fact that Derrick recognizes the voice, he pretends that he doesn't know who it is, just to buy some time to think about how right or wrong this encounter can go. His brother has the knife in his pocket, but just what Derrick has learned about Floss from their first meeting, if something does go wrong, Floss is sure to have a more brutal weapon on him. During the silence, he watches as Javis moves his hand closer to his pants pocket, and then he speaks to prevent the draw.

"Do I know you?"

"Yeah, nigga, this Floss. Tryina's brother. This my trail, lil' nigga. Stand down. Y'all look scared as fuck."

Javis looks at Derrick confused, but not saying a word because obviously who they can't see, can see them clearly.

"It's cool, man. It's Tryina's brother," he whispers. Derrick knows full well things may not be cool, but right now, Floss has the upper hand because he can see them, and they are totally blind. "We can't see you, Floss," Derrick speaks up.

"No shit." He walks out from behind the trees onto the lit trail, still unidentifiable, but made out by the silhouette. "I thought you were trying to ignore me for a minute," he pauses, "because you have something that belongs to me, and you might not want to give it back. You know I dropped that shit in your yard." The silhouette begins to move forward with the left arm swinging while the right arm is still. As he gets closer, the gun lying firmly gripped upon his upper thigh comes into full view. Javis detects panic in Derrick by the increased speed and heaviness of his breathing, so he doesn't hesitate to protect him. Little does he know that he's mistaken Derrick's heavy breathing for fear when it's actually the result of already putting together the pieces of a puzzle that left his father dead. It's this that makes him angry.

"Move, Derrick." Javis steps over in front of his younger brother, and when he does, Derrick's attention drops down to Javis' pocket where he knows the knife that Floss is looking for is located.

Floss tilts his head, and by now, his full face has come into view minus the eyes that are completely cast out by the cap he wears low on his forehead. It's beyond a shadow of a doubt Tryina's brother, and he now has the gun pointed directly at Javis.

"I didn't know I was going to have to kill both you young bloods tonight," he says with a grin. "This ain't personal to either one of you…"

"Go, Derrick," Javis orders his brother, but Derrick doesn't flinch. Instead, he walks out from behind his brother to stand on his side, ready for anything.

"You know you're cool with me, Derrick. My sister likes you and all that. Don't be mad at her because I overheard your conversation."

Javis's eyes become unsettled because now he knows he's missing portions of a story that's much deeper than a robbery. Prompted to ask Derrick on the spot about the conversation, the gun in Javis' face takes precedence over figuring it out and the argument that would coincide.

"I need that knife, Derrick. You have it." Floss continues, but then stops because he notices the look on Javis' face of total confusion. "Is this your brother right here? Oh, you didn't tell him?" he laughs. "Oh shit! My ass jumped the damn gun. Here it is I thought you were making your rounds to snitch on me over to the cops later after finding that shit in your yard from the drive by, and the only person you told is Tryina? Damn. I can't take that chance that you'll turn me over to the law, especially now. For the record, you a cool dude, and I didn't mean to have your father shot, Derrick. I'm gonna hate to kill you too…and him," he flicks the pistol up toward both their faces, forcing the barrel directly at their heads one at a time, then back at Derrick. "Just gimme the fuckin' knife, man. You got it on you or not. I gotta kill you anyway. You know too much."

"Derrick didn't find it."

"Nigga, was I talking to you?"

"I picked it up, and you're right. Derrick didn't tell me anything," Javis states eerily calmer than what he appears.

"That's a nigga for you! Your own brother hiding shit," Floss laughs, but then gets serious in a split second. "If you got it, hand it over. If you don't, like I said, I still gotta take you out."

"It's in my bag. I have to take my back pack off." Javis doesn't take his eyes off of Floss, and as Derrick listens to the conversation occur, he realizes that Javis has lied which puts him on higher alert for anything about to happen next.

"Go ahead then…take it off and get it out. I'm not touching a damn thing. We need to make this clean."

As Javis pulls his bag off of his shoulder, he holds it out in front of him as to prove he's going as slowly as he can go. Derrick is watching Javis' pocket, where he knows the knife really is, making certain that if it falls out, he can charge Floss with it. What his brother is doing, Derrick has no idea, but he knows he's ready for anything other than death.

Floss walks closer and the full depth of his face comes in, even revealing his callous nature, something very different from his sister Tryina. Derrick looks directly at the barrel of the gun pointing at them both as Floss' hands grip it tightly, ready to shoot as soon as the exchange takes place.

"Toss it over. Don't shove that shit on the ground. I want it to fall behind me," he states as Javis kneels slowly to the ground to unzip the bag. Floss then points the gun directly at Derrick, planning to shoot him as soon as he sees the knife leave Javis' hand.

"Floss," Derrick calls, but Floss isn't having it.

"Shut up and talk to the Lord, nigga," he interrupts, and for a split second, removes his attention from Javis who is on the ground with an unzipped book bag, and plants them on Derrick. Then he smirks, "I pray you make it in."

As soon as Javis catches Floss in that smirk and using the Lord's name in some sort of assassin's game, a gun goes off only one foot from where Derrick is standing, causing him to dive to the ground, hitting chest first on the trail to the right of him. Then he hears another gunshot that makes him shuffle again, closer to the trees. He stops to look back when he realizes that the bullet missed him. Before looking anywhere else, Derrick looks at his brother who is still kneeling with his hand inside the book bag. Then, taking a deep breath of relief, he glances Floss' way, and he has just hit the ground, but still moving.

As Derrick scrambles himself to his feet, Javis also gets up, but instead of running in the direction away from Floss, Javis lunges forward, grabbing him by his shirt, creating an elevation to his head. Derrick makes it over to Javis and decides to kick Floss' gun further away, and when he does, he sees Javis from the corner of his eye knock Floss' cap from his head. He knows things are about to get worse, but no matter what, he thirsts to watch Floss die for murdering his father.

"I ain't the bad guy, youngsters," Floss grins as he lies on the ground, pulling at Javis' clothing, causing the knife to fall from Javis' pocket as he struggles to live.

"My father wasn't a bad guy either," Javis says cringing in anger, tears falling down his face, wanting nothing more than to continue beating Floss in his face until he takes his last breath. "Why did you shoot at us that night?"

"You think you got yourself a good woman, ain'tcha?" he asks Javis but then turns his attention to Derrick. "Ask me where I got that knife from, Derrick?"

Quickly, Derrick snatches the knife off of the ground from beside Javis' pants, and shoves Javis out of the way, consumed with fury, so much so that he places the knife at Floss' neck.

"Just fuckin' say it, Floss, before I send you where you just tried to send me."

"Alexis," Floss states pronouncing every syllable in her name while planting a huge smile across his face. Then, he says her name again. "Alexis." Then he begins to hold on to Derrick's shirt, and suddenly gets serious. "She killed Bain. She shot him right in these trails by the red stone on two. Her ass came back in here, and she should've been rolled back out." He stares into Derrick's eyes and then he cuts a glance at Javis who is right beside him. "Your fuckin' girl got your father shot up. Truth is, I drove, but it wasn't me that pulled the damn trigger. I just led the way." Then he looks back at Derrick who is completely hovered over him, and almost like he's begging to die, he completes his conversation with a taunt and a weak smile. "Shit happens."

Derrick then raises the knife and stabs him in the neck. Blood pours onto the trail, and Javis tackles his brother, knocking him over onto the dirt as the knife follows, still held tightly in Derrick's grip.

"He led the way, Javis! He did that! He thinks it's so funny!" he screams, kicking his feet in the dirt and throwing the knife, trying to fight his way from Javis with his eyes glued to Floss' bleeding body. He's never been so deceived, and his heart continues to fill with a hatred that's unimaginable. "Now you go meet my God! You go meet him for the shit you did to my dad! That's the shit that happens. That's ..." He loses all strength and starts to sob uncontrollably as Javis comes to his senses behind his brother nearly losing his mind. He now has to save his brother and himself from prison.

With no other choice, Javis slaps his brother hard in the face twice and grabs him by his throat. "Come on, D. We gotta get out of here." Javis, then points back to Floss lying there with his eyes open to the night sky. "He's dead, now get up. Don't think about it, D. It's all self defense, but it won't look like it. We have to go, Derrick." He looks at his brother who has gotten specs of blood on his shirt, and he orders him to remove it. Derrick rushes to take of the shirt, and then he stuffs it in Javis' bag along with the gun as Javis runs to retrieve the knife that is now reminding him of Alexis.

The lawn mower is in the same spot facing the way that's closest to home, but Javis hesitates about coming out that way not knowing who may see them come out of trail number four. Derrick is clearly shaken, waiting on Javis to tell him what to do, so Javis decides on the next move.

"Where you going, Javis?"

He grabs the mower after putting his book bag on his back and dusting off his clothes. "We can't go out that way," he says referring to the end of the trail. Then he notices Derrick's hands. "Man take off your socks, wipe your hands down a little bit and then put them back on your feet. Do it inside out." Then he starts to walk again as his brother does what he told him. "We're taking another trail. Trail one. Wherever it puts us out, it puts us out. Let's go. People are gonna start coming out any minute."

Javis and Derrick leave Floss' body bleeding out onto the trail of which he claims ownership and exit at the beginning of the trail where they started. Upon crossing over to trail number one, Javis is tempted to go back to Alexis' house to confront her about the knife in his bag and all the things that Floss stated, especially about a guy named Bain. Derrick on the other hand is totally distraught, not talking, just walking with tremors running through his hands. As they enter the trail, Javis hands the mower to Derrick so that he can rest his power and anger on the bar of the mower as he walks, concealing the tremors from anyone who may be watching on the way to the house.

"You're gonna to have to straighten yourself up, D. Create that illusion, man. If we get caught, I did it. You hear me? I did it."

Derrick looks over at his brother, but says nothing.

"And it's not your fault. You had no idea about Tryina's brother," he pauses, "just like I had no idea about the story he told about Alexis. We're gonna figure this out." He watches as Derrick walks with his head low, nothing but dirt and grass beneath his eyes. Then he remembers his father's last words to him and repeats them to Derrick. "Things are going to work out, man. Everything's going to be fine. Just please keep it together...for mom and Joseph." Those words seem to work as Derrick snaps out of his trance. "Once we step on the inside of Gabriel's Trails, this never happened. Convince yourself and walk, talk like normal. Nobody knows but us."

On the inside of himself, Javis feels no guilt or a need to explain shooting Floss back at the other trail because despite the fact he was angry and desperate to watch him pay for murdering his father, he knows his part was more self defense. When Derrick jumped atop him and stabbed him in the throat, it made it something else more vicious. Either way, there's no way if caught, they are getting off, even if they call the cops. They're armed with weapons that don't even belong to them, and it's also two against one. If caught, they'll go down, and Javis won't let that happen.

Now everything is beginning to come together for Javis as he thinks about what the man he just shot said about Alexis. It explains why Alexis shouted those words when they were shot at in the driveway. Javis also puts two and two together about how she never wanted to make mention of herself to the cops while never once showing her face for his dad's cremation ceremony. Just like a criminal, she disappeared.

Javis' nerves are a pure wreck just thinking about how the girl he once cared about is the root to the evil coming after his family, and he stops walking. Derrick also stops when he hears his brother's footsteps halt, however, doesn't turn to face him.

"The knife, Derrick."

Derrick continues to look forward. "What about it, J?"

"The initials."

"M and B."

"Her mom's name?"

"Lorah."

"Her dad's?"

There's a silence between them both so thick that it sounds louder than the music that's starting to play near the end of the trail. They never met Alexis' dad nor did she ever mention him or his name except for the fact that he's a doctor, some major surgeon at the biggest hospital in the city.

Suddenly, the bloody knife in his bag becomes more real than it ever was when he picked it up from the front of the yard. He doesn't remember seeing the knife in the yard until after the shooting, then he thinks back to how Alexis disappeared when the knife fell out of his pocket.

There's no need to verbalize anything more to Derrick because they both know her last name – Balentine. The two walk through the crowd of people who have just come out to party, and they aren't even thinking about the two boys walking with the lawn mower. They get a few looks from the girls as Derrick is walking with his shirt off, however, Derrick could care less for the attention because his hands still have the sticky red tint of blood in the creases. Though the stains may be amplified to him, any stares from bystanders make him feel like the cops are waiting, and he has no chance.

"Javis," his voice quivers as the impact of everything that's happened starves his confidence that he'll get away with the crime.

"Stay cool, D. We're almost home. If by any chance the cops are there, we just won't go home. Keep it together."

Derrick is finally passing Tryina's house, and he reminds himself repeatedly to keep it together as his brother orders him to do on the walk back home. If that's not hard enough, Derrick can only hope Tryina doesn't see him as they pass by or their lives are over. Javis, on the other hand, has no idea that the home across the street is where the man they just murdered lives, and this makes him more at ease.

As Javis and Derrick enter the house, there's no sign of Joseph nor their mother, however, the food they cooked for them earlier is eaten and leftovers put up for the next day. Running back into their bedroom, the brothers remove their clothing, shoving them in one book bag but leaving only the knife and gun in the other belonging to Javis.

Derrick runs to jump into the shower while Javis goes outside to wipe down the lawnmower's handle with soap, water and bleach that he's poured onto the rag. Upon coming back inside, he runs the rag back to his bag, and then finds the telephone book where he looks up the one name he doesn't know from Alexis' family. When he finds it, he slumps onto the oven, and covers his face into his hands as the telephone book falls to the kitchen floor. Dr. Michael Balentine, and the home address matches that of Alexis'. The initials match the ones on the knife. The man he shot wasn't lying.

The telephone rings, but Javis ignores it at first until it rings again. On the fifth ring, he reaches over to pick it up.

"May I please speak to Derrick? It'sTryina."

MURDERS AT GABRIEL'S TRAILS V

Lies in the Crossfire

Murders at Gabriel's Trails V: Lies in the Crossfire

He hangs up the phone while Javis stares on intently, wanting to know every minute detail of the conversation that Derrick just had with his girlfriend, Tryina. They've only been at home for a very short while from trail number four where they left her brother, Floss, lying there dead from wounds they inflicted with bullets and a knife through the neck. Derrick is noticeably more shaken up than ever now that Tryina has called to talk to him, and Javis needs him to pull it together and recount each and every word she stated while they were on the phone plus the extra that he doesn't know about.

"Come on, D," Javis prompts him nervously, glancing back at the front door to make certain his mom and Joseph aren't coming inside to overhear the conversation or worse than that, the cops. "Let me hear it," he continues, sitting adjacent to him at the kitchen table. Derrick's whole head is spinning, and Javis can tell because after hanging up the phone, Derrick's eyes have been constantly shifting from left to right as if he's speed reading a book.

Before Derrick starts speaking, he places his trembling hands on the table. "When I got on the phone with her, I could tell something was wrong. That's when you heard me ask her if anything was the matter. She said that Floss roughed her up in the house while asking for me…"

"And?" Javis asks, persistent about hearing the rest of the conversation quickly.

"And she basically said that Floss was after me, so he probably went to the trails to head me off. But that's when I interrupted her to let her know that we caught a ride back." He glances up at Javis for his approval of the lie he told Tryina, but gets nothing but a concentrating and impatient stare. "Then she started to apologize for telling him where we were, and that she was scared. She said she hates him."

Javis stares at Derrick because he knows that's not the end of what was said. Derrick then looks at the floor and continues, "I asked her if she's going to be okay, and if she needed me to meet her somewhere. She said no. She said she'll see me in school and warned me to stay away from Floss if I see him because she doesn't know what he'll do when he finds me because of the knife he showed me." He, then, moves his eyes from the floor to the ceiling, worry taking over his body.

Javis glances back at the door quickly, banging his fist on the table. "Why didn't you say anything about it while we were at Alexis' house, huh?"

""Because, Javis, I didn't know if I should, man!" he yells, placing his head in his hands. "Floss showed me that knife when I went to Tryina's house the same night dad got killed." He begins to cry. "Why didn't you show me what you found in the yard, J? I didn't even know that you had that damn knife until today!" he sounds off, accusing Javis with his tone, but when Javis doesn't respond, he continues with his story solemnly. "Floss asked me if I knew anything about the knife, and I told him no. That's when he let everything go. He left and came back, we played video games, and then he left again. Things seemed fine. I didn't know he was going to go aiming at our house…"

Javis doesn't say a word, but his thoughts are running a mile a minute as he tries to understand far too many things, until Derrick speaks again.

"He must've heard me when I told Tryina that you and Alexis went out that night. That's the only way that he would know to come here and gun for her." Wiping his face down so that there are no traces of tears, he continues as he remembers what Floss did that night that now makes sense. "He came out of the kitchen right after I mentioned her name, then he got the knife, and his attitude changed, J." He looks directly at Javis. "It's the truth. Floss, he was telling the truth. That's who he was shooting at. Alexis." Feeling caught in the middle of everything by stabbing Floss in the neck, Derrick panics. "And I killed him, Javis. They're gonna come after me, J. They will, man…" he continues, squeezing his fists in an emotional fit atop the table.

"Hold yourself together, man! Just remember this - I killed him," Javis says, taking the blame. "You didn't, Derrick. I did, remember?" He stands up over his brother. "It was me. It'll always be me. That's the story if we're found out. Turn it over on me."

Derrick's eyes are fixated on his older brother. "He wouldn't have died if I didn't stab him?" Derrick moans, overwhelmed with fear.

Javis then grabs his shirt collar tightly, yanking him from the chair, feeling like he could beat the newly concocted story of what happened at the trails into him. "Didn't you just hear what I said?" He shoves him back down into the chair, but Derrick doesn't even respond with an attitude like he normally does when there's a disagreement. Instead he sits there like a rag doll on a string, hopeless and being controlled by his thoughts as

159

Javis continues to talk. "I stabbed him, Derrick. It was me, so that's how it is from now on." Suddenly, Javis looks at the door and sees the lock turn. "Straighten up. Be normal."

Entering the house are Karen, the boys' mother, and Joseph, their youngest brother. "Well, hello and hello! Just got back from the hospital with your brother here," she states appearing worn out.

Javis kicks Derrick on his foot hard on the way to the door, alerting him to get up and play it cool. "What happened?" he asks, looking over Joseph who appears fine, until he notices his knee.

"I twisted my knee, man, and it hurts, too!" he exclaims, throwing down his cane. "Man, my knee is all blown up like a balloon, but the doctor says it will go down in time, tells me to keep it elevated."

"How'd you do that?" Javis asks, taking his mom's purse and sitting it on the kitchen table as Derrick rises from his seat, staring downward pretending as if something is in his eyes.

"Trying to play ball at the church while waiting for mom. At first, there was nothing to it, but as I kept walking after getting home, the pain got worse and worse until I was out of commission. Now look," Joseph literally drags himself across the wall to the sofa and reveals more of the big, white wrap around is thigh and knee.

Mrs. Moores intercepts the big reveal by addressing her other sons. "When did you two get back from Alexis' house, cutting her yard?"

"About..." he pauses, "a half hour or so ago." He glances Derrick's way, and his mom notices something

160

strange in the air that she can't quite put her finger on, so she asks outright as she takes a seat to remove her shoes.

"What's going on?"

No one answers as Joseph leaves the room, a habit that he's picked up over his short life. He tries to mind his business to keep himself out of trouble after tending to always be the tag along for punishment that he normally had nothing to do with when dad was alive. Both Javis and Derrick watch Joseph's exit as he enters the bathroom, shutting the door behind him.

Believing the silence is a dead giveaway that something's going on, Javis carries the conversation further. "Nothing's going on," he states perkily. "As a matter of fact, ma, I'm tired." He picks up his mom's shoes, about to take them back to her room. "Alexis' parents have a big yard, and after me and Derrick went the extra mile of looking for more work before tackling her yard, I didn't know how tired it would make us feel, even after cooking dinner."

She looks over at Derrick oddly, and then asks, "What has your mouth glued shut, Derrick? It's generally the opposite…"

"I won the bet, ma," Javis blurts out, aware that Derrick is in no condition to conceal a secret so great.

"The bet? What bet?" she grins. "Thank you, boys, for cooking today, too. It was the best meal I've had in a while since I didn't have to cook it."

"It was?"

"Sure it was!" she affirms. "So tell me about this bet."

"He can't talk until tomorrow," Javis falsely grins, but the grin works, fooling his mother. "He ran his mouth so much on the way to and from Alexis' that I told him that if he could keep his mouth shut when we get home, ten extra dollars would belong to him from cutting the grass."

Karen looks at Derrick in disbelief. "And you want ten dollars that badly that you, of all people, is shutting your mouth for it?" Then she starts laughing loudly. "Well, Amen then!"

Javis creates a laugh to go along with his mother's and then turns to face Derrick, forcing him to loosen up a bit and shrug his shoulders while giving his mom a weak grin. As Javis walks his mom's shoes to the room, Derrick goes over and greets her with a warm embrace because feeling her love is what he needs the most right now.

As the night falls silent, Derrick and Javis end up in their beds wide awake. Javis has already peeked in on sleeping Joseph and his mother who appears to be completely asleep because her mouth is open. He's learned that if her mouth is shut while her eyes are closed, then she's actually awake and just resting.

"I don't know about keeping that knife and gun in the house, Javis, I don't…"

Javis bounces out of the bed like a spring, growing increasingly agitated because Derrick won't let him handle the situation. "You don't have to know, Derrick! How many times do I have to tell you that what happened didn't happen to you. The weapons are in *my* bag, and that's where they will stay."

"I don't want to go to jail, Javis, and I don't want you to go either!" he responds, raising his voice as loud as he can without waking anyone. "We left him there and probably left evidence…"

"And he left dad there," he says pointing in the direction of the living room, ignoring the part Derrick stated about evidence being left behind, "while he laughed about it out there on the trails, didn't he? We did him the same way he did pops. Besides that, D, it was mostly self defense."

"No it wasn't, Javis. I wanted to kill him…" He stares back at Javis with weary eyes. "I did. At that moment, I wanted to kill him, but after I did it, I couldn't take it back after I started thinking about the consequences. I didn't want to take it back because I killed him, J. Just the consequences, that's what I want to go away."

Javis doesn't know what else to say or do for Derrick, so he lies down, turns to face the wall, and pretends to go to sleep while Derrick lies awake watching himself kill Floss, regretting every minute because his father is still dead. Now, he has to look over his shoulders if people find out. As for Javis, he thinks about his next move.

"After being struck in the posterior region of the head and at direct center of the temple, this patient, Ms. Dawson, has suffered through not only a multiple day coma, but there was an infection detected in her kidneys that we had to treat along with high fever piled atop a blood test that revealed narcotics in her system, but everything seems to be leveling off right now, along with the patient being able to walk, talk and stool. She can be discharged." the doctor dictates as a reminder into his voice activated tape recorder before he makes his rounds for a previous doctor who had to leave on a serious family emergency. "Room four twenty-eight, end," he enunciates, alerting himself to that particular hospital room being the last room he is to enter for the night before going home.

As the doctor grabs his white lab coat, he takes down his coffee in four big gulps and then adds a breath mint on top of that before exiting to finish the rounds. Walking down the hall of the hospital, he puts a little pep in his step while passing the nurse's station while they smile at his knocking at the counter.

"Are we still alive here?"

"Sure are, doctor, how about you?"

"Didn't know I would be filling in tonight, but what the heck? I should be used to being on some sort of on call by now, right Nurse…" He looks at her nametag.

"Yolanda," she responds as the new nurse on the team.

"Good to meet you." He leaves the counter just as soon as he brings cheer in the middle of the night, and heads into room four twenty-eight.

When he enters the room, there's a woman there asleep with white, first aid gauze wrapped tightly around her head. There's no bleeding through the gauze, however, it's obvious she's been through some major trauma as the side of her eye is slightly swollen and discolored. The white bed sheets are pulled up to her waist as her bed is tilted upward. Her face is make-up free, and her hair is pulled up into a ponytail that hasn't been combed in days. She doesn't hear a thing when the doctor approaches her along with a nurse following him to check her vitals. As he watches the nurse follow through on the blood pressure, the patient wakes up, and the doctor drops the patient's chart to the floor, stunned by the patient's eyes. They're eyes that he's seen before, more than once in his lifetime, but he's never seen them without make-up and as bruised as one of her eyes is now.

"Excuse me, nurse," he beckons, resulting in her undivided attention. "That'll be all."

Although the nurse looks confused because she hasn't completed the full check, and it's customary for a nurse to remain in the room with any and all female patients while the doctor is examining, she complies with the doctor's orders. As the nurse aborts her duties and leaves, the patient's eyes follow her until they land on the doctor's white coat that reads Dr. Michael Balentine. Her eyes then follow the collar up to his face as the doctor removes his name tag from the coat.

"Too late," the lady states with an obvious pain in her head as she raises her hand to touch the bandages. Through the pain, however, she still finds the muscle strength to smile. "Well, look who's here. I would've never guessed that you're a doctor, Merle," she giggles. "Or is it really Michael as I read on the name tag from your little, white doctor's jacket?" she asks sarcastically.

Dr. Balentine, as he fiddles with the name tag in his coat pocket, clears his throat as he's in disbelief at what has happened to her. Soaking up the devastation lying in the hospital bed, he maintains his composure as a surgeon and nothing less, although the lady who lies before him views him as the man whom she'd been sleeping with for a very long time. Her name is Faye, and as he re-checks the chart after its retrieval, the name registers closely with her real name – Fayianne Dawson.

Nervously, Dr. Balentine sits on the bed, facing the door to watch who may potentially enter and exit during the secret conversation he's about to have with the woman whom he loved to have sex with when his wife wasn't around. He lifts the sheets slowly to find that her legs, along with the rest of her body, are in good condition, and she allows him to do so.

"Are you gonna to pay me for this sneak peek you're getting, or is this payment in exchange for the high ass doctor bill you would have given me?" The doctor doesn't answer, so she continues, more serious than previously. "You can put the sheets down now, doc," she stresses, as she's not into pleasuring on any level for free. "At least I know where you get your money now, huh?" she says, sitting up on her elbows to get a little closer to him. Then she turns her face to the bruised side. "How you like that? Some bitch gave it to me."

"Were you in a fight?" he asks, highly concerned for her because they'd become close over the three years that they'd been sleeping together on the weekends. Each time, he would land her, she would get paid up with five hundred dollars no questions asked because that's what she's worth for only one hour of pleasure. If the time runs over into two hours, Faye generally charges double and does double, leaving clients like the doctor satisfied and wanting to spend more. In the case of Faye and Dr. Balentine, their liaisons halted once Bain died.

"No, no fight. She just caught me from behind in her garage is all," she states as she lifts her knees, rubbing them with her hands. "In that mansion she lives in."

"Didn't you file a police report or was she arrested for the attack?" he asks, trying to be discreet as he struggles to stay in the doctor role, which is someone he never portrayed with her in the bedroom. All professionalism went out the door when he was ever with Faye. He reaches to touch the side of her eye, and she jumps from the pressure.

"Yeah," Faye responds to the painful touch. "It still hurts, and no, I haven't told the cops anything yet." Then she smiles, and leans over closer to Dr. Balentine's face. "Where I come from, we don't snitch. We settle. It's not an easy habit to break either," she continues, leaning back again on her pillows. "Especially when the law isn't on my side considering my way to make a living and all."

"Well, that's ignorance, Faye," he retorts, notating information in her chart.

"Why?"

"It just is. Surely, the cops have been here…"

"Fuck those cops. I was at her house, shit, and my ass kept my mouth shut through all those questions. All I remember is waking up in this room after she hit me. The cops came in here with the story all wrong, and I agreed to that wrong ass story they concocted. What the hell I'ma say? Some rich lil' girl hit me on my head after I was in her driveway confronting her, and what happened after that, I don't know." She closes her eyes and shakes her head. "No, Merle, I mean Michael, that would not be smart."

Dr. Balentine begins to flip to the admission paperwork and then reads notes on what happened with her from the beginning to end. It states that a security guard started rescue breaths on her until the ambulance picked her up from the scene with an extremely light pulse. As he continues reading through, he sees where Faye was in a coma for two days as they tried to remove illegal drugs from her system and cure a kidney infection that began to attack.

As he reads, he asks, "Where were you?"

Faye pulls the stringy ends of her hair that hang from the ponytail. "Why do you care so much, Merle?" she laughs, joking about the name that she's known him by for such a long time. "I like Michael better, but hell, if you have to know, I was in that neighborhood behind Gabriel's Trails at this chick named Alexis' house. That's the bitch the cops don't know shit about."

For a second, Dr. Balentine stalls, his eyes completely stagnant on the words in the chart. His guts nearly flush from his bosom at the sound of his teenage daughter's name coming out of the mouth of his call girl lover. Finding out that his daughter is accused by Faye of attacking her is about to cause another torrential downpour in his khakis because it isn't a simple misdemeanor fight on the table. It's attempted murder.

Dr. Balentine removes himself from the hospital bed, turning his back to her in the process, pretending that he's still engulfed in the words from the chart when in actuality, his entire body is flaked. He feels that he could crack at any moment, but knows full well that he can't because he has to save the one person he who has his direct DNA – his daughter.

"Why were you confronting this girl?" he asks, ready to calculate everything that comes from her mouth. He lifts his head from the chart as he stands at the foot of the bed, facing Faye, not as a lover, but as the sole woman who could bring unrighteous attention to his daughter along with a full scale attack of prison time or even blackmail along with it.

"Because she's the reason me and you don't see each other anymore. She shot Bain, and she didn't come back in there until she started dating some new cat on the corner. I never could contact you again to set up a date because Bain kept all his people in his head. When he died, our sex life died, too, with you being anonymous and all." As she speaks, she begins to pay more attention to the man she knows as Merle, noticing that his demeanor has altered ever so slightly. He's very stiff and distant, and Faye can feel it. That's when she notices his eyes. She's seen his eyes many times before, but this time she recognizes something similar to that of twins, an identical set of eyes like the ones on Alexis as she stared her down in the garage.

She starts to laugh, and it's a grin that disturbs everything about the doctor's camouflaged emotions. Being an excellent judge of moods and character with an impeccable memory for faces that she inherited from the street life, Faye has literally placed the eyes she saw in the garage atop the eyes standing in front of her, and they're a match.

"Oh shit," she sings from what has become her bed of discovery as she pulls every string of facts that she knows of Alexis and ties it to the doctor who stands before her. Faye then stares him directly in his eyes. "Alexis is your mother fuckin' daughter, isn't she? That's your damn mansion. You know the saying, once you go black…" she jokes, referring to Alexis' light brown skin tone, which blends her with the race of African American, and thus, an African American mom.

Dr. Balentine collapses his arms onto the metal posts of the bed to catch himself from fainting while Faye watches his breakdown. This is the weakest that she's ever seen the man who would flaunt his money like the biggest man in town while he slept with her.

"Here I am thinking I was maybe your first brown skin woman to lay with," she taunts. "Did you not know that your daughter is a cold blooded killer, Merle?" She lifts herself up from the bed's pillow while evil intent finds a home in her expression. "I guess this is where I'm worth more than five hundred dollars a lay, huh?"

Dr. Balentine knows what she's asking because he knows full well that though she pretends to be a woman who is only educated about sex and how to do it, she's also a woman who has had to make it on her own for a long while. When opportunity arises, Dr. Balentine knows with a woman like Faye, everything becomes a negotiation. He's not only felt but watched her give him a triple dose and take the extra five hundred for herself while hiding it from her pimp inside the private area between her legs. He's even heard her on the cell phone delivering strategies to other young women in the game to get more money for less while they bring a cut to her for the advice. Faye is very cunning, but while cunning, she's ruled by money.

At her words, Dr. Balentine reaches in his lab coat pocket and slides out the check book that he keeps on himself at all times. His wallet remains in his back pocket. He realizes that the pay off will be hefty, therefore, he doesn't think cash as he secretly grows into a rage by the second.

"I'll write you a check," he starts, nervously dropping his pen on the bed as his skin becomes stained with blotches of blood beneath it, changing the color of his white face to pink. Before he reaches to pick the pen back up, Faye, who appears to be in serious pain but proves she has high tolerance for it, lunges forward, nearly knocking over her IV pole.

She grabs his hand, and he doesn't pull away at all while her eyes gaze, contently angered, upon his face that's consciously willing to do as she asks. This is what infuriates Faye. "Your damn crazy ass daughter left me for dead to cover up her shit, and you want to pay me to leave her alone." She glances down at the pen that the doctor wants so desperately. "You think you can just write me a single check, and I leave you be?"

Michael snatches away from her grip, disgusted by her advance to criticize his motive to save his daughter and slaps her hand away during the retrieval of the pen. "I can't write you anything!" He shoves the pen against the check he has in the palm of his hand, rips it out and hands it to her. "You fill it out, Faye…and then you leave my child alone. You get no more money after this *single* check!"

Faye's eyes gloss over the incomplete check that holds his signature, and then she stares back at him with a cold blooded smile, wanting him to feel a grievous amount pain derived from the pain his daughter inflicted onto her. "You know your beloved daughter was sleeping with Bain, doc?" she asks, softening her tone from the harsh sounds that came from her mouth just seconds ago. "She got mad when she walked in on me and him doing our thing, and then she shot him out there in the trails. You remember that, don't you? The big time, dead pimp story on the news?" Faye slides the check across her mouth, and then she holds her hand out for the pen that he still has in his grasp. Instead of handing it to her, he tosses it so that it falls in between her legs on the bed. "You still know how to aim," she comments, and then proceeds to fill out the check. "You know, Bain wasn't tricking her out, though. She was Bain's own personal trick." She finishes writing the amount of her liking on the check, stalls to look at it, and then proceeds, "How's that?" She shows him the check's amount which reads seventy-five thousand dollars. Then, she antagonizes the doctor even more. "You have a nice three car garage, blue shutters…if I would have known you were that close to Gabriel's Trails, I would have paid you some free visits from time to time." Then she stares down at his platinum wedding ring. "Maybe your wife would like that," she states, adding fuel to her blackmail in order to secure the large amount written on the check.

With no argument, Dr. Balentine stares at the amount on the check and agrees, his stomach in knots while contemplating killing her as she sits in her hospital bed. "I'll clear it with the bank Monday morning. You're free to go. I'll be discharging you on behalf of your regular doctor for tomorrow by ten in the morning," he states, walking to the side of the bed. Suddenly, he grabs her by the face, squeezing as hard as is allowed for her injuries. "And you will leave this city!" Then, he shoves her head back while Faye manages to remain calm, knowing that she has him in the palm of her hand.

"Yes sir, Merle. I'm paid to obey," she laughs, ecstatic that the ball is finally in her court in a major way.

He fumes knowing that he has no choice but to pay her way out, so he exits the room. Ignoring the nurses who he spoke to gleefully earlier, he combats each emotion he has that wants to call the authorities on Faye because he knows full well that it may lead to his daughter's arrest. As he enters the office, he falls onto the chair, placing his hands on his head, not able to fathom how his teenage daughter could have been sleeping with a pimp, a pimp whom he got his girls from. Atop that, he cringes at memories of Bain's murder being splattered across the news last year, and as he moves to put things together in his head, he simply can't. He's never at home. None the less, Dr. Balentine takes Faye's story hook line and sinker because not only does she know his daughter's name, but she described his home, both of which he's never spoken about to anyone in the Trails, not even Bain who only knew him by Merle and nothing else, mainly speaking with him on a pre-paid phone from another side of town.

Preparing to reserve a hotel for Faye to stay outside of the city and then to stay away for good, he's devastated that he can't call his daughter and ask any questions. It would place accusations onto him which could potentially ruin his marriage and create such a distraught disposition between he and his daughter that it would completely kill their strained relationship because Alexis isn't stupid. All of the doctor's late nights and early morning arrivals on the weekends would be explained, even the times when he would ignore the cell phone.

He wipes the smooth, hairless skin around his face that's built like a model with a strong jaw bone while his deep set eyes graze over the tablet in front of him, locating a place for Faye to reside after discharge. He chooses the Golden Resort that provides the works only an hour away, but before reserving the spot, he stops. The credit card would be traced back to him, and he couldn't take any chances, therefore, he hesitantly chooses to send her via car and key to his place near the beach where it's secluded with hardly any passers-by.

There are anti-anxiety pills located on the inside of his drawer. He grabs them and swallows two down straight with no water, just his own saliva. The doctor's nerves are gone to no use as he formulates ideas on what to do next, especially when that seventy-five thousand dollars is withdrawn from the bank, alerting his wife. He starts to dial on his cell as he gets up to lock the office door, and then, he sits back down until he hears a pick up on the other line. The person doesn't speak, but Dr. Balentine continues.

"I need a favor."

The sun rises with its huge shine on Sunday morning as Mrs. Moores and her sons get ready for church. Sundays are especially hard for Mrs. Moores because she's so accustomed to her late husband, Trent, getting the family all ready for church with his beautiful singing. Trent had a voice that could soothe an angry giant, and it was on Sunday mornings that he would sing at his best.

Trent wasn't in the choir when he was alive, but he would always be the one to start the singing from the pew while the choir would follow. The only reason why Trent wasn't in the choir was because he could never make it to practice, having to pick up his wife from her job before he lost his. Again, the singing is what the family misses most on Sunday mornings.

The boys are all dressed in their dress shirts and slacks, going for a casual look this Sunday, while their mom is dressed in her favorite cool dress and heels. As they drive to church, Javis and Derrick, who just left a man for dead in the trails less than twenty-four hours ago, are suspiciously quiet while Joseph runs his mouth from the back seat. Mrs. Moores notices and attributes their dull moods to the death of their father who was always the leader of the family. Not having him alive is such a huge burden, and she decides to reserve speaking to the boys about their silence, unknowingly totally wrong about the issues the boys have managed to involve themselves in.

When they get to the church, Mrs. Moores continues to the section of the church she normally sits while she allows the boys to either follow her or sit, at the most, two pews in front of her. It's always been this way since the boys can remember, and this type of seating arrangement keeps them within reach and eyesight of their mother. Sitting two pews in front is what Javis and Derrick choose to do while Joseph does his usual and sits in place next to his mom.

As they stand for prayer, Derrick grabs the pew in front of him tightly, starting to scrape the wood with his fingernails. Javis reaches over and shoves his brother's hands inconspicuously as he pretends to reach for a hymnal. Everything is quiet except for the sound of the preacher and Amens from the crowd of brothers and sisters who agree with the prayer. When prayer stops, the choir stands to sing, and Javis begins to scold Derrick.

"Man, look, you have to chill out. This is church, and there will be a time when, if you need prayer, for you to go do that." He looks to his right as people pass up the aisle and then he turns back to look at Derrick. "We both need prayer and forgiveness. I'm with you, D. You're not alone in this."

Derrick stares straight ahead, his conscious eating away at him, creating so much pain that for the first time he seems to be crying from the emotion of the choir's song. In reality, the tear flowing down his cheek is from the guilt he can't shake for finishing off Floss instead of leaving bad enough alone.

Javis pulls a Bible out from the back of the pew in front of him, and then hands it to Derrick. "Just open it and read. Pay attention to that during church. Things will be fine." He doesn't dare look back to see if his mom is

175

watching because he knows she is. There is low tolerance from her with her boys talking in church, and Javis knows that if he doesn't settle down, she'll be at their pew in no time.

Soon the preacher begins to speak, and Javis isn't listening as he usually pays attention to every word. His mind is consumed with whether or not the cops will be at the house before he gets back home, and even if they are at his house, he needs to find a way to get to Alexis before any and all other things. Derrick is too distraught to tag along with him, so it's something that he won't tell him. He'll go at it alone. When church ends, he makes his move as he catches his mom stepping away from the other ladies of the church.

"Mom," he says extremely uneasy about the lie he's about to tell while standing on church grounds, so he takes one step off the curb and onto the street while making certain Derrick is still over near the car with Joseph.

"Yeah, baby," she responds, switching the Bible from one hand to the other.

"I need to go to Alexis' house. I left some school work up there I was finishing up for tomorrow."

"Well, how did you go and do that, son?" she asks, not seeming too serious about the question, but really just making extra conversation.

"I don't know, ma. Forgot."

"Well, I won't be able to take you until we…"

"You can drop me on the corner, and Alexis will drop me off back home," he interrupts. "So you guys go ahead and go to the store. I'll be fine, ma."

She trusts him, so she agrees, especially since he's been dating her for a while. "If Alexis can't drop you off, you go back home the long way. Your brother won't be with you, and I don't want you using those trails by yourself, understand?"

He nods. Mrs. Moores doesn't understand that the trails are the last place Javis wants to ever step foot again.

On the way leaving church, as Javis planned, Derrick has no idea of the conversation he had with mom on church grounds. Just like she promised him, Mrs. Moores drops him off on the corner on the way to the store, all to Derrick's dismay, and without looking into the backseat, Javis kisses his mom on the cheek, grabs his book bag that's located on the floor of the car in front of him, and exits the car heading to Alexis' house hardly able to contain himself. Derrick watches his brother from the back window as his mom drives off.

"Stop knocking so much, shoot! Pounding at my door so loud," she yells as she glances outside from the window to see her brother's right hand man, Chief, and two others at the front door. "I need to go grab a robe, so wait! Didn't I tell you that Floss ain't here, dang?" She walks to the back to snatch her robe out of the closet because she had to jump out of the shower with only a towel on to see what madness is going on at the front door. Before putting on the robe, she rushes through a quick dry, pulls up some black shorts and slides down a yellow t-shirt because she doesn't feel at all comfortable with only a robe on opening the door.

She rushes back up to answer their knocks as they seem urgent, and when she gets there, not only is she irritated but furiously curious as to what they want. Opening the door, she places her hand on her hip and speaks, "Yes?"

The young men standing at the door all hold straight faces as if they don't even know who she is, and immediately, she gets terrified as a result of their stares and goes to slam the door, thinking it's a robbery or even a attempt at rape because it was stupid for her to answer the door in the first place for them when her brother isn't around. Chief throws himself against the door as she's in the process of closing it.

"Tryina, it's cool. My blood on that, it's cool."

"Well, Floss isn't here, Chief, and I don't know where he is. He didn't come back home, so check somewhere else."

"Move from the door, Tryina. It's about Floss."

Faster than the blink of an eye, Tryina's stomach bottoms out, and she slowly moves from the door, allowing Chief's weight to open it. As Chief moves inside and the other men wait outside, he motions for permission to shut the door. Tryina only glances at his gesture, but doesn't give him a response. Therefore, he leaves the door ajar.

As she backs up, she's already far enough to hit the kitchen counter which disables her movement any further. All she does is wait. There's a moment where she opens her mouth, but only silence exits, so she shuts it. Her robe falls open, unveiling her wrinkled clothes, but she doesn't care. The only things she focuses on are the lips of the man she knows as her brother's good friend who has come to shed some news about her only guardian on earth, Floss.

"Sit down..."

"No," she interrupts quickly, leaping onto every word before they are completed.

Instead of contemplating how to say what he needs to say delicately, Chief feeds off of her anxiety and delivers. "Floss is dead, baby girl. He's dead, sis, and I'm sorry…"

Tryina's whole body hits the floor and curls up into a ball. "Oh God, why!" she screams. As Chief reaches to console her, she knocks his arm away, and he simply backs up, not knowing what to do next. She continues to call on God and ask the same question of why over and over again until she runs out of breath.

Chief sits on the chair, barely holding himself together, as he waits until Tryina's screams reach a minimum. Then he tries to speak again. "I'm sorry I…"

She angers and cuts him off once again. "And where were you? You're supposed to be his boy, everything … every single thing y'all do together! Look at all y'all, coming to my house together…" Then she screams her loudest. "Where the fuck was the group then, huh?" Then she stops screaming and gets up off the floor as Chief digests everything she's saying as if he deserves it. He wipes a tear from his eye, clears his throat and stands up.

While Tryina is still having a breakdown over her only brother whom she loves and hates at the same time, Chief calms his emotions and says, "No strings attached. Whatever you need, it's paid for. It's done." He pauses, "Now I got some shit to take care of."

"Wait," Tryina says, scrambling to touch Chief's scarred up and bruised hand. "What happened to my brother? Don't leave me without telling me what happened, please!" she pleads, holding her stomach as she finally allows Chief to touch her. He places his arm around her shoulder and sits with her on the chair, unwilling to let her go from his body as he proceeds to tell her how he found him this morning, shot up and a hole in his throat, like he was stabbed, on trail four.

As he tells the story, Tryina weeps tremendously in the cradle of his arms, squeezing his shirt as he rubs her back gently. To add a dose of justice to what he just revealed, he assures her that they know who did it, and they are on their way to settle it before the cops come knocking.

She lifts her head. "Who did it?"

"Those new mu'fuckas on the corner."

Tryina jumps back, stunned by the accusation he just made, but his arm stops her. "Let go of me!" she orders, and he lets her go, aware that she's friends with the family he's about to hit. She immediately moves off of the couch to stare down at the massive sized, hazel eyed, handsome dark and smooth skinned killer in her house. "What people on the corner are you talking about?" She points behind her in the direction of her boyfriend's family's home. "Down at the entrance?"

He stands up, ready to go. "Hell yeah. That's your man, but…"

"No wait, Chief, you gotta have it wrong. They're not killers!"

"How the fuck you know, Tryina?" he asks, angry at how she's taking up for the guys who killed her brother.

180

"Because I know!" she screams back, but Chief isn't convinced because he knows something that he's failed to tell Tryina. She gets a rush of adrenaline to prove that Derrick was nowhere around when Floss was killed, or there won't be any stopping Chief from cutting his life down or anyone else in his family. "He was cutting grass yesterday with his brother. Floss was with me when I was on the phone with Derrick yesterday, and on their way back home, they never went down trail four because they got a ride back home. I know because I called and they were at home. He told me they caught a ride, and that's why he didn't stop by the house." She runs back to get the cell phone from her room, and then shows Chief the times of the calls.

"They got a ride back home, huh?" he asks suspiciously, turning his eyes away from the cell phone as if it doesn't matter.

"Yes, Chief, yes," she pleads, but still Chief isn't standing down.

He then shakes his head, staring Tryina directly in the eyes. "That's a fuckin' lie, Tryina."

"No it's not, I swear, Chief. That's my boyfriend." She reaches for his arm to calm him down, but he pulls away in a rage, almost disgusted looking at her.

"I was on the phone with Floss, Tryina." As he speaks, his chest moves up and down like a wild animal ready to attack in battle. As Tryina stands there looking confused, he continues, "When those lil niggas came walking down trail four, Floss was talking with me on the cell phone. Those mu' fuckas did have a lawn mower like you said, cutting yard, but they walked back home. Floss got off the phone with me as they passed by his regular stoop behind the trees. That's where they killed him, right across from it on the trail."

Tryina's face is frozen in disbelief, but at this point, Chief doesn't care. He wants it to sink in that her brother died by the hands of her boyfriend and his brother, so he grabs her cheeks tightly and lifts her head so that she can get a good look at the words coming from his mouth.

"I knew about the hit that night, and your boyfriend ain't take no ride back home, baby girl," he states furiously and shoves her head backwards. "Say good-bye to your boyfriend. You know ain't shit you can do to stop it. Don't fuck up," he warns her before walking out of the front door, leaving Tryina to fall to her knees quietly, not knowing what to do next.

Mrs. Moores finishes changing clothes in the bedroom, and then goes into the kitchen to run water into a pot to begin stewing some chicken. Beginning to hum a hymn, she turns on the burner and tosses the chicken into the saltwater in the sink. Then she washes her hands, tears off a paper towel to dry them and then begins to hum a little louder.

"Joseph and Derrick, what are you doing back there?"

Joseph answers quickly. "Playing chess…and I'm finally winning!"

"Just checking," she responds as she picks up the wet dish rag and starts to wipe the counters down. She's worried about something, but so far, fiddling around in the kitchen is distracting her from what her instincts are telling her to focus on. Finally, she places the dish rag down and turns the stove's burner off. "Boys!" she calls, and they both come walking up the hallway, stopping at the doorway. She leaves the kitchen to grab her keys and purse. "Listen, I'm going to get Javis. I don't feel right, and don't ask me why but I'm going." Then she stresses, "Stay inside this house. Don't let anyone in and don't you dare go out. Something's not right, and I need all my boys in here with me."

Derrick's throat quakes as he suffers through keeping quiet about what he perceives as his mom somehow figuring out that about himself and Javis. Going to Alexis' house could bring her face to face with the reality of a possible bad situation going on there because Javis took that book bag, the same bag that housed the knife and gun used in the murder of Floss.

"Yes ma'am," Joseph answers while Derrick nods and moves to sink into the loveseat.

"Derrick, you hear me?"

He perks up, "Yes ma'am."

"I'll be right back," she continues, walking out of the front door. It slams behind her.

"You know mom is always right." Being the most prayerful of her sons, Joseph bows his head to start praying for Javis and his safe keeping. Derrick only stares at him, wanting to pray, but not sure if what he has to say will make it to God at all because of the guilt he carries.

Alexis turns around, shutting the front door behind her, confused about why Javis is heated while standing on her porch on a Sunday after church, still in his church clothes.

"Javis, what's wrong?"

"You tell me, Alexis," he states tossing his book bag down on the porch in front of her feet. Alexis follows the book bag as it hits the ground, and she quickly tries to diffuse a situation going wrong.

"Javis, we need to go around back because my dad is home and…"

"I could give a fuck who's home, Alexis!" He steps closer to her, almost daring her to turn the knob on her front door to go back inside as a result of his threatening stance. "Why the hell didn't you tell me about that knife, huh?" Alexis chokes in silence, but Javis persists, this time, getting only centimeters away from her face. Then he yells at the top of his lungs, "Why didn't you tell me about that shit when you saw it yesterday?" The air from his nostrils blow onto her eyelids as her eyes fill with tears, but Alexis realizes that she's trapped, scared that she has nowhere to go. If she goes inside, the information leaks, so she gives up, starting to swallow her worst fears coming to a head.

"Javis," her voice quivers his name as her fantasy world comes crashing down. "I'm sorry, but I didn't know how to…"

"Didn't know how to do what? Didn't I ask your lying ass if you had some shit to say about the shooting at my house?" He shouts, waiting for a response, but he doesn't get one, creating one of the worst rages Javis has ever had festering inside his body. "Pick up my fuckin' bag and dig it out." Javis doesn't back up from her face by any inch, forcing Alexis to back up to reach for the bag as he points to the bag with two fingers. His threatening tone reassures Alexis that he knows. Somehow, he's found out everything.

As she unzips the bag, there is dried up blood smeared on the inside, and she falls backwards onto her butt at the sight of it.

"Sit your ass up!" He kicks the book bag on top of her and out falls the knife and gun. Alexis kicks herself all the way back until she slams against the front door, and then she finally breaks.

"I killed him!" she cries, "Yes, I did it! I'm sorry, Javis, but I didn't know they would come back to kill me. His name was Bain. Bain!" she screams, and then quiets down. "He was my boyfriend, and I shot him in the trails with his own gun. That gun!" Alexis' retraces what happened in the concrete beneath her as she rocks back and forth.

"What about the knife?"

"It's my dad's knife. I gave it to some guy in Gabriel's Trails, but didn't get it back." Alexis stares into the eyes of Javis as she sulks on the ground and continues, "I swear, I didn't mean any harm. The knife was for my protection, but things went bad, Javis. They went bad, and I don't know why I shot him. I loved him…I swear it only looks like I tried to set you and your family up, but I didn't!" she cries.

Javis notices her partially open garage door, so he forces her to get up and go inside. She follows him willingly, not knowing if she's going to live or die. All Alexis knows is that she's tired of hiding and faking, lying about everything she knows at the expense of the lives of others. At this point, death would feel better than her life, and she even prefers it, especially if it means not going to prison.

As she enters, Javis knocks her down to her knees. Then he grabs the gun, placing it up against the back of her head. Alexis kneels in the same spot where she struck the death blows to Faye. Her hands are up in the air, and there's no weeping. Alexis is well aware of her end, and she has no choice but to take the bullet because she can't fight her way out of this one.

Javis holds down on the pistol tightly, dreaming of how his dad should be with him now but how Alexis' deceit stole his family, ripping it apart. He imagines shooting Alexis in the back of the head and just allowing the cops to come and get him, taking the blame for Floss' murder, letting the chips fall so that his family could get away free from the crossfire that keeps coming.

"Alexis!" a male voice from inside the house calls, but Javis doesn't move. The gun remains pointed at Alexis' head. Then, Javis leans into his bag and gets the initialed knife, placing it into Alexis' hand as she remains kneeled on the ground. As she feels the knife graze her palm, she cringes.

"Hold it and get up. Turn around and face me," he commands, breathing heavily.

Alexis does as he orders as the voice of her father calling gets even louder, meaning he's getting closer to the garage, possibly already standing in the kitchen. As Alexis holds the knife in her right hand, she stands, turning to face him.

"Now hold that knife up like the killer you are," Javis states, thirsty to pull the trigger on her for all the wrong she's brought his family when all she had to do is tell the truth.

Alexis hears the words coming from Javis' mouth, but she doesn't move. Instead, she keeps the knife at her side, in disbelief that he's about to set her up to kill her. As she stares back in his eyes, she sees Bain, an empty handed Bain that she shot down. Bain would never attack her for anything, and now she knows that Javis is a different man. He's out for blood.

She slowly raises the knife, doing exactly as he orders just as her father, Mr. Balentine, opens the door leading into the house.

"It's your move, Derrick," Joseph tells him as they sit back down on the floor to continue their game of chess after their mom left the home on the way to get Javis.

"I know it's my move." Those words mean more to him than Joseph could ever know. Derrick continues to keep his façade steady, not revealing too much anxiety about anything outwardly, but on the inside, he is a total wreck. The mental anguish is even causing him to make the worst moves in his history of playing the board game.

"What kind of move was that, D?" Joseph jokes at the fumble. "Check!"

Derrick looks back at his brother who has a huge grin on his face, clueless as to the type of trouble he's in. The telephone rings, and he's relieved to go answer it just in case it's Javis. He wastes no time jumping up to head to the kitchen, leaving Joseph in winning mode staring at the chess board.

It takes him no more than two seconds to reach the phone and pick it up. "Hello?"

The voice answering on the other end sends sickening quivers through his body, however, he holds it together by grabbing the counter with his free hand and breathing deeply.

"Derrick," the voice on the other end of the phone sounds off. Before Derrick can respond to the call of his name, the caller continues. "Did you kill my brother?"

There's a silence that's deafening as Derrick listens to his girlfriend, Tryina, weep the question about the man he stabbed to death in the trails. He doesn't know what to say nor think, but the one thing he knows is that he can't confess to anything. He starts to think about what Javis told him to do which is blame everything on him, but he refuses.

Sitting on the phone without speaking gives a crying Tryina the answer she needs, and she continues to talk without his response. "He was coming after you," she weeps, not fantasizing that her older brother was an upstanding citizen, and then she says something unexpected, "but you didn't have to lie to me. You let me lie around the house while my brother was out there dead on some fuckin' trail!" she weeps uncontrollably, creating a break in Derrick's composure that's unheard by Tryina. He removes the phone from his ear, as she keeps talking. "They're coming for you, Derrick, so you have to get away…"

Unfortunately, he doesn't hear her as he glances over at the window and sees movement. It's the movement of a gun, and then the blasts begin. Derrick drops to the floor as the telephone receiver hits the wall, swinging back and forth.

"Joseph!" Derrick cries as he dives to the floor, leaving the high pitched sounds of Tryina screaming in the background through the phone as she hears the horrifyingly loud gun blasts.

Derrick clears the hallway, throwing himself into the bedroom and then knocking Joseph into the wall next to the room door. Joseph finally hears the gun shots that have started exploding through the window while Derrick throws a small book shelf full of books toward the opposite wall to block them from the shots. Not more than a second later, Derrick shoves Joseph into the hallway, and they both lie on the floor while the house is riddled with bullets.

"Why are they shooting at us? They're shooting at us again!" Joseph yells, but Derrick covers his brother's mouth as he quickly becomes more afraid of the front door that they face as they're down in the hallway. Imagining a shooter coming through the main entrance, he rapidly slides, along with Joseph, into his mom's room, kicking the door shut with this foot.

"Get under the bed!"

Joseph is already there with his hands gripping his mom's Bible against his chest tightly. Derrick reaches up from the floor with his arm to lock the door and is hit with a bullet, causing him to jerk back.

"God!" he cries grasping his arm at the wound. "Please forgive me, Jesus. Please, forgive me." Derrick crawls underneath the bed where Joseph is hiding and

189

listening to everything his older brother just shouted to God while trying to figure it out.

"What did you do, D?" Joseph asks with tears in his eyes as he begins to tie the barrage of bullets attacking their home to Derrick. His whole body is shaking and as the bullets continue, he erupts in prayer, a prayer so fast that only he and God can understand it.

Blood runs down Derrick's broken skin, making a puddle onto the floor, staining the pages of the Bible that are touching the scratchy hardwoods. As he watches Joseph pray, he tunes out the bullets and makes a request.

"Pray for me, Joseph. I killed somebody…"

The prayer stops as Joseph lifts his eyes only to meet his brother's as they lie in his spilling blood.

"And I did it for dad. I killed him."

Joseph can say and do nothing. The bullets stop finally, and the brothers lie there in complete silence with Joseph left in a state of fear of his surroundings and disbelief of what his brother just confessed. Joseph now knows that the shooting going on is retaliation and that his brother isn't lying when he says he's a killer. He can feel the truth of it all in his bones.

Derrick grabs Joseph's hand and continues, "They're going to keep coming until they kill me, too." The blood from Derrick's hand washes Joseph's hand like soap and water lathered together on a rag, and then Derrick let's go of Joseph's hand while he slides out from underneath their mom's bed. When he stands up to open the bedroom door, the silence of no gunshots is enjoyable because along with the protection inside the walls of the home and the confession he made to Joseph, he finally feels eerily at peace.

As he turns the knob of the bedroom door, figuring the scene is safe since the shots have stalled for a couple of minutes, a bullet cracks the bedroom window, shooting him in the back. Instead of watching his brother peek out of the room door, Joseph reaches his hand out from underneath the bed to Derrick as he watches him fall against the door handle from the power of the bullet hitting his body. Derrick finds the strength to turn completely around to face his killer who is standing at a small opening at the window through the curtain. Then he falls to the floor dead, with no parting words to his younger brother who is under the bed safe and sound, bound by sorrow, watching his brother take his last breath while finally hearing the strange sounds of faint screaming from the kitchen.

Mr. Balentine walks out onto the garage floor and zooms in on a young man holding up his daughter with a pistol. Without a second to think about it, Mr. Balentine lunges forward to move Alexis out of the way, but things don't go as planned because Alexis intervenes.

"Daddy, no!" she yells, the knife quivering in the palm of her hand. Instead of pointing the knife at Javis, she turns to aim the knife at her father.

"Alexis!" Without another word, all the things that he learned from his ex-lover Faye come to memory, displaying themselves before his very eyes as his daughter holds a knife to his chest. He stares at the knife from the tip of the blade to the uncovered portions of the handle, and he realizes that the knife belongs to him. "Alexis, put my knife down, baby. It's okay. I already know, sweetheart, I already know," he states calmly although he truly isn't, using the training he has as a doctor to mitigate harmful situations and remain in control. That's the one thing he can't stand to lose is control.

"I killed people, dad! Me! Just leave him alone. He's not a killer, it's me! Just me!" she pauses, "Leave him alone. Let him go. His dad died because of me," she states soberly, fully persuaded by her own guilt that her time has finally come. She can't live with herself anymore because things seem to just be getting worse.

Dr. Balentine's wrath continues to grow as he can't believe his own daughter not only has killed people but has a knife pointed at him as well, ready to end his life, too. His eyes immediately rise to the young man holding a gun to his daughter, and though he's never met him, he now recognizes him by the story that Lorah, his wife, told him about the yard cutter's father getting shot to death on their anniversary.

"Are you Javis?" His eyes move back and forth between his daughter and Javis who is still holding the pistol tightly in his hands. Dr. Balentine actually begins to feel remorse for the young man who's before him in church clothes, obviously hurting behind his own daughter's evils.

Javis doesn't answer. Instead, he stares back into the eyes of the man he now knows as Michael Balentine. His urge isn't to pull the trigger and run, but more to drop his gun and force Alexis to tell why he may go to prison for murder when it should be her going in his place. Before Javis makes up his mind on what he will do next, Dr. Balentine reaches out slowly, not to take the gun, but in surrender. The doctor has heard nothing but good about Javis from Lorah, and the last thing he believes is that this young man is a cold blooded killer, siding with Alexis in her opinion of him as well.

As he reaches out to bond with Javis to lessen the situation's severity, Alexis makes her move. "Give him some money! He needs some money!" she screams, and her dad leaps from his trance. "Don't dare call the cops, dad, or I will slit my wrists right here and right now. Just do it, dad. Go to the safe…I know how much is there. I know the combination. Give it all to him, all forty grand," she states, glancing at Javis quickly, then back at her stunned father. "So he can leave the trails, him and his family, before what I did comes back on them any more than it already has." Alexis then looks at Javis who hasn't removed the gun from pointing at her, and then she takes the knife from pointing at her father, placing it onto her left wrist, pushing hard enough to begin the wound.

Dr. Michael Balentine nearly drops to his knees as he watches the knife's first cut create blood from his daughter's wrist, but instead of fainting, he rushes back into the house to get the money. At this moment, the money isn't about anything else except keeping his daughter and Javis alive. He's very much aware of the guilt she's feeling after hearing some of the story from Faye, and there isn't any amount of money that would keep him from fixing his daughter's pain and making the damage go away. Unfortunately, he also knows that Alexis is very calculating and must maintain control were she can, a trait she picked up from him. The doctor is aware that she's using the belief that she's been raised to live by and that is the falsehood that money cures all ills and pays off broken promises. Either way, in his contempt for Alexis' ways, he still loves her dearly, just doesn't like her, especially now that she's aimed a knife at his chest. For all he knows, Javis could be in more danger than Alexis as they stand in the garage, so he hurries before anything goes wrong either way.

Arriving at the safe in his office, he spins the combination lock to the appropriate numbers, and the safe opens with one tug from the doctor. There are two rings, a watch and then there is cash, the full amount of cash that Alexis spoke of while she threatened taking her life in the garage. Dr. Balentine reaches in and only grabs twenty five thousand dollars, hoping that this will be enough to retain secrecy and eliminate the threat of having Javis go to the authorities on his daughter. So far, money has solved all his family's other problems, and this should be no different.

He races downstairs with the money in hand, only glancing at the telephone for a split second, not completing the thoughts he starts to have about calling the cops. His daughter could get shot or even killed, even arrested for life, and he can't take that chance.

Entering the garage once again, Dr. Balentine holds the bag of money out toward Javis. "It's all there." He looks over at Alexis who has moved the knife from her wrist. "Not forty thousand, but the rest...all I had left. There's twenty-five thousand there to leave Gabriel's Trails and never look back. You don't know us anymore, and you know nothing about Alexis. You hear me? Nothing!" he yells, furious about losing his money but his anger misdirected at Javis who points the gun at Dr. Balentine and then snatches the bag.

While Dr. Balentine was getting the money, Alexis already somehow maintained control of the out of control situation by convincing Javis that killing her or getting her arrested for any crime wouldn't help him nor his family get out of Gabriel's Trials. They would still have to fight off the sins of another, that another being her. The money would put them onto a better start away from Gabriel's Trails, making good out of the bad. During the one sided conversation, Javis made up his mind or Alexis made up his foiled mind for him. He would get his family out of there, not having to worry about being found out because if he is found out, Alexis is found out. He feels confident that she nor her family will snitch on anything at anytime.

A car pulls up on the side of the road, and a door slams. Quickly, Javis lowers his gun, placing it inside the bag while Alexis drops the knife and kicks it underneath her parked car. The car that pulls up is Javis' mom, and as Javis exits the garage with the money, he watches his mom run to the front door frantically. Before calling to his mom, he looks back at Alexis and her father.

"If you talk, deal's over." He stuffs the money in his book bag, and leaps from the garage. "Mom, I'm over here. Let's go."

Mrs. Moores turns away from the front door and walks quickly to Javis. "Do you have your stuff?"

"Yes, ma'am. I was just about to start walking home."

"Well, that's where I need you. Something's not right. I can feel it." She looks him over as they walk to the car. "I just gotta get back to the house…I left Derrick and Joseph. I tell you, something just isn't right, Javis."

Javis looks back at where he used to work, making just over fifty dollars a week cutting the lawn. It's a beautiful home which makes him feel better about getting his family out of Gabriel's Trails with the money he just secretly collected for not a rich, but a better way of living.

Faye is already lounging in her new temporary beach house and things feel right for her, even though her head is still patched up from the wounds. She was out of the hospital by ten thirty in the morning being that Dr. Balentine wasted no time getting her an approved ride to his beach house. The town car pulled up to the hospital's front and the staff wheeled her to the car where she was able to stand and let herself in. Dr. Balentine was nowhere to be found, but he described the town car in targeted specifics that let her know it would be her ride.

On the way to her new life, she ended up passing by what is now her old home in Gabriel's Trails. As she rode by, she even blew it a kiss while shouting a *"Bye, bitches!"* as she looked down at the seventy-five thousand dollar check that she will deposit in her brand new and very first checking account. She supposes that she'll give him at least a full business day to clear it with his bank to avoid any banking hiccups that would flag security. Faye has also decided that as her funds run low, she'll hit him up for more hush money, especially now that she knows his real name.

There's a small chance that she can't swindle him out of more money, but she bets that she can being that he doesn't strike her as the fight fire with fire type. Dr. Balentine, in her mind, seems more the type to pay his way out of a bad situation, similar to what he's doing for his daughter and reputation, and from Faye's vantage point, that's a very weak man that she can take full advantage of in the future. That's far better than telling the cops anything about any murder or an attempted one. It's also far better than getting Alexis killed because as long as she's alive, the more money Faye can get.

Living at the beach house of one of her main paying customers is a dream. She's always had enough money coming through to buy her own place, but never enough to be comfortable signing on the dotted line. She never came from a place of ownership so ducking and dodging paperwork and ties is all she knows. Money, whether she kept it all or spent it, would remain on her at all times. The rest she would bury. So far, Faye's money is in several memorized spots in the city and on the less traveled trail number one in Gabriel's Trails due to its dead end.

As far as the beach house bed, Faye loves it. The window gives her a clear and extremely close view of the water, and she waves back as the waves from the water greet her with full openness, coming extremely close to the house that's held up on stilts. There's even a small motor boat with the doctor's name on it at the water's edge that she's thinking about taking a lounge in later. Faye's life is brand new, and she's going to make every moment count with seventy-five thousand dollars to spread her wings.

There's no television, but Faye doesn't need the entertainment as she glosses over all the fancy furniture that only a rich woman would love as it's obvious that Dr. Balentine's wife chose the décor. She opens the fast food that she had the driver pull over to get for her on the way and lays it out on the bed, placing a towel underneath from the bathroom's cabinet.

"This is the life," she says to herself, expressing her preference for this life versus her other at Gabriel's Trails. As she holds the drink in her hand, she notices that there isn't a straw. "Damn. Those damn people…" The paper cup is full to the very top, so to prevent wasting it on the white, fluffy and noticeably expensive bedspread, she gets up and goes into the kitchen hoping to find a glass to pour it over into instead of tossing a portion down the sink.

As she places the cup on the counter, some of the ice that layers the top spills when she begins to search the cabinets for empty glasses. Upon opening the second cabinet, her search ends, but then she hears a crack on the floor, forcing her to turn around quickly as she feels that she's not alone.

"What the hell?" She scopes the small area, but doesn't notice anyone or anything. "This damn place must have rats. Merle needs to get an exterminator," she kids and continues to take the glass from the cabinet until she's suddenly yanked from her stance from behind by her neck. Faye's eyes spring back and forth searching for who has her by the throat, and in the process, her flaring arms knock her drink to the floor. Her feet skate on the icy drink as she's dragged down to the floor screaming and scratching, trying to pull at the face of the unseen person attacking her.

As she grows weak by the choke hold, from the corner of her right eye, she watches the attacker place a gun to her head. Then he pulls the trigger. The last thing she sees is the drink falling from the counter, but the last thing her body does is fall into the ocean, weighed down by huge dumbbell weights tied to her waist.

Javis and his mom see smoke rising high as they continue to ride toward their home in Gabriel's Trails. At first, they don't give a second thought to it, but as they get closer to the entrance, they notice that the rising smoke appears to be coming from their condo.

"Mom, mom!" Javis yells, about to jump from the moving car's seat as it enters into the Trails. What his mom sensed earlier is right, and she steps on the gas, grabbing Javis by the arm so he won't jump from the car.

"Oh dear, God, save my children. Save my babies. Oh, Jesus, help us, Lord, help us." She continues to pray as she races the car onto the grass. Without turning the car off, she jumps out as Javis leaps from the other side. They both run to the front door as Javis kicks it in, hoping to see his brothers alive.

"Derrick! Joseph!" Mrs. Moores screams with tears covering her face, but she sees nothing beyond the hallway due to the thick smoke. Javis runs into the house at the kitchen, but there's no sign of his brothers at all. He shouts for them, but the smoke starts to consume his lungs causing his mom to pull him back outside.

"Get the water hose, Javis! Somebody help!" she screams as she runs around the back side of her burning brick home, going from window to window to see if she can get a glimpse of her escaping sons. Javis is in the front of the condo, turning the water on full blast as he begins to drench the inside of the house with water, aiming down the hallway. Suddenly, as he still sees no signs of his brothers, he inhales deeply and then runs inside to the kitchen to dial emergency, noticing that the phone is already off the hook. He picks it up to listen, but no one is on the other end, so he quickly dials emergency before losing all his breath, runs back outside, and allows the water to pool the home as the hose lays on the floor.

Javis runs to the opposite side of the condo in search of his brothers through the windows, but he can't see anything until that changes. Javis stops in his tracks, and then falls to his knees, crawling to the sight of death again as he sees Joseph cradling his brother, Derrick, by the head as he lies there dead.

"God, no! No!" his mom screams in agony as she lifts Derrick by his neck trying to pick him up from his sleeping position in an attempt to get him to walk or talk again, but she's failing. Javis rapidly crawls over to his mom and tries to help her stand Derrick up, but his legs are limp with no motion.

"Come on, Derrick, come on! You can do it, man, you can. You're stronger than this, bro," Javis encourages, but it's too late. At this moment, he chooses to believe that Derrick has only passed out because of fire injuries and smoke inhalation, however, he finds out the worst.

"He's dead." They don't hear Joseph as he speaks, but he needs for them to finally hear him. "He's dead, ma. Javis, he's fuckin' dead!" he yells, cursing for the first time in his life while throwing the rocks that are balled up in his hands. "They came back for him! He told me, Javis. He told me that he killed a man for dad. He told me, and then they shot him down dead. They killed him, and I had to drag him out here through the window…and his back…" Joseph weeps, not being able to continue, pointing to Derrick's ripped skin that was caught on a nail as he pulled him out of the only opening he had to save his life. The bullet wound is right above the split.

Mrs. Moores lifts her dead son's shirt and sees the blood dripping from his back, causing her to become delirious as she tries to patch his wound up with her hands. "No, baby, no," she continues to whimper as she wipes and rubs the gaping hole in Derrick's back as Javis pulls him onto his shoulders to lift him back to the car. Joseph gets up, more saddened than he's ever been before in his life because he didn't have the ability to help his brother in his death. Joseph has a crippling limp, some days it's better than others for him to walk, and today is the worst day due to his knee injury at the church as it hindered him from a better escape than through the window. All he can visualize in front of him, as he follows slowly behind, is the harm he brought to Derrick as he tried to save him from the fire.

Javis lays Derrick in the backseat as his inconsolable mother climbs on the other side of him, holding his head and breathing in his mouth as Derrick's head repeatedly falls to the side. Mrs. Moore's screams echo through Gabriel's Trails, and more people come outside to see the bullet ridden and burning death trap that has taken the life of her son. Joseph climbs into the front seat while Javis pulls out of the yard to get his brother to the hospital. He looks down at his book bag that sits between his brother's legs on the passenger's side floor, and he hits the steering wheel over and over again as he cries, eyes blurry as he speeds out of Gabriel's Trails.

Upon arrival at the hospital, Javis jumps from the car in front of the emergency room and requests help. An emergency room team rushes out as fast as they can with a stretcher, and when they reach the car, Mrs. Moores must be detached from her son by three men trying to calm her down. Joseph sits inside the car watching the scene and weeping as they handle his mom and remove his brother from the backseat.

Javis rushes to his mom's side and sits her back in the car, explaining to her that he has to get a cane or something for Joseph to help him walk faster. Being aware that he must have his hands empty for his mom's sake, he runs inside the hospital again and asks for a cane or walker. A walker is provided, and he rushes out to Joseph who has already started walking toward the doors slowly, ready to get to Derrick.

"Come on, ma, let's go," he urges as he hands Joseph the walker he usually refuses to use, but now is different. Joseph is able to keep up, appearing as if he doesn't even need a walker now as the strength of his arms holds his limp steady as he moves his legs.

As Mrs. Moores chases behind Derrick, Javis remembers to grab the book bag as he heads inside the hospital with his broken family. They follow Derrick's stretcher as far as they can, and the nurses plead for Mrs. Moores to have a seat, explaining to her that the doctor will be out soon. Mrs. Moores is so loud that they move her to a closed room away from the crowded emergency room, and she sits there wailing with her sons paralyzed by the grief of their dead brother and what seems to be their mother dying from mounting grief.

The doctor enters the room after thirty minutes go by, and Mrs. Moores is in the midst of praying, rocking back and forth, unable to be still as she begs the Lord for her son's life back. Her begging continues as the doctor gets on the floor with her telling her the opposite, that they tried everything but her son is no longer alive. Mrs. Moores doesn't hear him, and he must repeat it three times before she suddenly stops and looks up at him, her face plagued with despair, horror and grief before the loudest wail of sorrow comes pouring out of her. She falls into the doctor's arms, and he begins to cry, too.

The embrace between the doctor and Mrs. Moores ends as Javis and Joseph get on the floor to comfort each other with intermingling tears, and the doctor leaves the room to allow them time to mourn as the nurses prepare Derrick's body to be viewed by his grieving family.

There he lay as Mrs. Moores enters the room that holds her deceased son. The white sheets are pulled all the way up to his neck, fitting tightly around the bed. Derrick's eyes are completely closed, but his expression looks unsettled. Javis and Joseph enter the room together while their mother lies her cheek atop her son's forehead, kissing him on his eyes and telling him that she tried her best and that she loves him.

Joseph breaks down in tears holding his brother's hand, and Javis stands at the foot of the bed, staring directly into his brother's face, out of tears to shed. His devastation, however, is overwhelming, and he longs to be there in the hospital bed dead in place of Derrick. Derrick was not only his brother, but they were best friends. They did everything together, except for die.

After saying their good-byes and waiting on Mrs. Moores to get paperwork signed pertaining to Derrick's body, they leave the hospital. When they get back to their burned down home, Mrs. Moores is questioned thoroughly by police who end up asking her about the events that took place before the fire, enemies and more to which Mrs. Moores can't pinpoint anything to help the cops.

Javis stands back in silence as he realizes that he doesn't know who it was that actually shot their condo up. All he knows is what Joseph told him about what Derrick revealed – that he killed someone over his dad's death and there was retaliation that ended in his brother's life. As Javis stands back while another officer talks to Joseph, finally the tears come again and they continue until the cops leave.

"We got nowhere to go, babies," Mrs. Moores addresses her sons. She's drained and doesn't know where to take her family now that they've lost everything, including her son. "There's a free house up the street, and we can go there until in the morning to see if we can rent it out…"

Javis interrupts. "We can't stay here anymore, mom."

"Well, we can use a phone and call the…"

"Momma, no," he stresses, already on edge. "Please, mom, let's go. We can't call anyone anymore. We just have to get out of here…" Javis chokes back his words as he cringes his fists, and his mom catches the look on his face that tells her that he knows more than what he's saying.

"Javis, tell me what's wrong here, dammit, tell me!" she screams frantically as her instincts tell her more than her own son tells her as he stands before her, face to face.

Finally Javis gives in. "It wasn't just Derrick, ma!" he yells, rejecting her hand from his face as she reaches out in agony over secrets hidden under her nose. "They're gonna come for me, too, and I don't know who," he pauses. "All I know is they're probably going to keep coming until they kill me."

Saddened and distraught, Mrs. Moores sobs, cutting Javis off, as she puts the pieces together that are missing. "No, Javis, please, baby, don't tell me that you and Derrick…" she pleads backing away from her oldest son, but Javis cuts her off by grabbing her tightly, concealing her words because he still can't allow those words to be heard by anyone nor himself. Joseph collapses onto the car at the sound of what his mom is muffled from saying, and he can only glare at his older brother as if he never knew him.

"Yes, ma," he weeps, placing his head into her hair as she squeezes him tightly as if she's about to lose him next. "And if we stay here any longer, they could be back, so we have to go." Javis gathers himself, as he looks around in the yard. It still isn't nightfall. He knows that he can't stand around now that the cops are gone because, as he told his mom, if whoever killed Derrick isn't satisfied, he'll be back. They take one last look at all that was lost inside the home, and Joseph poses the question about dad's ashes.

Immediately, Javis moves his mother out of his way and heads for the living room where his dad's ashes are kept. When he enters, the home is encased in black smoke, but there it is. His father's ashes sit on the wrought iron stool in front of the window, and Javis begins to sink inside.

"I'm so sorry, dad. I couldn't stop it from happening, and I have to get us out of here. It wasn't supposed to happen this way. Derrick didn't know, daddy, he didn't know, and I should have been here," he talks to his deceased father quietly hugging his ashes in his arms, then he yells so loudly that his mom comes running inside. "I should've been here!"

"Javis," she calls, reaching him and pulling her husband's ashes from his arms. She sits them down on the stool, and then holds him by his face tightly. "You aren't a murderer, baby. I don't even have to ask you, and you don't have to tell me. You said we need to get out of here," she continues, her eyes carrying enough tears for a funeral, "then let's leave. Your dad didn't get the chance to get us out, but he left the chance with you. Let's go. It's gonna be alright." Mrs. Moores' encouragement comes from realizing that she can't live losing another son, and she'll even sleep next to dumpsters overnight to keep her sons alive. "We don't have any money, and what was left is burned up, but we can sleep away from here, in the car if we have to…"

"I have money, ma," Javis reveals to her as he lowers his head in shame. "I have more than enough money for us to get a place to stay and clothes for a month and food, too."

Mrs. Moores doesn't understand what money Javis is talking about and where he got it from until he gives her a name. As he stares back into his mother's confused eyes, he responds verbally to her questioning expression. "Alexis. Alexis…she gave it to us. She gave it all to us, ma," he states as his voice starts to quiver, looking around, imagining Derrick laughing in the hallway and his dad sitting down on the recliner reading the paper and telling a funny joke. Then he breaks down, falling to the burned floor, facing outside the door as his mom falls with him and holds him tightly, not letting go, despite her confusion about the money and Alexis. She knows that she'll get the full story later, but now she's worried about her remaining sons.

Then, Javis sees a girl as he looks upward toward the car where Joseph is waiting. Tryina sits on the curb, starring at the house, in tears. He beckons his mom to get up. She grabs the urn, and they both walk from the house, enter the car and leave.

As Javis pulls out of the yard, he stares Derrick's ex-girlfriend directly in her eyes, but he feels nothing. His brother is dead, and so is hers. They now have to live with it, and Javis knows that she's probably the only one who would believe him if he says it was self defense up until the very end. He turns his eyes from her, continuing out of Gabriel's Trails, never to return. As he looks back in the rearview mirror, he watches as she stands, grabs her stomach and weeps.

Alexis and her father look each other in the eyes as they stand inside the garage. She regains possession of the knife that she kicked under the car and hands it to her father, but he refuses to take it, afraid of what's possibly been done with it. Instead of mentioning what he already knows about her, Bain and any murder along with the attack on his ex-lover Faye, he walks toward her with open arms as she drops the knife back on the ground. Instead of a hug, he has a change of heart and provides her with a huge slap to the face. Alexis' face immediately turns brownish red as a result of the penetrating slap that causes her father relief.

"Daddy, I'm sorry! I'm sorry!" she screams, clinching her fists like she needs something else to murder in order to release her rage. No matter how much she apologizes, she knows that there's no turning back the hands of time.

"You're a fucking whore and a fucking liar!" Then he walks closer to her and scolds her with the worst, demeaning name of all, "And you're a fucking murderer. Don't you ever point another damn knife at me again!" Then he grabs her arm and snatches her so close to his body that they're attached at the chest. "Because if you do, slitting your wrists will be the easiest pain you'll deal with because I'll kill you." He throws her arm down and storms inside the house, slamming the door, leaving her inside the garage alone, the knife at her feet.

Dr. Balentine is boiling over, and his cell phone rings. "Hello," he angrily answers while thinking of all the money he lost behind trying to save his daughter from prison in less than twenty-four hours.

"It's done. She's in the ocean, and I found the check. It's burned. The place…it's cleaned. She was shot on the kitchen floor in the head," states the man on the phone.

"Pick up is outside the hospital at my car on Monday morning at 4am where we've met before." Dr. Balentine answers, referring to the payment location for the murder.

The call ends as Lorah, Alexis' mother, enters the garage with a bag full of clothes wearing the most expensive pair of heels to match her purse. Before she speaks to her daughter, she drops the bag to the ground at the sight of Alexis' face bruised and teary face. She rushes toward her daughter, dropping herself to the ground along with Alexis who is in the process of falling to her knees as well.

"What happened, baby?" Mrs. Balentine asks, moving Alexis' long hair from her face. As she does, she notices the knife on the ground and picks it up. "What's this? Why is your dad's knife out here in the garage?" When she gets no answer, she tosses the knife back down and shakes Alexis violently. "Talk to me! Who hit you?"

At that question, Alexis glances up at the door that leads into the kitchen. She doesn't take her eyes from the door as the feeling of hatred overcomes her in response to her dad slapping her in the face when she feels he should have been hugging her, something he hasn't done in a long time. The words he called her, whore, liar and murderer, repeat over and over again in her mind, and she finally stares back at her mom, whom she knows loves her husband very much. The only person her mom loves more than him is her, so she takes advantage of the situation and the secrets that she's confident her mom won't find out about because Dr. Balentine isn't willing to burst her bubble. Mrs. Balentine believes that he's the most perfect, hardworking man while Alexis dominates her mother's emotions by being her only child. Besides, her dad never talks about things he's not asked about.

"Dad did it," Alexis states.

Mrs. Balentine is stunned. "Your father?"

"Yes ma'am."

"What the hell…" she exclaims, standing up from her kneeled position with her daughter to go and confront Michael, but Alexis stops her.

"No, mom, please," she pleads, tugging at her mom's arm. "Just let it go! Mom, I don't want any arguing. Look at all he's done for us," she continues, triggering another monetary way to control the situation, but at the same time, purposely building a wedge between her mom against her dad. Her mom loves the life she leads, and it's up in the air if Mrs. Balentine will let this go for the sake of a false sense of happiness. "Promise me, mom. Let it go. He works hard, and I'm fine. We just had a misunderstanding."

It works. Mrs. Balentine wraps her arm around Alexis' neck and soothes her pain, rubbing her fingers through her daughter's hair. At the same time, Alexis continues to face the entrance to the house, turning her pain into a seducing smile, drawing hatred for her father from the fact that she got a hit instead of a hug along with a thank you for clearing things up. Then, she pushes gently away from her mom, confirming to her that she'll be okay.

For the rest of the night, Alexis' parents don't speak to one another as Alexis knew they wouldn't. She's aware of their silent treatment, which gives anger the time it needs to set in and find habitation. As her dad returns to work on Monday morning, her mom cooks breakfast, and she sees Alexis off to school, delivering the appearance that everything is fine at the Balentine residence when it never is.

Alexis drives, unsure of where she's going, but the one place she won't go today is school. She ends up across the street in the parking lot opposite Gabriel's Trails, ending up stunned when she sees the home where Javis' family once lived burned to the ground. With the car still running, she feels pushed to ask any passer-by across the street what has happened, but her better judgment tells her to remain silent inside her car. She doesn't know if the family is alive or dead, but they definitely aren't there.

She pulls out of the parking lot, continuing down the street with a lone tear rolling down her face, her dad's knife on the passenger's seat along with a photo of her broken family laying underneath it.

MURDERS

AT

GABRIEL'S

TRAILS

bonus

SINS OF BAIN

Murders at Gabriel's Trails Bonus: SINS OF BAIN

"Now that you lay down to sleep, I pray the Lord your soul to keep."

"Daddy, is Jesus going to be with me?"

"Going to be with you? He is with you, baby. Goodnight."

"Night, daddy."

They kiss each other goodnight, and then he goes into the other room where his twenty-six year old wife sits inside the living room with her hair fully pulled up and ready for bed before he leaves for work. Tim is a hardworking man who saves every single penny he finds or works for, and it would seem that he should have enough money to make his goal of moving out of Gabriel's Trails, however, it's not so. There's some sort of imaginary hole in his pocket. Everything he works for ends up gone on something, either illness, the mechanic, or his baby daughter who he has in private school to keep her in the books and hopefully in a more stable school surrounding versus where she's zoned.

Tim's daughter, Shyla, is only seven years old, and he wants to keep her mentality at that age. She's never allowed to step foot outside except for one hour with a nice little girl next door. Other than that and school, he has a rule to keep her away from the windows in the evening and throughout the night when she should be sleeping. It's been this way since she was able to walk at one year old. Shyla is Tim's heart outside of his body, and the fact that he wanted a son doesn't change the way he feels about his baby girl. He plans to teach her all he knows and then some.

"I have to get out of here in one hour, Pretty." Some people think that Pretty isn't Tim's wife's real name, but it is. The story she tells those who ask is that when she came out of her mom's womb, she was the prettiest baby in the nursery. That's why her mom named her Pretty instead of the name she originally was going to name her. The original name was derived from her dad who is now deceased. He was a rough man who would cheat on her mom constantly, therefore, her mom didn't second guess naming her something not derived from her dad's wishes. It was the best slap in the face she could give him since he wasn't even in the delivery room showing support to his wife in labor. Instead, he was in the arms of another woman. How accurate the story is, no one knows, but that's the story that everyone got about how she ended up named Pretty. Pretty's mom is now suffering from a mental disorder. It's that mental disorder that left Pretty alone for years until Tim came along.

"I know. Do you want me to make you some more food before you run?"

"No, no, sit down," her thirty year old husband insisted. He was so in love with her. They'd dated since she was eighteen and he was twenty-two years of age, meeting on common stomping ground – the church. He was a member, and she was a passer-by each Sunday until he stopped her after church let out. She's been a member ever since. "I just want to relax with you a little bit, you know, kick back while our little angel is asleep. I miss you at nights."

"I know you do because I miss you, too," she replies back as she endorses his desiring lips with a passionate kiss. Her small diamond shined on her finger as she caressed his neck while his hand reaches up during the kiss and removes her hand softly. Their eyes meet so passionately that if in a crowd, it would cause onlookers to believe they were newly infatuated.

Tears stream down Tim's face. "I'm doing my best, Pretty. That's why I accepted more work at the job, ya' know? The results should be coming on the next pay check."

"Tim," Pretty says in a panic at the sight of her husband breaking down before her face. His eyes stray away from the agonizing gaze of his wife who is acting out every fear in the world in her composure as she grips her arms across her oversized shirt and bounces her legs in jogging pants. Her feet are bare on the wood floors as her toes curl up, revealing the amount of tension she feels about her husband's tearful situation.

"I've been feeling sick. I haven't been feeling too good, Pretty. It's been going on for a while now, but I tried to, you know, drink water, stop worrying, and I've even been napping for lunch overnight so that I can get extra sleep. Nothing's working, and I just can't seem to keep it together. I'm stressed out, but…"

"No, no, no," his wife interrupts, grabbing his face in the palms of her hands. "Everything's gonna be okay. I'm able to bring money into the house if you just let me, Tim. I can work as well, even if we have..."

"You know you need to be at home, Pretty, so I can sleep for the next work night and you can take care of Shyla. If you went to work, no one would be here for her and then I wouldn't be rested enough to work all night. It wouldn't work, babe. We already tried that remember. It just doesn't work out because that last job wouldn't let you leave on time all the time to get Shyla from school. We only have one car, Pretty. Come on, now."

Pretty stands up and walks toward the wall, fed up with him not wanting her to have any job or help with the bills. She's fed up with the way their household is falling to pieces financially ever since they put Shyla in private school. It just costs too much, but they refuse otherwise. They both made the decision to struggle for her well being. "I see you everyday looking weaker and weaker. It hurts, baby. It just hurts when I can do something."

Tim walks over to his troubled, young wife who can see no means to an end, and as he walks over, his arms are outstretched. She falls into them weakly because she's at her wit's end. The bright smile he once knew on Pretty has been broken little by little for a while now, but she still finds a way to cock her head to make it appear the same as it used to be. In reality, her head tilt is just her hiding the emptiness she feels inside.

"I have an appointment to see the doctor. This time, I'm not going to the clinic down the road. I have a physician at the hospital I'm going to see. I hear he's real good. Just keep praying for me, okay?"

"Yeah, baby. Okay."

"I'm good. I'm good." He kisses her again on her cheek, and then heads off to work. Pretty stares on in silence while locking the door behind him. The dark brown strands of her hair blow from the fan that's elevated onto the window sill as she looks at him get in the car as the sun goes completely down. As the car pulls off, she wipes the tears from her eyes while she walks to the bathroom clearly upset. When she gets there, she pulls some tissue from the roll and peers down into the toilet.

"Oh shit," Floss laughs as he chases a man through the woods into trail number one from trail number four. He pulls his gun out in a taunting manner and slows his pace as he watches the young man, about twenty-two years old in stature, trip over all the rocks and fallen limbs that are camouflaged by the darkness of the night under the umbrella of trees. Not even the moon can be seen. Floss knows the trails like the back of his hands though, and in the thick of the woods, he slows, knowing that the frightened young man is headed for destruction on the dead end of trail number one.

"Help me!" the young man screams, but quickly silences again figuring that his noise will attract more harm his way because when he looks behind himself, he sees no sign of his chaser anywhere. There's complete darkness as he halts crawling to feel his way around on the ground before standing back up on his two feet. He doesn't know his way out. Spinning around only twice has gotten him lost, so he continues to walk slowly, jumping with the sound of every leaf, limb or rock beneath his feet.

As he plants his feet down, one by one at a snail's pace, his eyeballs are opened to their limit. This doesn't help however, especially when he steps out into trail number one. He realizes that the only way to go is to the left because running to the right would place him in front of a mountain of dirt and debris so thick that it creates a trap.

His breathing is caught between faint pants and rough groans as his legs move him into the full openness of the trail. He's never been on this end before, and most people don't come because there's nowhere to go. Looking side to side, he steps out and starts to speed up, looking at the opening far down the trail which is brightened by a street light in the next neighborhood. It's the first sign of hope he's had since running from the trouble he put himself in.

Nearing the halfway point of the trail, shreds of confidence start to push through the overwhelming dread on his face. He starts to run again, and the pace is faster than he's ever run before. Nothing but adrenaline pumps through his blood, and he feels nothing but freedom ahead until he falls to the ground, knees first, at a sudden sight in front of him.

The man holds his hand out in a welcoming gesture from the side of the trail. Tears start to roll down the fleeing young man's face as he stares at the man who appears to be setting him free. Therefore, he stands up from the soiled ground, quivering despite the warm temperature in the nighttime air, and takes his chances, praying to God for forgiveness and a way out. Staring back at the man allowing him to pass, he walks by him, only five feet from the man's outstretched arm. The man has a calmness about him, not threatening at all, so the young man makes another break for it and runs, keeping his eyes on the man with the outstretched hand until he hits something in front of him which causes him to fall to the ground.

"I don't have it, but I can get it. Floss, I can get it, please, Floss, please!" he begs, recognizing the man he just hit as being Floss towering over the cowardly position of his body on the ground.

218

"Man, you just ran right into me. I could've sworn you were looking for me. Weren't you looking for me, man?" Floss asks jokingly although life and death is no joking matter. He gets a high off of making those around him feel reliant on his mercy even though he isn't God.

The grounded young man shakes his head vigorously back and forth, pulling on the dirt and patches of grass for a grip to help him move backwards faster, away from the man who is now his enemy. As he's moving however, he bumps into the man who welcomed him this way.

"Don't look scared, my man," Floss continued to taunt. "Hey, Bain, what you say about him, man?"

The young man makes a fast switch in bodily direction, now facing the one and only Bain that people outside of the trails generally only hear about but rarely see. If they do see him, they don't even know it's him. This is this newcomer's first time, and it may be his last.

"Bain, Bain," the young man stammers as Bain grabs him at his elbow, helping him up from the ground.

"The first rule is never to talk to another man from the ground. You are a man, right?"

"Yes. Yes, I am, Mr. Bain."

"Mister Bain? Fuck is this?" Floss interjects in a high pitched tone. Bain just looks at him, and he silences.

"How old are you?"

The young man looks back at Floss who is now patting him down from the chest down. Then, he answers Bain. "I'm twenty- three this week, sir. Just twenty-three."

"This is a grown man, Floss. Back up off him," he orders Floss. "Let the man pat himself down. If he has a gun, let him choose what to do with it. Tell me this…what's your name?"

"Simon."

"Your last name," Bain continues. Asking a last name gives Bain more of a feel for family ties, just in case he needs it later. The young man hesitates to answer because he doesn't want to reveal his whole identity.

"I asked for your last name." Bain speaks calmly. He has a gun in his belt, however, he hasn't reached for it at all. He enjoys entering the head of each individual he comes in contact with for a bout of manipulation and power. Bain is a different type of man, some would call a gangster, dealer, or even a pimp. Some call him all three because he's been known to do all three in the same night. The man part of Bain gives every human being an opportunity when faced with life or death. The animal side of Bain could care less about their life or death. Tonight, there's an even split between his animal side and the side that could be called a man.

"Duke. That's my last name. It's Duke."

"Would you say that this was all a mistake, Duke? Being that you're a grown man now, would you say that you slipped up and you really do have the money you owe me for all those nights?"

"Bain, I didn't know she was yours. I didn't know, and yes, I made a mistake. I did, but..."

Like night and day, Bain immediately goes from calm to extremely frustrated in a matter of seconds. "Gin!" he calls angrily.

Out steps a female in a leopard cat suit from the woods. Immediately, Simon Duke glances toward the movement, and when he sees her clearly, she's visibly shaken, not the jovial and loving woman he clearly fell in love with over the joys of her mattress.

"Give me the recorder I sent you in your bedroom with tonight, baby." Gin didn't move fast enough, so Bain calmly turns her way. "Gin, don't play with me now. Go ahead and give me the recorder. Did you find the spot for me because when I press play, I don't wanna wait."

She pulls it from the top of her cat suit, but doesn't hit play. "Just tell him that we're in love, Simon." She looks over at Bain. "Bain, I love him. Just please let him go. He'll pay, just let him go, please, Bain." She looks to the ground, afraid to speak anymore because the silence from Bain is killer. He's allowing her to ramble, and he's not one for rambling. Bain simply waits on her to finish, and he then politely takes the recorder from her hand. She starts to walk toward her lover, however, Bain quickly reminds her of wisdom.

"Stand still, Gin."

Once he orders her still, he presses play, and she freezes in her tracks. They all listen as the recorder reveals a conversation between her and Simon Duke prior to another session of making love. It's obvious on the recorder that Gin tried not to bait the conversation in Bain's favor, however, her lover didn't need the bait. He admitted he knew she was one of Bain's girls, but when she comes to lay with him, she was to no longer consider herself a whore. Instead, she was to consider herself a woman in love with a man who loves her back. That's when Gin started crying on the recording, and Simon Duke proceeded to comfort her, confused about what she's crying about.

Gin never answered him about why she was sobbing, but she continued with her regular service, this time making love with the man she's servicing for what could be the very last time. The recording stops.

Bain starts up again. "I know the recording isn't rigged, Simon, because Floss was outside waiting on you to exit. His time matches the time that passed on the recorder. You said that shit, didn't you?"

"Who doesn't want his woman to feel like a queen, Bain? Gin is right. We're in love."

"Did you just lie to me about not knowing she was mine?"

Simon Duke doesn't answer.

"Nobody sleeps with my girls for free. I'm owed the fee. Either you owe Gin some money and that's why she didn't pay me," he says, reaching for his pistol. "Or you paid Gin, and she's hiding a stash of cash that she owes to me. Which one?" When he finishes speaking, he points the pistol at Simon Duke. No one responds to his question, so he speaks again. "Twice no answer, twice the bullets."

"I'm in love with her, Ba..."

Simon Duke doesn't even get his sentence out. At Bain's nod, Floss shoots him in the back of the head. He falls to his knees in front of Bain. He steps out of the way to allow his whore to cradle him.

"I asked him a question. That mo' fucker evaded it. The next time you go making a man fall in love with you, get my money, and I'll set you free. Gin," Bain calls because she's too busy holding her dead lover than listening to him. She glances up unable to even cry, in a

222

river of disbelief, as she holds Simon's head from behind, shocked beyond repair. "You know the rules. I don't hold you here, but you will respect the game you signed up for, baby. You want me to say I'm sorry?" he asks with no chance of empathy. "You were under contract…my verbal one." He looks up at Floss. "Take care of Gin for me. Make sure she gets back home safely. The debt's paid how, baby. You're free to go now, Gin."

"Alright, man," Floss answers.

"My name is Hazel. Hazel mother fucking Walker, and I hate you, Bain!"

"I didn't kill him, Gin. He killed himself, then Floss shot him." As he begins to walk back through the woods, he warns her in a low tone. "Watch your mouth until you die, Miss Hazel Walker. I got no problem with you. Just watch your mouth."

Hazel Walker knows what that means coming from Bain. Watch your mouth means more than shouting at him in anger. The meaning goes much deeper. Watch your mouth coming from Bain means to not speak one word about this particular murder on trail number one and to pretend that her former life as his whore never existed. Gin is no longer Gin, and she can no longer make the same living that she used to because Bain holds all the cards. If she's ever caught taking money from a man for sex as long as she lives in Gabriel's Trails, she'll be killed. He just ended what's been her only source of income for over five years.

"I've seen you around. Come on over here and sit down. I don't eat humans, so you're fine," she explains, laughing while sucking on a hard piece of candy.

The woman begins to approach her from the sidewalk. Instead of walking up the steps, though, she went to the side of the porch, choosing to stand on the grass, completely ignoring the invitation to sit down.

"I see you have your own mind or either you're too afraid to talk to me level to level. Instead of making this a full out conversation, let me just cut to it." The woman with the candy in her mouth lifts her leg up on the rail so high that anyone walking by could see up her short skirt. Then she leans over and asks the timid woman, "When do you want to start, sweetheart?" She waits on a reply, and when there's no answer, she shouts, "Talk, dammit! Got some damn problem?"

"Bain," the lady stammered. "I need to talk to Bain."

The lady takes her leg down from the rail, stands tall and looks out into the darkness. "Well, Bain's not here. I don't see him either, so you have to talk to me for now. I'm Faye. What's your name?"

"Pretty."

"So that's who I've been seeing with that cute little girl every now and again? Little Mrs. Pretty. You're married, right? What do you need with Bain, Pretty?" She lights a cigarette. "You can't wanna be one of his tricks, right? Your husband will slit your damn throat." She laughs, but when she glances back down at Pretty, she watches the tears fall down her cheeks. The cigarette that she just lit, she puffs on twice and flicks it away. Then, Faye jumps off of the porch, swings her hair back away

224

from her eyes, and then warns her, standing two inches from her face. "Don't be fuckin' stupid. Get the hell out of here before I beat your ass or before your damn husband does."

"No, I really need to talk to Bain."

"Not about this shit, Pretty!" Faye yells, rejecting Pretty's response altogether. She, then, examines Pretty's clothes and shoes. She's wearing jogging pants, but on her chest she wears a skin tight tank top, her breasts up in the air. "So you can tuck those in and go back home. Bain don't wanna see you." Faye then rolls her eyes. "And you look like a piece of walking ass shit." It wasn't the truth. Faye's only reason for criticizing her is to break her, to make her give up and leave. Outside of all the harsh talk, Faye knows that she's looking at a beauty, with or without the jogging pants on. This is one of the reasons Faye doesn't want her there. Faye, when she looks at Pretty, sees the innocence she lost a long time ago, so she's attempting to preserve Pretty's good thing whether Pretty knows it or not.

"Please, I need some money."

"How much?" Faye lights another cigarette as she moves back onto the porch. Pretty is confused, so she stalls on a response. "I said how much!" Faye shouts.

"I don't know!" Pretty nervously retorts. "I don't know, but my family needs it now more than ever. I don't have anything…I mean we got nothing."

"Shut the hell up. You're too late. Don't fuckin' say I didn't try." Faye straightens her body up, fixes her clothes despite the fact that they're too tight to move, and smiles, "Hey, baby! Back so soon?"

Bain walks up the sidewalk and then up his porch as Faye grabs his hand to stop him and give him a kiss on the lips. He allows her to enjoy herself, and as they kiss, his eyes remain on the other woman beside his porch. He then motions his eyes, allowing the uneasy lady to follow him inside after backing away from Faye. Bain backs away from Faye who is all smiles, and then he goes inside. Pretty follows as Faye's eyes follow her.

"Stupid ass trick," she whispers and takes a seat on the rail. "Can't tell hungry ass people shit."

"I need to sit down a minute. Just feeling a little dizzy is all, probably my electrolytes down."

"Are you sure you're alright? I can run and get you a juice, water or something from the canteen, man."

"Appreciate that, Dice."

"No problem. I got you." He walks off, and Tim sits there on the stool as he places his head on the wall. It isn't the cleanest place to lay his head being that he's sitting right outside of the bank's bathroom, but it feels just like a pillow to Tim's head. He and Dice are in charge of cleaning two four story banks overnight every night, and they are the last men standing who do a good job with the privately owned business. The others were cut because they weren't cleaning up to par, and their duties were given to Tim and Dice. Tim jumped at the opportunity because handling buildings such as these could lead him to management in a shorter amount of time if he proves himself, and more buildings means more pay.

"Here ya' go, man. Some water and some orange juice. Take that down, and if you can't move right now to help me with the cleaning, I got it, man. Knock it out just like if you were on your own two feet beside me. I got skills like that," Dice brags.

"No, Dice, I can do it. Feel better already." Tim stands but winds up falling straight to the floor, his eyes rolling back into his head.

"Tim, man, Tim!" Dice kneels to the floor and lifts Tim's head, but when Tim doesn't come back, he pulls out his cell phone to call the boss on speaker. "Yeah, Mr. Robertson, it's about Tim. He just fell to the floor, passed out. He's breathing, but hasn't got up yet. What do I do?"

"Did he complain about being ill?"

"Yeah, dizzy but other than that, I gave him some juice…wait, wait a minute." He puts the phone down. "Tim, it's me, Dice. Wake up." Dice taps him on his cheeks, and then he watches as Tim wakes up, weakly shaking his head until he comes back into full consciousness.

"Send him home, Dice. Tim, Tim…if you can hear me, I am ordering you to rest at home for at least two days until you can see a doctor with a diagnosis. Dice, he hasn't been feeling too good as you probably already figured."

"Yeah, I know, but he looked worse today. He could barely stand, and now look what happened."

"Dice, I'm on my way up to help you with the building. When I get there, we'll either take him to the hospital or home. He is awake now, right?"

"Yeah, yeah, he just sat up."

"Well, give him some more of that juice. You know what to do. Put on the doctor's hat, and we'll take him home after I get up there, then I'll come back up and help you."

"Cool." He hits the end button on the cell and puts the juice up next to Tim's lips. Tim sips slowly, wanting to vomit it all up. "Tim, man, Mr. Robertson is coming up to take you to the hospital or home. Which one do you want? I'm driving behind him in your car."

"I have an appointment already. I'll be fine if I just get back home. I'm sure this is just stress." He strains out a smile, but it's really weak.

Dice looks over his friend and co-worker in doubt of everything he just said. Instead of arguing with him though, he pretends like he takes him at his word when in the back of his mind, things are quite opposite. After helping Tim rest his back against the wall while remaining seated on the floor, Dice goes back to work again, periodically checking on Tim to make sure he's still conscious.

The inside of the condo may be dusty in appearance from the outside, but inside it's as clean as a whistle. As she moves around inside the living room, her nervousness increases, causing her to contemplate walking back out the front door. She doesn't take a seat, but just stands there like a lost little girl in a strange place while the man who lounges before her on his couch simply stares.

"What's up, Pretty?"

"Bain…"

"Sit down," he interrupts to offer her a seat. She starts to walk over to the same couch he's on, but he stops her. "Not over here," he instructs, pointing his chin over to the chair by the window. "Right here. Now tell me what's up?" Atop the center table is a small cooler filled with bottled water. Bain reaches in and tosses her one. She accepts with a catch, but she doesn't open it.

"Thanks."

"You're welcome." He stares at her body, but waits on her to respond to the question he asked.

"I need some money, Bain. I know this isn't cool for me to stop in and ask for some money being married and all that with our history…"

"Money for what?" he interrupts again. He removes his shirt, revealing all the manpower any woman would want, then he tosses his shirt on the back of the couch. Although Pretty is in love with her husband, she isn't blind to Bain's muscular frame, but she's quickly distracted by the gun in his waist, causing her to get back to the reality that she almost left.

"My family. I need money for my family."

There's an awkward silence between them after her admission. The tension is so thick that Pretty rushes to get up, heading for the door, but Bain restrains her with words.

"Pretty, sit down. You don't have to be afraid of me. You're running up outta here like you're about to cross me. We go back, all the way back to grade school. Sit down." He reaches over and hits the side of the chair.

Pretty responds in obedience as Bain never moves from the couch. He removes his pistol, placing it at his side, but assures her that it's just for comfort's sake, not to take her life.

"So you need money for your family?"

She looks down to the floor ashamed and answers, "Yeah, yeah, I do."

"Look up at me."

She does as requested, but as she does, tears begin to flow down her eyes as if she knows what's coming next. Instead of allowing the sadness to show in forms of streams down her cheeks, she wipes her face with her wrists, calms herself down and sits there, staring hopelessly back into the eyes of the man whom she once knew as her school yard friend.

When they were small children in elementary school, it was Bain who was the class clown. Back then, no one called him by his last name. He was known in school by his first name Davon. As a matter of fact, it was in elementary school where Pretty had her first kiss. The kiss wasn't adult like in form, but it was with a boy whom she adored and had a crush back on her. Her first kiss was with this same Davon, and she was his first kiss as well. They were in fourth grade. Their relationship changed when people started to call him Bain, and that was when the crush ended. They were only one year away from leaving elementary school for good.

"My family needs money, too, and you know that, Pretty."

She knows exactly what Bain is referencing, and her soul starts to ache. Fighting with every ounce of herself to hold back, she loses it and lashes out. "That had nothing to do with us, Bain! It had nothing to do with me," she painfully explains, holding her hands against her chest, looking at him with sore eyes. "I didn't know anything about anything, Bain, and you know that! It's not my debt."

"Well, whose is it then?" Bain isn't shaken nor is he moved to compassion by her sensitivity to the matter that only they know about. It's been so long ago that his dad shot her father to death, but it's still fresh in their minds. Bain seeks loyalty to his father, not friendship with Pretty. Pretty seeks the same friendship she once had with the boy she knew as Davon, but wants nothing to do with the man now known and feared as only Bain.

She gets up to leave, but he stops her again. "Pretty, you better sit your ass down while I'm talking. I asked you a question. If you want to leave after I'm finished talking, then you can, but don't interrupt me by walking out when I'm waiting on an answer." He takes a gulp of water and sighs. "Now, I asked you," he restates while leaning over as to let her know just who serious he is, "whose debt is it then?"

Frustrated because she has no choice, she sits and remembers to look back at him because he hasn't taken his eyes off of her yet. It's disrespectful to look away from Bain when he's talking, at least that's what the word is in the Trails. Bain is getting to know her again, and with every second that goes by, he learns more and more about how to manipulate her and what makes her tick. He does this to everyone by watching them, and it doesn't ever take him too long. He's only failed in reading people and situations a couple times, and those couple of times were times where he could have lost his life. He was trained by his now dead father, Johnny Bain.

It was Johnny Bain who taught him how to make the most and take the most out of people when they're in his visual. It's all about watching. Weaker people are easier to read, but it's the people who rarely show emotion who are harder to break down, but even they show signs if watched close enough.

On the day Johnny Bain was shot and killed, it was the same day Davon was with him. They were very close, and although his dad was caught up in much bad business, he kept blood from his son's hands and blood off of his son. He taught his son life lessons in dealing with people of all walks of life before he entered the fifth grade.

This deadly day Davon walked into a house with his dad, he felt secure. His dad was well respected by many out of fear, but some people didn't fear him at all such as his wife, Jeneeva. There was nothing that those two wouldn't do for each other.

It was on this day that Davon overheard his dad speaking about collecting his money from a guy who didn't pay up. This only happened every once in a while, but this day of collection, his dad chose not to leave him at home with his mom. When Davon and his dad reached the debtor's house, he jumped out before his dad did. There were children out playing, and he was about to run to join in. His father stopped him, grabbed him by the shoulder, and took him to the front door.

Davon was still watching his peers play a game of dodge ball, but when he turned around, he watched Johnny Bain pull out his gun. Johnny Bain didn't even knock. He just opened the door and pushed his son behind him. With each step Johnny Bain took, Davon took the same. Then out steps a young girl around Davon's age. It was Pretty. She came out of her room with a doll and hair brush. Not even looking up, she simply walked down the hallway to a back room. Davon looked up at his dad, about to tell him that he knew the girl from school, but that was when a man walked out of the bedroom. Pretty followed behind. The man stopped in his tracks when he saw Johnny Bain.

"Now isn't the time, Bain. My daughter's mom isn't home, and I have things to do. If you wanna talk something over, let's do this without others around." His eyes turned onto his daughter and then onto Davon.

"You've had weeks. She said the last time you didn't pay her, so today is the day. Pay me because there won't be no other day to do it."

"Davon!" the man's daughter shouted, recognizing Johnny Bain's son. Davon didn't respond like he wanted to because he knew that when his dad was conducting business, he was to remain silent and watch.

The man looked down at his daughter, and then, back up at Johnny Bain who'd already lifted his gun at about thirty degrees. "You can put the gun down now, Bain, because my daughter is here. I got the money, but…" That was when Pretty's father reached down, pretending to reach for his daughter, but quickly changed the direction of his hand, went down to the back of his waist, drew and then shot the gun. Johnny Bain fired back at the same time. The bullets hit each man in their chests.

Pretty started screaming and covering her ears, her doll dropping to the floor while her dad fell lifeless onto the toes of her feet. Up the hallway, Davon watched as his powerful dad fell to his knees, his hand still on his son's shoulder.

Struggling to look at his son due to the jolting pain taking over his body, Johnny Bain still drew the strength to speak. "I love you and your mom. You know where all the money is, so use it. This is your last lesson because I messed it up." Johnny Bain struggled to get his words out. "Never talk too much to anyone, especially those that owe you your money. All that does is give 'em time to kill you so they don't have to pay. This was my mistake, and you better keep it in your mind, boy! That man owed me. Get my money because it belongs to us! It belongs to us Bains." Then, he fell closer to the floor, pulling his son down with him. "Don't you fuckin' shed one tear for me. Not one. Remember your name because I worked hard for it. Remember your name."

In the background, Davon heard children screaming along with Pretty who'd never stopped her wail, but Davon wasn't permitted to shed one tear. He kneeled there, crouched over his father as his dad pulled him in closer, striking so much fear in him with his stern eyes, he felt that if he cried, he would fail his father. Therefore, Davon stared right back at him, right back into his dad's eyes, until his father took his last breath. He didn't quiver nor did he shed one tear. This is how he learned to swallow sadness. This is when he became Bain.

As Bain sits there watching and waiting on Pretty to answer, he answers for her. "Since you can't tell me whose debt it is, go get your money tonight. Faye'll show you how." Bain leans back on his couch, knowing full well that he has the upper hand in more than one way, still in a disbelief that Pretty really came to him asking him for money.

Pretty, despite her coming to a pimp's house, was hoping on her walk down that her old friend wouldn't be so hard on her, but her hopes go unanswered. "Bain, I'm married. You know I'm married, and I have a little girl…"

"No, baby girl, it's *you* who knows you're married. *You* came here. I didn't take no vow, baby, and I don't break 'em. But you, you just broke yours." He pauses, checking out her willingness to perform the task about to be handed to her. Pretty, although she changed into a more revealing shirt before leaving the house, now feels that she must have been out of her mind. Thoughts race about how to get out of doing this, but the front door seems so far away with Bain only inches from her reach. "How's your baby girl?"

"Leave her alone, Bain." Tears fall only half a second after he mentions her daughter.

"How's your man, then?" he smiles, but she doesn't answer which sets him off. "Hey, Faye!" he calls loudly, and she comes inside, glaring at Pretty. "Go tell her how to earn double by doing double. She tells me she needs some money." Bain then leans forward, terrifying her with his pistol in front of him although he hasn't even touched it. "And I need my money, too. I'll set that shit up tonight."

Pretty just looks on as Bain removes himself from the room. Her eyes full of tears, she gets up and leaves with Faye, her mind still on her husband, daughter and on asking Jesus for forgiveness. There's no turning back now. Before she exits the front door, she gazes down the hallway through her soaked eyes, and watches as Bain callously walks into what looks to be a bathroom and slams the door behind himself. This used to be her very best friend.

Opening the door for Tim, Mr. Robertson hands him his keys and then helps him down.

"I'm fine. I'm fine. Thank you, Mr. Robertson, and the car is fine parked right there on the street for now. Let Dice know I'm good when he pulls up, and I promise to go to the doctor, Mr. Robertson. It's just a little rough spot. I'm good."

"Don't let money or anything keep you from your health. Take the bill. If you can pay it, fine. If you can't, it's still fine. Just don't get so sick that you can't survive. Not good, Tim. Take care of yourself the best way you can." He knocks on the wall before he leaves. "I'm checking on you tomorrow. I'm not a hard knock boss. I love my people. Go to the doctor."

Tim raises his hand high in efforts to say bye because he really doesn't want to open his mouth. He feels sick to his stomach, so he limps as fast as his feet can carry him into the bathroom. As he leans over the toilet, he receives the reminder that something is terribly wrong.

There's a toilet full of blood. He then remembers that he forgot to flush, so he does. A feeling of hopelessness overwhelms him as he sits on the floor, thinking about Pretty and if she's seen what's been coming out of his body for weeks. Standing back up, he decides to walk into his bedroom, but before he moves toward the bedroom, he peeks inside his daughter's room. Shyla is fast asleep, and in his eyes, she looks heavenly. He walks into her room, kisses her on the cheek, and double checks the window locks. Then, he walks into his bedroom, and while he approaches the bed, he blinks because he can't believe what he's seeing. His wife isn't at home.

"Pretty?"

He peeps inside the small closet that they share, but still, Pretty is nowhere to be found. The bed isn't made up, and when he looks for his wife's purse, it's still there. Panicking, he goes as fast as he can to the backyard from the back door, but there's nothing. He shouts. "Pretty!"

Tim's eyes begin to tear up in disbelief that his wife isn't at home with their daughter. He reviews the situation in his head. The door was locked when he came inside. As he looks around, everything appears untouched. It's starting to look like Pretty left the house purposely, leaving Shyla in the bed.

"Pretend like you're in your bathroom and just take your clothes off," she tells the terrified woman whom she brought to an old abandoned condo at the farthest side of Gabriel's Trails. She motions her fingers, rushing her along to undress. "Go ahead. This is easy, and plus I got other shit to do besides monitor your ass on a man's ass tonight. You better work the shit, too. Bain's money is his money." She plops down in an empty chair. "Don't worry about the bed, baby, the sheets are clean. Bain makes us change and wash those things, plus buy new ones when we come here. Smell 'em. Go ahead."

Pretty leans over and sniffs the sheets in different areas. The sheets smell like fabric softener, and there aren't visible stains anywhere. The thought of lying with another man still makes her feel filthy, but she has no other choice. Her only grasp of sanity is knowing that her husband and child will never know.

Faye has someone going over to Pretty's house, sitting outside her daughter's bedroom window to make sure no one goes inside. It's Bain's orders. Pretty has no idea, but Faye knows that once a woman comes to work for Bain, Bain protects the flock. None have fallen yet as long as the flock sticks by the rules.

"Hello?" Faye picks up her cell. She doesn't put it on speaker, but when she hangs up she lets Pretty know it's time. Faye spits her gum in the small trashcan in a mad rush. "This is where the condom goes. Use two since you're married and two if you ain't I always say," she advises, placing the condoms atop the side table. "Now, look, when I open the door for him, I want you to have those clothes off, so drop em. Stand up like a school girl on the playground, your leg out with your hand on your hip."

Pretty starts to undress quickly as she imagines being a school girl once again. She knows the stance that Faye speaks of, that one stance that every girl enjoyed doing because that was the 'in' thing to do. It's not fun anymore because she realizes that this isn't for fun and games. She has no choice now but to do this, whether she likes it or not. It's too late to pull out. Bain would possibly force her back inside or kill her if she even thought about jumping from the window, and besides that, she has to get back home for Shyla and Tim before he finds out. It's either run and die or hurry and hide it from her man. Those are her only two choices, and only one of those choices brings in the money.

Faye walks over to her. "Relax. I'm not giving you anything to take because the last thing that child needs is a junkie for a mom, so you're gonna have to phase out the best way your ass can." Faye sees her tears layer Pretty's deep brown eyes, so she places her hands over them, presses softly and wipes. "I'm outside. Don't act like you're enjoying it because you're not. This is a service.

Make him feel good. It's not about you. This is a job. Now…I'm gonna tell you something, and don't say shit about what I'm about to say to Bain, got it?"

Pretty nods her head and answers, "Yes."

"He said to do a double. Do a triple. Stick the extra money in the socket and leave the room. Got it?"

"The socket? Which one?" Pretty becomes confused.

"Pretty, wake up." She slaps her on the side of her head lightly. "Your socket," she stresses, looking down at her hips. "But here's some olive oil. Pour that in there first. That way, nothing sticks to the walls. I'm sitting it underneath the bed, and then I'm outside the door. You should pull at least fifteen hundred dollars tonight. If you don't, knock and I'll show you how." Before she walks out, she turns back to look at Pretty. "If you say shit to Bain about that little extra I told you to help your ass out, I'll tell your husband and your child plus all these other mother fuckers that you're just like me, and a woman like you, I can tell, won't like that shit." She pauses at the door until she hears the knock. "That's him. Now take all his money, ask God for forgiveness after this and don't you ever come back. Bain will free you, at least you better hope so. This ain't the life for you or nobody else. I just got too used to it."

Faye opens the door, and before her stands a high priced clientele. She looks puzzled because she normally gets men like this one, but instead of questioning it on the spot, she submits to Bain's authority on the matter to let a virgin to the game tackle a hard knock and leaves the room. She sits in a chair that's parked in the hallway. Her pistol is loaded and ready. Faye knows Bain is outside watching, but the client has no idea what he looks like. Her job is to watch the front door, but to mostly, watch out for little Mrs. Pretty just in case the man she's with gets out of hand.

"I can't believe this high priced loon came inside the Trails," she comments to herself and waits. "His ass might not make it back out."

"Hey, hey! Get away from my house!" Tim demands as he gathers the little strength he has left to fight off a couple of ladies leaning up against the side of his condo. When he went back to check on his daughter asleep in the bed, he heard the ladies talking from outside. They were laughing loud, cursing, and just portraying the life that Tim has tried so hard to shield Shyla's eyes from.

The ladies watch as Tim comes around his porch, holding his stomach. Then, they look at each other and laugh. "Oh hell no! This chick's husband is at home."

Tim hears their words, but he isn't truly listening. He doesn't tie their words to the wife he loves so much, so he continues to walk toward them, forcing them to leave their current leans against the brick.

"I am telling you to leave. My daughter is asleep in the room."

"We know that. We can see the night light from the blinds." Then one of the ladies walks toward Tim. "Listen, it's not like we have a choice to be here. We're babysitting your daughter tonight."

The other lady interjects. "Oh what? You didn't know?"

240

"Babysitting?"

"Yeah, and if we would've known that you were in the house, we sure wouldn't be here either. We were told you were at work."

"Told I was at work? Don't you see my car?"

"How the hell are we supposed to know that's your car? It's not pulled up in your driveway, now is it?"

"Where's my wife Pretty?"

"Getting ugly."

"Shut up! Don't say that! Damn, have some tact."

Tim watches them argue for about fifteen seconds, and then stops them both. "Again, where is my wife?"

"She's making some fast cash, if you must know. She needed help, so Bain helped her."

As soon as Bain's name travels into Tim's ears, a pain hits his heart. His body falls inward as if someone just hit him inside his chest, and he nearly falls backward. The girls run forward to try and catch him, but he catches himself. A groan comes from the pit of his stomach like an animal dying, and his knees slowly rely on the grass as cushion for his sorrow.

The two ladies don't really know what to do, so they just stand there until, finally, they call Faye. When Faye picks up, they walk over to the side of the adjacent condo and let her know that Pretty's husband is at home and that he knows that she's under Bain's eye now. When they hang up the phone, they prepare to take off, feeling anxious after the call.

"We have to go. Your wife, she'll be back home. It's probably a misunderstanding, right, CeeTee?"

"Yeah, a misunderstanding." The ladies know that Bain is going to have to come and lay down the law since the husband just found out that Pretty is sleeping with another for money. Not wanting to wait around and see what happens, the ladies leave in spite of Tim yelling after them for more answers. There's no use. The ladies disappear into the crowd up the road.

The car is running. Faye has already relayed the message to Bain about Pretty's husband being home as well as knowing that she's out making money with her body. Although Bain wants to leave to approach Pretty's husband before he does something Bain considers stupid like call the law, he continues to wait in the car. The one thing he will do is make certain Pretty gets out of the house safe. All Bain's other watchers are busy watching other people tonight, and Pretty is something spur of the moment. This is one reason why he is personally waiting, because she can't handle herself without help which is his normal situation with the newbies. The other reason why he's here is much more personal that what anyone knows.

Bain watches as the customer walks outside first. Then, he receives a text from Faye saying that things are cool before the client gets into his car. He then leans back and turns on his car lights. The client becomes aware that he isn't alone, so he rushes to get into his car and leaves, driving right by Bain, never seeing his face.

Back inside, Faye is rushing Pretty to get washed up and dressed. She still hasn't told her about the phone call

242

that she got while she was sleeping with the client who happened to pay her more than planned. He left her two thousand dollars, expecting to see her again.

"Listen up," Faye starts as she walks into the room to a shamed Pretty as she sits in the bed curled up like a small, afraid child. Faye starts to snatch Pretty's clothes up off the floor along with ripping the sheets off the bed from underneath her as she lies there sulking. "Get up, Pretty. This ain't the time. We don't lounge. There's water. Bain pays it. Go shower." She slaps her on her naked behind. "Get up!"

Pretty doesn't move as she stares at the money that takes her husband practically a whole month or more to earn. She just earned it in less than two hours. She also earned a terrible conscious and a corrupted feeling all over her body while others know what she just did. She just became a whore.

Faye continues to clean the room, and since Pretty won't get up the easy way, she walks by the bed, tosses her clothes on top of her and says, "Either wash now or after your husband smells you because he knows where you are and what you're doing already."

Pretty shoots a terrified look at Faye, but Faye simply shrugs and looks back at her, continuing to talk before Pretty opens her mouth to get a word out. "Your plan got fucked up, and ain't shit you can do about it but wash the mud off and keep going, baby."

Pretty leaps from the curled up position she was in weeping and trembling. "You're lying, Faye," she cries. "How did he find out? He's at work. Did something happen to Shyla, my daughter? Oh Jesus, God please forgive me, but I…Faye, answer me!" she screams hysterically, noticing that Faye isn't paying any attention to her rambling.

"Looks like he ain't at work, pretty lady," she sings with a side smirk, but that's quickly replaced with a grave seriousness when she leaps onto the bed in front of Pretty, grabbing her by the throat and shoving the back of her head into the pillow. "I told your ass not to do this, so don't you ever fuckin' raise your damn voice at me again. I'll take this damn extra money right from under your sorry ass. Should be home with your baby anyway instead of fuckin' some damn stranger for cash. You need to feel like a whore," she smiles, "because that's exactly what you are now, lil Pretty. That's exactly what you are." Then, Faye leans back, hands still around Faye's neck as she loosens her grip, and then, hops off the bed. "Walk your own ass outside. Bain's waiting." Before she leaves, she grabs the one thousand dollars that Bain expects from the encounter. Then she hands Pretty the olive oil while she rolls up the extra money in a tight enough roll to be hidden. "Say some more smart ass shit and I'll take it for myself. I could have given you this chump change, but your ass didn't answer me."

Pretty moves from the bed to go wash, and after she's done, she tries to escape from her reality by making an attempt to locate her previous self, the woman who she was before the encounter. Unfortunately, she can't find her. Although her brown eyes, shapely eyebrows and spotless brown skin tone look the same, they all feel different on. They're not what they used to be, and she doubts she will see that same woman ever again. She doesn't even want to go home because her only way there is on foot or via the one man everyone knows can't be crossed – her old first kiss – Davon Bain. He's outside waiting. Either way, she must report back to him.

When she gets to the door, she takes one step outside. She smells fresh. There was some perfume, powder and even toothpaste and a packaged toothbrush in the room. Her clothes smelled the same, retaining the scent of her daughter who she held in her arms before she left the house. Pretty's hair is brushed up into a nice bun on the very top of her head, and if no one knew it, it would only look like she's on a stroll in the middle of the night. Nothing about her screams whore except her insides, and it pains her as she moves closer and closer to the car because she knows that the one thousand dollars she's hiding from Bain isn't enough to last the family. Her efforts will have to be repeated, but now, she doesn't know what or how to go about earning anything because her husband, according to Faye, is privy to everything she's just done.

Faye sits inside the car beside Bain as they both watch Pretty walk down the driveway. Bain even rolls down the window slightly to zoom in on her face a bit better, and Faye notices. She becomes a bit bothered by what she reads on his face as his concern. Then, Bain opens the door to get out, but she grabs his arm.

"Where you going? You don't get out and do shit like this. You could get nabbed by the police or somebody else! Sit down, Bain. She's coming! What's wrong with you?"

Bain remains silent when he turns back to look at Faye holding his arm, and due to the severity of his facial expression, she lets go of him quickly, allowing him to get out of the car, leaving Faye to her own temper tantrum. She fumes watching Bain walk over to the woman she just helped out behind Bain's back, and she suddenly regrets every moment of it. Envy eats at her because of the look she saw in Bain's eyes before he got out of the car because she plans never to lose what she sees as control with the man she wants all to herself, especially behind Pretty.

Bain stands there in the darkness at the end of the driveway as he watches his old friend from long ago walk down the pavement so slowly that her gait could almost be confused with a person about to halt. During the slight stall of Pretty on the driveway, Bain remembers the pain he saw when he was a boy in elementary school, placing himself and Pretty back inside that same path at her parents' house. The only people missing from the recollection are their fathers.

As Bain continues to watch her with an expression void of emotion, the way he feels isn't as stone as what it may seem. Pretty comes to a complete stop, staring back into Bain's eyes once again, broken down to nothing. This time, instead of watching her dad die, shot to death at her side, it's herself who is dying on the inside, and Bain knows it. They both just stand there, aware of each other's pain although neither will admit to it. Bain remains completely still, and Pretty, absolutely too weak internally from everything, falls to her knees. Bain simply watches her take hold of the hardened ground as the sky begins to drizzle rain. The wet drops of rain fall, but they fail to interrupt what's going on between the two who share so much history together from an early age.

"You could've just given me the money, Bain. You could've given me the money!" she screams, slapping the pavement with the palms of her hands while moaning as if she's lost everything that ever meant anything in her life. Bain stands there watching, unable to feel anything overtly. All he can do is remember the past which makes him walk forward until he reaches her body weeping on the pavement.

"Stand up," he says to her in a tone that's relaxed but demands respect. Pretty wants to attack him, but fears she'll lose the little hope in her life that she has left, therefore, she holds in her anger and gets up. She doesn't even look him in the face, and even though she's looking behind him, just over his shoulder, she can feel his eyes penetrating hers. Her lips are quivering from crying, and just before she leans over to her knees to start crying again, he touches her face.

"Look over here."

Pretty finally finds the strength to stare back into the eyes of Bain. When she does, he says nothing to her. He only looks back into her saddened eyes, listening to her holler at him like he's the worst man on earth.

"I hate you! You know me, Bain! You know me! Look what you did to me!" she screams, pointing at what she sees as a shameful shack. Then, she brings up even more raw memories that still ache her until this very day. "You and your fuckin' father!"

Bain allows her to say it all, still not moved by anything she's doing. The only thing that is beginning to exert its strength over Bain is the same thing that's exerting its strength over her - memories. At that moment, he reaches into his pocket which causes Pretty to freeze in the midst of her commotion, afraid that he's going to kill her. Then Bain, with his other hand, reaches and grabs her wrist. She yanks back, but he's holding on too tight, but she suddenly feels okay when she sees what he's pulling from his pocket.

Breathing deeply, she watches as the man she now hates delivers a huge roll of hundred dollar bills into her hand. When she opens her hand to allow Bain to place the

247

money in her palm, he then reaches for her other hand.
This time, she holds it out herself. Bain then reaches inside
his other pocket to place even more money in the other
hand.

"You paid off your father's debt to mine. I got that
money in the car. This is my money that I give to you, and
it doesn't have anything to do with anyone else but us."

"My husband's not gonna want me anymore, Bain.
He knows, and when you take me home…"

"I'll fix that shit." He continues to stare back into
her eyes. "He won't let you go. Ain't nobody in the Trails
gonna say shit about this either, you understand?" Before
he starts to walk back to the car, he brings her more
reassurance. "There's more money where that came from.
Whatever you need, you can have. You won't have to do
this again. Now come on."

Pretty doesn't move. "Why did you make me in the
first place?"

He stops in his tracks. "You never said no."

"You're lying, Davon!"

At the call of his first name, Bain turns back around
and becomes as honest as he will allow himself to be about
the incident when his father died because she still doesn't
know what he told him to do that day which is get the
money. He answers her, "Johnny Bain. I made you do it
for Johnny Bain, my father." He stands there strong as
ever, in allegiance to his deceased father. Then, across his
face comes a softness not seen by Pretty for years. She's
finally reminded of the boy she once knew. " Now, I'm
setting you free for myself, baby girl. I'm setting us free."
Looking around at this empty section of Gabriel's Trails

until his eyes land back onto his first girlfriend, he holds out his hand in peace. Pretty walks up beside him and lightly touches her wrist over what could have been, and they both walk to the car together.

Faye stands outside the car, leaning on the hood, her eyes bulging from the sockets. "What the hell?" she exclaims. "And your ass is still sitting in the back!" she yells angrily at Pretty as they approach the car.

Tim sits worried on the porch as a car pulls up behind his on the street. His eyes are too blurry from crying at the thought of his wife doing only God knows what to see exactly who's getting out of the vehicle, so he stands up and wipes his eyes, still weak from his unknown illness that's been giving him bloody stools.

"Pretty," he calls, recognizing her in the short distance from the porch to the end of the driveway. Pretty runs to him with a plastic bag in her hand and falls to her knees when she reaches his feet, crying and saying I'm sorry continuously.

"Please, Pretty, tell me you didn't do this," he begs while kneeling down before her as he brings her head in to his chest. As he holds her in his arms, rocking back and forth, he watches Bain approaching the porch. Then, he pushes Pretty gently aside. No matter how weak he is, he refuses to stand down to any man. His manhood is at stake. Since he's been sick, that's the one thing he feels he needs to maintain – his manhood and his family.

"Hey, man, hey! Don't come up here, Bain. This is my home, and you're not coming up in here disrespecting it, man! This is my wife. She ain't one of your whores you can just come through and take." Tim starts to laugh hysterically for a moment during his ranting threats. "Man, I'll kill you, Bain. I'll take you off the face of this earth before I let you have my wife and daughter, too."

Bain pays no attention. To Bain, those are only words. He continues to walk to his destination which is Tim's porch because he already knows what he's there to do.

When he reaches arm's distance of Tim, Tim swings a solid punch toward Bain's face. Bain simply backs away, realizing that the man has a right to be angry, therefore, Bain doesn't retaliate, especially after watching Pretty's husband fall to the ground after the missed punch and start giggling like something's funny.

"He's sick, Bain! Please, don't … please. We have a daughter!" Pretty isn't understanding what's going on with Tim, so she falls on the ground in between her husband and Bain.

"Don't beg this man for nothing, Pretty!" her husband demands, but Bain interjects quickly, knowing he has to get off the streets in the open with all this commotion.

Trying to smooth things over, Bain begins to speak, "We go way back, man…me and your wife right here. I fell short on a drop and knew she was free, so I took her. Just came and got her. My bad, man." He smirks down at Pretty's husband who is struggling to get back on his feet, then he stares at Pretty who is on the ground in need of him to fix the situation faster. "She didn't really have a choice. I left some people over here to watch your daughter. It didn't take too long. No man touched her. Didn't mean to upset you, man. That's the cash I gave her for her trouble." Bain tosses his hands up in the air. "No harm, right? I won't come back. Deal's done."

He snatches the bag of money from Pretty's hand, and throws it at Bain as he's walking away. "I don't need no help from the next, man! I got my family!"

Bain turns back around after being struck in the back with the bag of cash. His walk is like a bulldog thirsty for revenge, and Pretty's heart grows numb, completely engulfed in so much fear that she no longer feels it.

"Bain, no!" Pretty cries, so loudly that the sound is heard over the music that's playing up the road, but Bain doesn't hear her. What was over in Bain's eyes has now reversed itself with the retaliation from Pretty's sick husband when he threw that bag. Tim just denied the truce. Bain remembers what he's lived by for so long. It's what his dad told him before he died and that was not to talk to the enemy too much or you make fatal mistakes. With that in his memory, he whips out his gun, kneels and shoves it at Tim's chin.

"Daddy!"

Bain hears the little girl at the door but doesn't look her way. Instead, he puts the gun in the front of his pants and drapes it underneath his shirt while not taking his eyes off of the man cowering beneath him. Bain then leans over closer to Tim's ear. "Your daughter wants her father. Be a man about this shit. Be a fuckin' man. What man hits another man in the fuckin' back?" Tim can only stare back at him, trying not to lose his manhood, but inside, he feels he already has. Tim glances at his daughter looking at him beneath another man, and then he looks at his wife who looks petrified, and who has already heard the words come from Bain's mouth about him being a real man. He dwells on his unknown illness and knows that he's already hopeless, even dead. Then, he quickly snatches the gun from Bain's waist, points it at Bain's face, and as Bain falls backwards guarding his face, Tim turns the gun into his own mouth and pulls the trigger.

"No! Oh, God, no!" Pretty desperately screams.

"Mommy!"

Faye comes running up to the porch. In her hand, she has wipes and gloves. "Is it dirty? Is it dirty, dammit?" she asks, referring to the gun and if it's been used in a murder already.

"No, no. Clean the shit and let's ride. Be quick." Bain looks up at Pretty who is visibly shaken at this point, shaking the chest of her dying husband who is still twitching on the ground. Everyone on the block who witnessed the shooting scatters at the sight of Bain memorizing the scene and the people around, including Pretty's daughter who just missed what her dad did to himself because Pretty was kneeling in front of him, blocking her view.

"Mommy, what's daddy doing?"

"Go call 911, baby girl. Your daddy's sick." Bain advises little Shyla before he runs to the car.

"Okay, hold on, daddy!" she encourages. "I'm hurrying. God is with you, just like you tell me when I get sick, daddy," she continues, running back into the house.

Pretty is zoned out, holding her husband's face together by trying to seal up the holes with her hands. He's still breathing as Faye places the gun back between the fingers she took it from. Then, she stares directly at Pretty.

"This ain't no murder. This is a suicide. Now, this gun wasn't clean at first because Bain's prints were on it, and now they ain't, so you got only one choice – shut the fuck up about us being here because we weren't here! Got it? Put that money up that your husband tossed over there. As a matter of fact…" Faye snatches the bag up by her fingernails and throws it inside the house since the little girl left the door wide open. "If you want more of that money, you'll shut up. Bain didn't do shit. If anything, your husband assaulted him because I saw it with my own eyes, and you did, too." Pretty simply stares at her with an empty look, and that's when Faye realizes that Pretty isn't fighting back at all. When Faye's adrenaline comes from off its high, she sees clearly that Pretty isn't at all angry. She just wants her husband back. Faye then leans down and apologizes for her loss, realizing that it isn't the time nor the place for a bitter scolding. "I'm so sorry this happened to you… you and your family." After that, Faye runs back to the car with Bain, and they take off.

When the cops come along with the medical personnel, they load the still breathing Tim into the back of the vehicle. The cops question Pretty about what happened. She tells them that he was outside when she heard a pop. When she came outside, that's when she saw him. She never says a word about Bain, and Tim survives the gunshot wound. He dies several weeks later from terminal cancer. It's Bain who moves her and her daughter out of Gabriel's Trails, a request made by a dying Tim who had no choice via a letter from his death bed. Shyla's private school is also paid up for two years while she lives with her mom Pretty who has steady income in a fully paid for small house and brand new car, all courtesy of Davon Bain.

"Man, what's up with this shit? You're hardly out in the daytime. Get the fuck outta this mo'fucka, man. This can't be real!" a young man laughs at the brand new sight he sees.

Bain leans on a tree at the back entrance of Gabriel's Trails. Only a few of his partners are out and about, doing their normal thing, but for Bain, this is something very new. He never sees a full day because he sleeps through it, conducting all his business when he can barely be seen in the crowd that usually comes out in the nighttime. There's been a slight change in Bain since the night he encountered Pretty and her family. He wants to feel love once again which was a part of him that he lost in the home where his dad died. There was a resurgence of emotion when he had those moments with Pretty that he just couldn't shake.

It feels good to him to finally break free from what choked him up since he was a young boy. No one ever knew about what exactly happened in the house, and he never released the information. Doing good for Pretty and her daughter for Tim's sake makes him feel like he finally has a way out of the pressures of being Bain. He wants to live a somewhat normal life to someone who doesn't know anything about him, someone who doesn't know his deep past nor present, nor about how much money he's stashing in one of the least rich neighborhoods in the city. A glimpse of kindness takes Bain from ice cold to just cold with a bit of lukewarm in the weeks that pass. Now, he's spotted in the daytime, when most of his crowd is asleep, and he isn't as afraid to feel the one thing he's run from since Johnny Bain got shot to death – his true emotions.

In the distance, he watches a young lady walking down the street in the middle of all the mansions that surround Gabriel's Trails. She looks like a rich kid that doesn't know that she's walking the wrong way, and she seems unphased by the small group of territorial men standing at the Gabriel's Trails sign. The rich always remain out of what is called the slum because the neighborhoods are separated by the trails and the dense woods. They never come through Gabriel's Trails unless it's through the front entrance and for business only.

"Bain, that's one of your girls, man?" one of the guys ask that are leaning on the sign. He reaches back for his pistol because trust doesn't go far beyond the trails. What happens in the trails, stays in the trails, so all the fellas move back near the woods at the sighting, closer to Bain.

"She's not one of mine. Stand down though."

"Man, Bain, she could be a cop."

Bain realizes that he's taking a risk, but she doesn't look like a cop. On the other hand, she looks like some girls that he's come in contact with before, the type of girl who lives the good life but wants a taste of the bad because they feel like they're missing something, something that they can only find in the trails.

"If she's a cop, when I talk to her, unload your clips. I'll give you the sign." There's always a sign with Bain. With Floss, it's a wink. With others, it could be anything, but they've been with Bain for so long, until they know what he means by almost any gesture. This is a new Bain, however, and as he waits on the female to move in closer, they wonder what Bain is doing without speaking another word to him out loud.

255

Her hair is long, draping around her shoulders as she wears a short, checkered skirt and a semi-tight T-shirt with white sneakers on her feet. Bain is enjoying what he sees and makes her out to be a teenager, maybe new to the area, and is innocently wandering. Either way, if she's coming to Gabriel's Trails, she'll be coming with him. He's made his mind up on that fact already.

Bain remains leaning on the tree, not making any sudden movements as the young girl walks closer to the Gabriel's Trails sign. Then, he watches her glance his way, all the while learning her personality by what she does. After stalling, she looks at the various entrances to the trails, and then chooses to turn toward trail number one.

"Psst!"

The young girl stops and turns around flirtatiously, lifting both hands to her waist. Bain doesn't know who she is or why she's here, but he yearns for simple conversation with someone who isn't afraid of him. Someone with whom he can be Davon again, just to recapture the time he's lost as he grew up under his dad's inherited fame and name. He calls her over, not with his voice, but with a welcoming posture that she accepts.

When she reaches him, he's already learned that she's fairly innocent, no matter how she tries to hide it. She's also curious and naïve, a girl who likes to live through experience and not exactly be told. Bain can almost smell her defiance as he glances above her head at the entrance to trail number one.

"That's a dead end." To Bain, the girl looks about seventeen but no younger based on her build.

"It is?"

"Yeah. What's your name?"

"What's yours?" she quickly responds with a smile that sends Bain into an immediate attraction, but then he falls silent and looks around. His eyes are drawn back to her clothing, and this makes the young girl smile. Bain isn't looking at her clothes for anything sexual, however, because he isn't exactly out of control in that area being that he sees women every night and makes money off of their bodies as well. The reason he's examining her clothes is because he's aware that his boys are hidden and ready to fire if she's mimicking a youngster but really undercover. She has no idea of the danger she's in.

"Why are you looking at me like that?" she asks.

"No reason. Aren't you too young to be over here like this?"

"Not if you show me around, nameless man."

"You're too young to walk around here with me."

"And you don't look that old either, but to make you feel better, you don't have to touch me. I just feel like I need to know what's back there, beyond the trails."

"Are you a cop?"

She laughs. "Is that why you were looking at my shirt? No! See look," she says, lifting up her shirt and then busting out laughing. "I'm not a cop."

"Pull your shirt down," Bain requests. "Don't do stuff like that in public. Keep your beauty to yourself or for your man. Anything else will take your beauty away, baby girl."

She allows her shirt to fall, embarrassed by her actions but impressed by his response. He didn't bubble up with excitement like a schoolyard boy would have, and this is what attracts her to him instantaneously - his authority over himself and over her without force. His nice brown skin and well built frame was a plus as well.

"Alexis…that's my name. Will you tell me yours now?"

"Name's Bain. Let me show you around, and I promise I won't touch you. You won't send my ass to prison."

"Ha, ha. Funny!" she responds sarcastically, but he was serious, more serious than what she knows. Bain would choose to perish or kill first before going to prison.

Bain reassures her that he won't let anything happen to her while inside Gabriel's Trails, and nothing does. He doesn't lay one finger on her nor does anyone else. He's found his freedom in Alexis to at least try and be someone new.

THE

END

Remain updated on all upcoming books by Mirika Mayo Cornelius at mirikacornelius.com. For upcoming Akirim Press books, visit akirimpress.com.

More Akirim Press Books

Books by Mirika Mayo Cornelius

Secret

Colored Lily: Poppa Took My Innocence

Paton

Ain't Quite What I Thought

Ain't Quite What I Thought 2!

Sunny Sides of My Shade

Murders at Gabriel's Trails: The Complete 5 Part Series with bonus Sins of Bain

Inside the Gates of Doons

Books by Rod Cornelius

Diggin' Gold

The Trusted

Single Again

Ugly

Ghetto Eyes

The Best Kept Secrets

Books by Cyan Deane

Dead Man's Mayhem

Execution's Karma

Preview SECRET by Mirika Mayo Cornelius

"I told you your aunt is resting, didn't I?"

I reach my leg back and kick him in his mouth. He yanks his head back and stares at me like he's gonna kill me, so I kick him again with both of my legs swinging like a wild bat. He jumps on top of me holding my right leg with his hand and ducking away from my other leg while its kicking. He starts to unbuckle his pants with his other hand.

"Yeah, it's present time now. You done asked for it. I heard about your momma. A nice piece of work there."

He rips off my pajamas after he gets his pants down. My heart fills up with scary feelings when I just now figure out why my Aunt May said what she told me all the time. Where's Aunt Janie?

"Aunt Janie! Your friend is in my room! He's not supposed to be in here, Aunt Janie!" I yell the loudest I can yell.

Sam reaches back with his right hand and hits me on the side of my stomach. I curl up in a ball.

"Guess what, Secret. She ain't coming so ain't no use in you calling for her. You act like I'm about to hurt you. I wouldn't have hit you like that if you didn't try to wake up your aunt, so I'm sorry. Now hold still."

He feels up my back with his naked hand. My stomach is aching. He keeps acting like he ain't gonna do nothing to me, but this don't feel right. I keep thinking about Aunt May while his hand is going up my leg. I feel something wet on my leg, too. I yank away, but he jerks me in front of him. Jesus, please, help me, Lord. Tears are falling every which way down my face, but then I see it. I fell asleep with my pencil beside me in my bed. It's halfway covered up with my sheets.

"Touch it."

I look back at him, and he closes his eyes.

"Look down and touch it."

That's when I look down and see what he's talking about. I panic.

"Get off of me! No! I'm not touching that thing-ever! What is that? Aunt Janie, please!" I reach for the pencil real fast, but I don't know what to do with it yet. My hand grips the pencil like somebody else got it for me. My other hand grabs that long, ugly thing, and my hand, with the pencil in it, reaches all the way back and stabs that big, ugly thing right in the center.

He lets out the loudest holler I ever heard from a man in my life, and his eyes fly open. I jump up off the bed, and run towards the other end of my room. I look back at his ugly thing and see that the pencil is still stuck in there while he's tumbling around on the floor. His hands are around it, but he ain't pulling it out. It's hurtin' him so bad that I pick up my lamp so that I can aim for his head so I can bang some more pain into him. He justa hollering. Betcha he won't come in my room no more.

Preview Diggin' Gold by Rod Cornelius

She wanted him just as bad as he wanted her, but just not bad enough to get it on in the car. She also realized that another round with Trent meant another day of lying to Jimmy, but what he doesn't know wouldn't hurt him, she thought. Besides, she was trying to come up and Jimmy's stock was falling fast. Trent had tangible assets, and she was almost ready to go all in.

"I told you earlier that I had a lack of patience for you. Now how about let's get up out of this ride and take a no-holds barred tour of my humble abode. There won't be a piece of furniture off limits. I promise," he said as he continued feasting on her neck.

She observed his house again, "I don't know if you got a back strong enough for the kind of tour that you're talking about. Your place looks like it has a lot of ground to cover. It could take the whole night to get it all."

He pulled up and backed away from her. "There's only one way to find out."

"Then why are we still in your Jag?"

He backed away further with a smile as she smiled right back at him. "Baby, it ain't nothing but a word."

"Then what are you waiting on?"

"Shiiiiiit!" he said. She finally told him what his ears had been waiting all night to hear. The green light was lit. He knew he could have pretty much any woman he set his sights on but Kizzy carried an extra spiff. Not only was she sexy and a freak in between the sheets, but she was

Jimmy's lady. She was the last thing he could take from Jimmy and that was worth more than its weight in gold.

He quickly hopped out of the automobile and danced around the vehicle to open her door. He grabbed her hand to assist her on her exodus. He shut the door, not releasing her hand as they made their way to his front door.

As she stood behind him, she looked up and admired the huge brick home. She had never been in a house as big as his, and she couldn't wait to serenade it with him. "This really is a nice place, Trent. I could see you making me some pancakes in bed here," she joked.

"Oh we 'bout to make something, but it's not going to pancakes, that's for sure." He pulled her into the dark house and slammed the door shut. Then he pulled her into him and gave her a passionate kiss.

"So I guess you mean business," she said as she pulled away from his lips and rested her arms around his neck.

"Do I?" he smiled. He placed both hands on her rump and gripped it tightly, pulling her up off of the floor as she wrapped her legs around his waist. As his tongue ran its slow, slippery course up and down her neck, he walked her through the dark living space and carried her to the leather couch. He laid her down and his tongue twirled around her bosom as his hands made their way down her legs as he began to inch her dress upwards.

Preview Dead Man's Mayhem by Cyan Deane

What the hell was that? If they don't get their little southern asses out of my viewing! Rest in peace? Mary made my life a living, breathing, stinking hell, and she has her sweaty panties coming in here trying to start some real shit while I'm still trying to wake myself up from this doomsday nightmare.

Mary – she's the lady that built the straw house that I wanted to crap on each and everyday to make that thing fall down right on top of her ass. When I would walk into her bar, for some reason or another, she would always be there. What owner is always at their establishment? That's the purpose of hiring people to work for you while you sit your ass at home and play golf in the middle of lunch time traffic so everyone can see what a grand life you have. She would make her baggy eyeballs twitch at me, and she's only forty one years old, looking and sounding like a grandma of eight hell raisers.

Truth be told, Mary would constantly talk shit, but it was shit that I could never hear. Call me paranoid, but she was ten words from getting popped in her mouth the day I supposedly went cold. I still don't even know who knocked me over my damn head in her nasty ass bar, but I swear it was probably her ass that set me up. She hated me, and I could tell. Her raggedy bar wasn't even that good for anything, but I was determined to go inside each and every week to make her life-long dream of store ownership reek of irritation with my presence.

I'd come to find out that I dated Mary's second cousin, Barbara Sue, back in the day for like three minutes tops, and Barbara Sue had gone and told her whole felon ass family that I was the one who broke her heart into pieces. First off, what they didn't know was that I would have never dated anyone seriously named Barbara Sue. Let's get that out there right now. Secondly, all I did was kiss her after talking on the phone with her for about one week.

When I met up with her, Barbara Sue wasn't really my type, but hell, the date was still on. We went to see a movie, parked it at the park, kissed and I took her snaggle toothed mouth home. It's true I never called again, but it was a damn shame how she ran my name in the mud about it.

Preview Ain't Quite What I Thought! by Mirika Mayo Cornelius

I hit the floor. Hard! My credit card flew out of my hand, only to land underneath the display counter. As I reached for it, I found out quickly that I was louder than what I thought I was because everyone was looking at me. Everyone, including the man that just walked through the door - Andre'. Thus, in order to avoid more embarrassment, I scooped myself up off of the floor. Andre', who was now watching me get up from off of my butt, walked over to me, as if he didn't even know me at all, grabbed me by the hand to play like he was helping me up even though I was already halfway there.

"What are you doing here, Andre'?" I whispered.

He gave me the eye, and I knew what it meant. Shut up.

"My gosh, Jeena? Jeena, are you okay, honey? What happened? I heard that big thud over here, and I thought, my God, someone must've fallen and broken their neck!"

Shut up, Kyaiki. At the same time Kyaiki started running her mouth, my situation got to the worst stage imaginable. Tina came over, and touched Andre' on his pinky. That's how they ended up before my very eyes, holding hands by the pinky fingers. Somebody should have stabbed me in the chest before their next physical moment of pure passion came up. Oh wait, never mind, too late for the stabbing. She kissed him dead on his lips. I wasn't jealous in the least bit. They were married, but dog, Andre' could have had some mercy on me! Shoot, he kissed her right back! He could've given her a side lip or something to make me feel better.

"Kyaiki, my credit card. It's under the display

count…"

"I'll lift it up for you," Andre' stated, butting in while deciding he was going to take this time to play credit card rescuer. Thus, he went and lifted up the display counter just enough for me to grab my card.

"Aren't you the girl from the hospital?"

While I was stooped over, Tina's question sent a chill down my spine. She recognized me, even with those big behind sunglasses on. Why on earth was she wearing them in the store anyway? Crawling under a rock wasn't an option nor was crawling under Andre' while he was holding up the display, so I rose once again to the unpleasant occasion.

"The hospital? Do I know you?" I asked, as if. Of course, I knew her. Tina, I'm having an affair with your husband, I thought. You know, the man standing right next to us that sent me 24 red roses today and told me he loved me. Yeah, the man on your pinky finger. What you are tasting, so am I, I thought while feeling slightly ill at the taste of her in my mouth as well. "Yeah, now I remember. What's your name again?"

"Tina." Her teeth were even perfect, no plaque, tarter, grill, nothing. Those had to have been fake fronts in her mouth, and if they weren't, I've got to do better.

"Yes, good to see you, and this is Andre'!" I gawked at him like I hadn't seen him since the hospital as a fully equipped and well built human male. "Wow! You have come a long way."

Andre' didn't even respond right away. He just lowered the display case, and looked over at Tina. Then, he glanced back at me. "Yeah, I got better really fast thanks to all your help."

He was damn right thanks to all my help.

"Anytime," I shakily stated, quickly looking at the garment that I was planning on sharing with him dangling from Tina's arm.

"You like this, baby?" She held up her choice of lingerie.

"Nice to see you," I gagged. I didn't even wave bye-bye, but ignored Kyaiki and left. Fast. Forget the white sheets and lace. I was gonna toss those roses in the garbage.

Humiliation was what I felt. Like a complete dumb ass for the cause. I couldn't believe I fell on the floor in front of Andre' and his wife! My forehead hit the steering wheel and while I rolled it around on top of it, I stuck the key in and started the ignition. As I started backing up from my parking space, I caught a glimpse of Andre' staring at me through the window. I pressed on the gas harder and drove off. Asshole!

I didn't even know why I was raging mad. Over him and her? Ha! I stopped at the stop sign and looked in the rear view. The signage for my favorite store was still within view. I slumped. Man, who was I fooling? I was still in love with the man, and my feelings were all broken inside. He was all up in my face and sending me roses…and all up in his wife's face buying her lingerie. I was the idiot buying my own! At least she got her stuff paid for!

www.ingramcontent.com/pod-product-compliance
Lightning Source LLC
Chambersburg PA
CBHW060535260626
47161CB00003B/904